Chapter 1

Life would change completely for Siswan on her twelfth birthday. She had enjoyed a wonderful day. Her family and friends had all turned up to celebrate and it seemed as though most of the village was in her front garden.

She wore the secondhand, but pretty yellow frock her mother had bought the previous day and her long black hair was tied back into a ponytail. She would have preferred to have worn the sandals with the flower design, but her mother had insisted she wear her black lace shoes with white ankle socks.

'Your feet will get too dirty, Siswan,' her mother told her, as she bent to tie the laces.

'But my feet look too big now, Mama,' she argued, but to no avail.

Siswan had learned from an early age not to argue for too long. Her mother would only tolerate so much and would end further discussion with a swishing stick. The long, thin canes that grew alongside the broken fence were always within easy reach and the swishing noise they made, as her mother used one across her legs or arms, had earned them their name.

Actually, her feet didn't look too big at all. At just twelve years old, Siswan was a very well endowed young woman. Over the previous twelve months she had shot up in height and had started developing some of the feminine curves that, within another few years, would give her a body that men would desire and women envy.

Even though she played and worked in the heat of the sun, her skin remained a light coffee colour. Like honey.

She had started her periods just a few months before and, although they were light, she was glad she wasn't having one on this special day. The uncomfortable pads her mother had shown her how to use would become sticky and smelly after just a few hours.

Despite the fact that she attended the local school, Siswan had learned most things from her mother. The school was ill equipped and, to be truthful, she didn't go that often. Her mother usually needed her help in the fields or with the housework.

From her mother she had learned how to show respect to the monks who lived in the temple a few kilometres from their village. Every week she and her mother would visit to pray and wish for better luck in the future. The monks would look kindly enough upon her but they refrained from getting too close. A monk was never allowed to touch a female and, even when she once bumped into one accidentally, she had been scolded with the swishing stick when she got home.

It hadn't really been her fault. She had only been ten at the time. She had run around the corner straight into the yellow robed figure. Her mother had told her to purchase some more incense sticks and, whilst she continued to prostrate herself at the alter, Siswan had raced outside with the energy and eagerness of a young child. The monk had reacted as though her touch was poisonous.

She had learned long ago how to deal with the big black scorpions that sometimes entered the small garden in front of her house, and she feared for a moment that some part of her body would need to be cut off in the same way she removed the scorpion's sting from its tail. She ran back to her mother with tears streaming down her cheeks. Her mother had marched her home and used a swishing stick until it broke.

'You cannot touch a monk, Siswan!' she had shouted.

The cane had left dark red welts on her legs, arms and back that took weeks to fade away and Siswan was left in no doubt that what had happened had been her fault.

Her mother had also taught her to show respect to her father, and she would shrink away in fear if Papa even so much as looked as though he was going to lose his temper. She had seen his foul moods before and, whenever he came home smelling of the local whiskey, she and her brother would hide themselves away in their bedroom until they heard the snores of his sleep. They had both felt the strength of his blows.

On many of those occasions, when she was very young, she would climb into the same bed as her older brother, Bak, and they would lie still, holding one another. The sounds of their father shouting and hitting their mother could be easily heard through the thin walls of their small wooden house.

Sometimes, the sounds of crashing furniture or the cries of their mother, would make her cuddle tighter into her brother's arms. She never understood why her father behaved the way he did, but she began to associate the smell of the whiskey with the cries of her mother.

Bak was almost three years older and, as he grew, he developed the same traits as his father; a foul temper and a complete lack of respect for his sister and mother.

'You must remember your place, Siswan,' her mother told her, after her brother had hit her.

'But we used to be such good friends, Mama!' she had replied, through her tears.

Her brother had slapped her across the face when he caught her looking at the comic books he kept beneath his bed. The books were only drawings of people without their clothes on and she didn't think they were that important. She hadn't thought the drawings that good either. They were just black and white sketches. Bubbles were drawn near the character's faces and she had wanted to read what they were saying. Her brother had walked into the bedroom they still shared and hit her.

It wasn't the slap that made her cry so much as the fact that her brother obviously no longer looked upon his little sister as a friend and playmate.

'Why do men hurt us, Mama?' she asked.

'When they think we have done wrong, Siswan,' her mother answered.

'But what do we do that's wrong?' she asked.

'Sometimes we don't know. But the men are stronger and cleverer, so we must listen. Life is a test, Siswan. It is a harder test for women than it is for men, but we have to learn. We have to be good in this life so that we can go to heaven and not have to come here again.'

As Siswan grew, she learned that all men had to be respected. One of the villagers, who lived a short distance up the road, was a policeman and everyone respected him. He wore a dark brown uniform that was far too small for him because it stuck to his skin and didn't hide his large belly. He also wore a gun on his belt and would threaten to shoot the young children of the village if they played too noisily when he wanted to sleep. Siswan and her friends stayed away from his house. He was angry all of the time. With or without whiskey.

When the first guests arrived, Siswan ran down the old wooden stairs to greet them. She was an excitable young girl, despite her strict upbringing, and needed little encouragement to laugh or to smile.

Her auntie had arrived with her three children and they all gave wais to Siswan's mother upon entering the home.

The house itself was perched on tall wooden posts that afforded it some protection from the monsoon floods and offered a shaded area below where the family would sit to eat or to work.

Her mother had taught her how to tie the bundles of sage that they grew in their small allotment. Each bundle would sell for a pittance, but Siswan and her mother would sit in the shade of the house and tie so many that the family earned enough to survive.

Her father worked in the town but never seemed to have any money of his own. He was always demanding more from her mother and would lose his temper if none was forthcoming.

Siswan sat on the old rattan mats and talked happily with her cousins who all exclaimed how pretty she looked in her new dress. No one mentioned that her black shoes made her feet look big so, in the end, Siswan decided that perhaps her mother had been right after all.

More and more guests filed into the small garden and each of them brought some small offering for the birthday meal. One dish, when it was uncovered, revealed roasted chicken and another, boiled pork. All manner of vegetables were placed in a neat arrangement on the bamboo table and piles of freshly boiled rice were laid out for everyone to enjoy.

Although the village was poor and could never afford extravagant birthday gifts, food was plentiful. If ever anyone in the village was hungry all they had to do was walk a few paces away from the road and they could have their pick of all manner of fruit and vegetables.

Food grew everywhere and a diet of rice could easily be supplemented with insects of every shape and size. Siswan's brother would spend a long time digging up the root beetles he was so particularly fond of as an in-between-meal snack.

In the early evening, her father, together with some of his friends, came home from work and the women all busied themselves making sure the men-folk had places to sit and enough food to eat.

Siswan spent most of her time sitting and talking with her young cousins as the adults ate and drank. One, in particular, was her best friend and she and Ped would discuss the most intimate of subjects.

'I started my periods last month,' Ped exclaimed, with great delight.

'Mine started ages ago,' Siswan told her.

'Yes, but you are older than me,' Ped pointed out.

'Only by a month. Anyway your bumps are bigger than mine,' she laughed, and poked Ped's developing breasts.

'Yours are bigger,' cried Ped, and reached over to grab Siswan.

The two girls playfully pretended to grab each other's bumps, as they called them, until interrupted by Bak.

'Neither of you have got boobs. Just little bee stings,' he said, with disdain.

At fifteen years old, Bak was already practicing the manner his father and friends showed toward women and, laughing, pushed his sister hard so that she rolled backwards into Ped.

'Leave us alone,' Siswan said, as she sat back up.

'Shut up little girl or I'll hit you again,' her brother threatened, as he walked off to join the older men.

'He's horrible,' Ped said, quietly.

'He never used to be,' Siswan said.

She regretted the fact that her brother was turning into a man. They used to play so happily together down by the pond at the edge of the village. He would run around trying to catch fish by hand and she would laugh so much her sides hurt as he dove and splashed in the muddy waters.

After drying in the sun, they would wander into the cane fields to look for lizards and scorpions and Bak would be scared when she carefully picked up a scorpion by the tail to show him how easy it was. Things had been different between them when they were children.

Later, when all the guests had eaten their fill, Siswan was called to her father's side. She was worried that perhaps she was in trouble again and gave him a long and low wai as she approached.

'You aren't in trouble, Mia,' he laughed, as she came to him. She didn't know why her father insisted on using the nickname 'Mia' when he spoke to her, but she was pleased he was in a good mood.

'Here you are. This is for your first adult birthday,' he told her, and handed her a small box wrapped in brown paper.

Inside was a silver chain with a small silver image of Buddha swinging loosely from it. She couldn't believe her eyes as she looked at the small ornament. The image looked up at her with a smile on its face. He looked happy. This was the only birthday present she would receive but it was the best one she had ever known!

Her mother helped her, and showed her how the small clasp worked so that she could attach it around her neck.

'Thank you very much, Papa,' she said, and gave a wai so low that she felt the small silver Buddha bump gently against her chin.

'Now that's over with, let's have a drink.'

Her father had dismissed her already and was talking to the rest of the men. A bottle of whiskey was soon produced and the female guests made their excuses to leave, taking their children with them.

Siswan had said her goodbyes to her friends and family and had taken herself off to her bed. She showered, using the small bucket to throw cold water over herself, and carefully hung her dress on the rail that sufficed as a wardrobe.

Lying quietly in her small bed, she listened to the noise of the men below as they consumed more and more whiskey. Her father was the loudest of them all. She prayed that he wouldn't hurt her mother tonight.

She fingered the small figure that still hung around her neck. This was the first piece of jewelry she had ever owned, or worn, and the chain felt strange against her skin. Not uncomfortable exactly, just strange. She wondered if the small figure minded being in contact with a female.

Despite the raucous shouts of the men below, Siswan fell asleep clutching the small silver ornament in her hand.

She awoke a few hours later when Bak entered their shared room. He stumbled through the doorway and she could tell he was drunk. She pretended to be asleep. She heard him undress and curse, under his breath, when he fell against his bed.

Their father was shouting downstairs. She could hear her mother's quiet replies. She hoped she wouldn't hear them fighting again. Why did men become so angry, she thought to herself? Why couldn't they just be quiet and get on with life like the women?

'Siswan?' Bak whispered.

He was standing over her bed. She didn't open her eyes but she could sense his closeness. He had been mean to her in front of her friends and she didn't want to speak to him.

'Siswan,' he whispered again, more insistently.

She continued to pretend to be asleep. She didn't know why, but she felt a little scared. Her brother was no longer her friend. He sounded so much like their father these days. Hard and cold.

'I know you aren't asleep,' he hissed, close to her face.

She could smell the whiskey from his breath and felt afraid. She kept her eyes closed and continued to pretend. Her hand, beneath the single sheet that covered her, tightened on the small Buddha. Make him go away, she thought. She felt his hand on her shoulder.

'Siswan. I have something for you,' he slurred in her ear. 'A birthday present.'

She could feel his foul smelling breath waft over the side of her face. He was so close she imagined she felt spittle spray on her cheek as he spoke.   His hand slid down her arm and, as it reached her elbow, slid onto her waist.

'Don't worry. You can stay asleep if you want,' he told her, as he slipped into the bed behind her.

His hand slid down to her hip and she felt the hem of her nightdress slide up as he gathered the material with his fingers. She trembled at his touch. What was he doing, she thought?

Bak felt her thigh. He slid his hand down the length of her leg to her knee and then stroked back up again. She held her breath. She felt something hard in the small of her back. He moved up and down against her. She didn't know what to do. This felt wrong. Very wrong.

Still pretending sleep, she shrugged away from him and moved further away in the small bed. She was almost on the far edge. Another move and she would fall out.

'Don't make a sound. Papa will come and you'll be in trouble,' Bak told her, as he shifted close to her once again.

She wanted to shout. She wanted to tell him to get out, to leave her alone. She couldn't. She was frozen with fear. If she shouted, her father may come into their small bedroom. She would be in trouble. Big trouble. She wasn't sure what was happening but she knew it was wrong, and she knew, with all her heart, that whatever it was, it would be her fault. Men were never wrong.

She felt Bak push against her again. Shifting back and forth, up and down. His breathing was becoming louder. More rapid. The stink of the whiskey washed over her. His hand was between her legs. Feeling. Touching.

'It's alright. Just a few more minutes,' he whispered, into her ear.

She screwed her eyes tight. She could hear the shouts below. She heard the first slap as her father struck her mother across the face. She clung to the figure around her neck. The little Buddha smiled in her hand.

*****

It would be another year before Siswan did anything to stop her brother's attentions. Sometimes he would abuse her two or three times a week. Sometimes he wouldn't touch her for a fortnight. But, however long the periods in-between, he would always come back eventually. She lived in fear of him. Fear of what her mother and father would do to her if they ever found out about Bak.

'I'll tell Papa' was all he had to say if she tried to fight him off. If she tried to stop him. He just smiled. She would never tell.

Her father declined into an almost full time drunken stupor. He was always angry. Always shouting. Most nights, if he wasn't so drunk that he just collapsed, he would beat her mother. She could hear her cries. Hear the thuds of her father's fists.

Some nights, when the cries were at their loudest and the thuds could be felt through the thin wooden walls of the house, Bak would come to her bed and touch her. He told her he would take care of her, comfort her whilst their father ranted and their mother cried.

It wasn't the same as when they were young. He didn't comfort her as he had then. Now he just took, never gave. There was no comfort or warmth in his touch.

During the day, Bak treated her no better, and no worse, than he treated his mother or any other female in the village. He behaved with complete indifference. It was as though he saw nothing wrong in what he did. She was just there to clean, cook, work and give him pleasure when he wanted it.

Siswan didn't tell anyone what was happening. She saw no reason to ask for help.

Who could help? Perhaps this was normal? Perhaps all women lived the same way? She didn't know.

She worked hard and tried to take care of her mother as best she could. The woman was taking beatings from her father so often she could hardly work. Her face was swollen and her stomach a mass of blue and black bruises that never had a chance to fade away.

The rest of the villagers never spoke to her about her mother's plight. They could see and hear what was happening, but they never said a word. It was unfortunate, they said to each other. Maybe, in her next life, she would meet a kinder man, they said. Maybe, in her previous life, she had not had a good heart.

Her mother increasingly hid within herself. She spent her time bundling the small crops that Siswan harvested from their fields and withdrew more and more from the world around her. As time went on, and the fists continued to land, she would seldom cry out. Just accept the punishment as just and well deserved. She declined in health.

Bak had introduced Siswan to some of his friends and, on occasions, she would be made to give pleasure to them in the fields away from the village. The first time, when she had refused, Bak had beaten her so hard and so fast, she was stunned.

He had never beaten her before and, even though he threatened her often enough, she had only ever felt his hand hit her once before. This time it had been different. No longer a boy, he hit her hard again and again and again.

'You make me lose face, Siswan,' he had told her. 'You must not make me lose face.' And he punched her so hard in the stomach that she was sick in the field.

Bak stood over her, waiting. He still wasn't finished. Grabbing her by the hair, he pulled her head back and spat into her face. His saliva ran down her cheek.

'I told my friends you would be a good girl,' he shouted at her. 'You will do as I say. Mama and Papa can't help you now. Only me.'

She did as she was told. She pleasured his friends with her hands and her mouth and Bak left her alone. He no longer touched her or came to her bed in the night. He had passed her on.

'Don't let any of them enter you, Siswan,' he told her. 'You can do anything else for them but don't let them enter you.'

She hadn't understood exactly what he meant but as time went on, she learned. She learned a lot. It was very seldom when a day went by without her having to leave the field where she tended the sage, and walk into the cane with some boy or another. It became just another job. Another chore she had to perform.

Over the course of the next year her father lapsed into a continuous drunken stupor. He became bloated and indolent. He lost his job and sat around the home mumbling incoherently. Her mother washed him and tried to feed him but all he wanted was the whiskey. The foul smelling local brew that was slowly, but surely, killing him. Siswan's thirteenth birthday came and went without notice.

The only good thing that came from her father's increasing ill health was that he no longer had the strength, or inclination, to beat her mother. He became like a truculent child that needed constant attention. Too lazy even to use the hole in the ground that passed as a toilet.

The family became more and more reliant upon the money Bak earned. Siswan didn't know what he did, but without him they wouldn't be able to live. What he told her to do for his friends seemed a small price to pay in return.

Bak provided just about everything the family needed. The few coins Siswan earned from the allotment were pitiful in comparison. He paid the household bills and even bought the whiskey his father craved. When he turned up one afternoon on a brand new motorbike he seemed, for a moment anyway, like the brother she had known so many years ago.

'Where did you get it?' she asked him.

'From the garage in the town,' he replied, with a grin. 'It's the latest model. It even has an electric starter.'

'It must have been expensive,' she said.

Siswan was careful to keep the tone of her voice light. She didn't want to upset Bak. It was good to see him looking cheerful again.

'I bought it on credit,' he looked at her. 'It wasn't much.'

'Well, I'm pleased for you. Maybe you could take me for a ride?' she smiled.

'Maybe later,' he said. 'I'm going out with my friends tonight. Make sure you give Papa his whiskey.'

She did as she was told. Sometimes Bak would go out all night and she would help her mother take care of her father. Washing him was the worst.

'Where does Bak work, Mama?' she asked, as she rinsed the cloth they used to wipe away her father's waste.

'I don't know,' her mother replied, quietly.

Siswan looked at her mother closely. The woman was old. Older than her years. She never smiled and her eyes seemed far away. She no longer taught Siswan anything new and seemed reluctant even to talk to her. Without the beatings from her father her mother's previously swollen face had become loose. The skin sagged under her eyes and chin. She looked like a woman that had lost. Whatever it was that she had been fighting, had won.

'Are you alright, Mama?' Siswan asked her.

Her mother looked at her and, for a second, there was recognition in her eyes. A look that scared Siswan. A look of condemnation.

'Everyone knows what you do,' she spat the words at her daughter. 'Everyone!'

Siswan looked at her in shock. The words cut through her. Each one left a welt in her mind much worse than the swishing sticks on her skin. For a moment she didn't know what to do or say.

She felt stunned. What was it? What had she been doing that would make her mother speak so cruelly?

'What, Mama?' she cried.

'You are a whore, Siswan. A dirty whore!'

The sound of her mother's voice cut into her. What she did with the boys had made her into something bad. Something worse than all the foul names she had heard her father call her mother over the years.

It must be what she did in the cane fields. There was nothing else she had done that would make her mother speak to her in this way. Suddenly, she felt dirty. Sordid. Feelings that she had never experienced before, welled up inside her.

'I only do what Bak tells me to do,' she shouted back.

'What you do is wrong.'

Her mother was drifting away again. Her voice became tired and frail once more. Siswan wanted to shake her mother. She wanted her to stay with her. To talk to her. To tell her what she should do.

'Mama!' she cried.

The woman who was too old, too tired, turned back to dress her husband. The eyes withdrew, leaving Siswan alone once more.

'Oh, Mama,' she cried, quietly. 'Oh my poor Mama.'

It was all her fault. What she had allowed Bak to do, what she did to the boys, was wrong. She felt dirty. Alone. Scared. She had made her mother ill. Made her father ill. She didn't know what to do. The enormity of her understanding threatened to overpower her. She felt sick. Powerless to do anything. She cried into her hands.

*****

Once she had accepted her role in the life Bak had chosen for her, Siswan had learned to switch off her mind to what she did. It had been very easy after all. She had quickly learned what it was that they wanted and she had performed the tasks easily enough. The young men wouldn't take very long most of the time.

When they had finished most of them quickly pulled their trousers back up and walked away. On those occasions she would just go back to the fields and work. Sometimes the boys would want more. They would want to touch her, or even kiss her. She let them. It didn't matter to her what they wanted as long as they didn't enter her.

Once she had learned what it was that some of the boys wanted to do, especially the older ones, she had found it easy to convince them not to get carried away.

'I'm having a period,' she would tell them.

If that didn't work, she would struggle just enough to stop them from pushing into her and, after squirming away, would be able to control their passions with her mouth. Most of them seemed to prefer that anyway. She had been surprised at how quickly their passions had died once they had shuddered and trembled under her caress.

One or two had wanted to talk. Mostly afterwards. It seemed as though they wanted to offer some kind of explanation. A reason for having done what they had, up until a few minutes before, insisted upon. They acted like guilty young children trying to explain their reasons to an angry parent.

She hadn't understood why they needed to talk. Why they had wanted to explain. She just listened and smiled. She hadn't cared, or minded, that much. A smile, or a word or two in the right places, and they seemed satisfied until the next time. She had just accepted her life. Got on with it as best as she could.

Now it was different. Now she knew it was all wrong. Her mother's words had stung. Hurt her deep down. She couldn't walk through the village, or go to the temple to pray, without feeling eyes upon her. Without feeling the stares. Hearing the whispers. Everyone knows, her mother had told her. Everyone knows.

She took to looking at the ground directly in front of her. She averted her gaze whenever a neighbour glanced at her. She felt ashamed. Her whole demeanour changed and, as if in confirmation of the gossip, she walked with the heavy burden of guilt pressing on her shoulders. At thirteen years of age, Siswan walked through the village as a fallen woman. Her mother had called her a whore.

Bak noticed the change in his sister. He felt the change in her personality. The cheerful and happy little girl was gone. In her place stood a broken young woman. A woman who, he knew, would gladly watch him die. He didn't care. As long as the money kept coming in, he would never care.

'You have to work, Siswan,' he told her one evening. He had been drinking again. His words were slurred. He was sitting in his father's place at the head of the table under the house.

'I work in the fields,' she answered, not looking at him. She continued cutting the stems off the bunches of sage she had prepared. The small knife was sharp and she took care not to cut her fingers.

'That's not work,' he shouted. 'You earn nothing!'

'But with the money you earn,' she had started.

He reached across the table and slapped her hard across the side of her head.

'Don't be stupid,' he smiled. 'Where do you think I get the money to pay for everything?'

'I don't know,' she was holding the side of her face.

His hand had stung her. She felt the jolt of his blow run through the bones of her face. Her ear rang with pain. Her cheek felt as though it were glowing red under her hand.

'The boys pay, Siswan. They pay to do what they do to you,' his voice was cold.

He was enjoying this, she thought to herself. He was enjoying telling her. She couldn't believe what she was hearing. He didn't work. He did nothing.

The boys in the village had been giving him money! The household bills, the food, clothes, even the motorbike he took so much time cleaning, it all came from what she did in the fields. Everything. The small knife lay on the table beside her.

She looked at him. Saw the laughter in his eyes. Saw the grin spreading across his face. He found it funny. He was watching her. Laughing at her shock, her horror. He laughed aloud.

'And, my little sister, you have to keep doing it. Mama and Papa need us now. We have to take care of them,' he told her.

Their father lay upstairs in bed. Too ill even to come downstairs anymore. Their mother sat with him and was past caring. The last coherent words she had spoken were to condemn her daughter.

Bak was right. She had to take care of them. What else could she do? The tears began to fill her eyes. She wiped them away angrily. She wouldn't cry in front of him. Not again. Not ever. She clutched the handle of the knife.

'How much do they pay?'

The question caught him off guard. Bak had expected her to cry. Had expected the sobs. In a way he had been looking forward to them. He liked to see his sister cry. Something about a girl crying in front of him gave him a feeling of power. He was more like his father than he knew.

The question she asked was unexpected. He took another drink of whiskey before replying. She was looking at him. Her face was red from where he had hit her. He wanted to hit her again but he didn't want to spoil her looks.

'Why?' he asked.

She had caught the fleeting look in her brother's eyes. He had looked shocked for a moment. She fought down the urge to cry. Something inside her hardened. A cold tremor ran down her spine. Her mother had condemned her!

'I want to know,' she said, calmly.

'Not a lot. More later,' he answered.

'Why more later?'

'You have something that men will pay for, Siswan,' he sneered. 'They will pay a lot.'

'What?' her voice was cold. 'I want to know everything, Bak.'

'All in good time,' he said.

She looked at the arrogant young man sat cross legged in front of her. He was reaching for the whiskey bottle. There was a knowing smile on his face. He knew something that she didn't know and it annoyed her.

From somewhere deep inside her an anger grew. A slow and purposeful anger. Something that she had never felt before. She wouldn't allow it to explode into a sudden burst of temper. That would be a waste. She had to control this feeling. Control the anger. Use it. Her mother had condemned her!

'No,' she said. 'Now. I want to know now.'

He looked unsure. A hesitation as he poured more whiskey into his glass. A fleeting look of something. Worry? Fear? She didn't know.

As she watched him she remembered the young boy who had chased the fish in the pond. How she had laughed and how he had smiled in the sun. A young boy who had held her at night when their parents fought. A young boy who had been so scared of the scorpions in the field.

She didn't see that boy now. What she saw was her father. A spiteful, mean man whose only kindness had been to give her the silver chain and Buddha that still hung around her neck.

She concentrated on the fear she saw within him. A young boy who had been so afraid of scorpions. So afraid of their sting. She had learned to be quick when dealing with the scorpions. Her mother had condemned her!

'And what if I tell you? What will you do?'

Although the smug grin spread across his face once more, the uncertainty she heard in his voice was all she needed. She controlled the anger.

'You will tell me everything, Bak. Tell me what it is that men will pay for.'

He leaned forward across the table. His hand flat on the surface ready to reach out and hit her. She needed a lesson again. He smiled. He wouldn't ruin her looks. A small slap to startle her then he'd give her a beating she wouldn't soon forget. He'd leave her face alone but there were other places he could hurt her. The whiskey made him feel confident. Arrogant. He wanted to see her cry.

'You are so much like her,' he spat. 'No wonder Papa had to deal with her.'

As soon as she saw the tension build in his arm, she struck. Before his muscles had a chance to lift his hand, she moved. The anger was controlled. The speed of the knife a blur in the glow of the single light bulb. She knew exactly what she was doing. She had seen the look in his eyes. She had seen the young boy who was scared of the scorpions.

Long ago she had learned to deal with their venom. Now it was her with a sting. She didn't stop looking into his eyes as she brought the knife down. How dare her mother condemn her!

He screamed out in pain. The voice of a young boy. A scared boy. He stared in disbelief at his hand. The pain raced up his arm. Siswan had brought the knife down so hard and so fast that it went straight through his flesh and imbedded itself in the wood of the table.

Even as she had struck, his arm had been lifting to hit her. The sharp edge of the knife had ripped back towards the knuckles. Blood flowed dark and hot over the back of his hand.

He clutched at the handle with his other hand but couldn't bring himself to pull the blade free. The pain coursed through his body. The blood. So much of it!

Siswan looked into his face. Into his eyes. She saw the fear now. Not just a fleeting glance but outright fear. Wide and open. She had no right to condemn her. None.

'Tell me everything, Bak,' she said, when his sobs had subsided enough for her to be heard. 'Tell me everything.'

Three days later Siswan left the village. Bak had told her everything she needed to know. He had been saving her virginity to get the best price. He had told her how he was negotiating with three of the men in the village. One of them was the policeman she and her friends had been so scared of when they had played near his house.

In a way it had been good to learn. Some of the things he told her had horrified her but the most important piece of information had stuck in her mind. She had listened to everything.

'Women have power, Siswan,' he had said, through his tears. 'Men will pay anything for the right woman. Anything.'

She collected her few small belongings together. Parcelled them in one of the sheets from her bed. It wasn't a large bundle.

'Where are you going?' he asked her.

'Away,' she replied. 'Away from you. Away from this village.'

In truth she didn't know where she was going. Her need to leave was not brought about from fear or the looks from the other villagers. She didn't care about them. She didn't care about anyone anymore. She needed to leave to feel clean.

'But what about Mama and Papa!' Bak cried. 'What about me?'

She stopped folding her clothes onto the sheet and looked at him. The bloody bandage on his hand, the frightened look in his eyes, the open-mouthed look of disbelief.

The memories of what she had done to him, for him and because of him flooded into her mind. The nights she had endured his touch. The times spent in the cane fields. She despised him for what he had become.

'I don't care what happens to you, Bak,' she answered, coldly and truthfully.
She had removed his sting. He was nothing to be afraid of anymore. No venom.

She walked along the road that led away from her home. She walked with her head held up. Her shoulders were straight. Tears threatened the corners of her eyes, but she hardened her heart against them.

There was an air of confidence surrounding her. Her body was that of a woman and she knew far more than a young girl should know. She walked past the small dirt track that led to their allotment and the cane fields beyond. She wouldn't go there again. Not ever.

She had informed Ped that she was leaving and told her cousin to look after her mother.

'I'll send you money, Ped,' she said. 'But never give any to Bak. Never.'

Her cousin hugged her. Ped was the only person in the village that was sad to see her leave.

'I'll take care of them,' Ped told her. The young girl had heard all the gossip. All the stories. 'Where will you go?'

'I'll head to the town first,' Siswan answered.

The look of determination in her cousin's voice, the look in her eyes, stopped Ped from asking anymore.

'Remember, Ped. Nothing for Bak.'

'I'll remember,' Ped answered.

As she approached the pond at the edge of the village she stopped. This was a place filled with memories. Where she had played as a child. Where she and Bak had played. Even as she looked out across the still and stagnant water she thought she could hear his laughter. See him running through the mud to catch the fish he had thrown to the banks before they could wriggle their way back down the slippery slopes.

It felt as though she was remembering someone else's life. Not her own. She had never been there. Never laughed or smiled in the sunshine. Never splashed in the water with her brother. She closed her mind and shut off her thoughts.

She put down her small bundle of clothes and reached up to the clasp of her necklace. Taking it off she looked into the smiling face of the silver Buddha. Her twelfth birthday present. A birthday that she would remember for the rest of her life. A birthday that had marked an ending. And a beginning.

She balled the chain into her palm and, without further thought, threw the necklace far out into the pond. It hardly made a ripple as it sank beneath the muddy water.

Picking up her bundle of clothes, Siswan walked along the road. Away from the village. Away from her home. Away from the memories and away from her childhood.

She told herself that she would never again subject herself to the attentions of men. Never again would she allow them to touch her. Never again would she administer to their desires and passions.

'Never again,' she told herself, aloud.

Chapter 2

Mike sat on the stool at the end of the bar and looked along the line of regulars. They were the same faces. They came just about every night. He sipped his whiskey. It was the same brand he always drank. The topic of conversation was the same. The music coming from the stereo was the same bland music he always played. Nothing much changed. Always the same.

'What do you think, Mike?' A voice asked, bringing him out of his spell of reverie.

'What about?' He asked, trying to concentrate. Another few whiskies and he'd be okay.

'Have another drink, Mike.' laughed one of the others. 'You'll wake up eventually.'

The regulars all laughed before returning to their favourite discussion. Mike didn't need to wake up. He knew what they were discussing and didn't have to be focused to know that it was all bollocks, anyway. They'd never learn, none of them.

He'd been the same when he had first arrived. The land of smiles they called this corner of Asia. The land of smiles. That was a good one. It made Mike smile anyway. He'd discovered why they smiled. He reached for another whiskey.

Twelve years he'd been here. Twelve years of drinking and sitting in this bar. He knew he drank too much. Smoked too much. He didn't much care anymore.

He had spent the first few years trying to understand the locals. Trying to get to know their ways and their language. He had tried really hard. It wasn't until he gave up that he started to find out more about them.

The conversation was beginning to get heated. It always did. Everyone had their own opinion and were certain it was right. It wasn't. They were never right. He lit a cigarette.

The only thing that concerned Mike these days was how much his customers spent. Nothing else mattered. He needed them to pay the rent. The electricity. The stock. That was all. Just buy enough to keep me going, he thought to himself. He didn't need anything else. The room upstairs was good enough to sleep.

'But that's not it at all!' A voice shouted.

Mike concentrated long enough to recognize Barry. Barry always started shouting first. He was a big man with a big voice. Mike didn't mind him. Barry drank well.

'So what is it then, Barry?' Tim put in.

Tim was okay too. Once he'd had his fill of beer he'd move on to the whiskey. That was where the profit was, Mike thought to himself. Drink the bloody whiskey.

'What you have to remember is where these girls come from.' Barry stated.

Mike looked at Barry. The big man was getting onto his soap box again. He loved to voice his opinion. Don't talk so much, he thought, just drink.

'They come from a poor village, most of the time. They can hardly read, let alone write, they can't speak our language and all they know about is sex.' Barry was well on his way. 'It's the only way they can make money.'

'Yes. But that's not what we're saying, is it?' Tim stated. 'We were asking if they can love. Really love.'

'No,' Barry shouted. 'That's my point. They can't love. They think sex is love. They don't have any feelings. No emotions.'

Mike left them to it. As long as they were drinking he couldn't care less what the conversation was about. He'd heard it all before, anyway. Always the same.

He turned to look at the girls sat outside the open front entrance. All of them looked young. Not all of them were. All of them dressed in their sexiest outfits. They all looked the same to him now. The only time they smiled was when new blood walked by.

The land of smiles. That was a good joke that was. More like the land of guiles. It wasn't the first time he'd cracked the same joke to himself. It wasn't funny anymore.

One of the girls looked at him. Tam was her name. She was the eldest and therefore, by default, the leader of the group of five. She was the one he always had to deal with. The others barely spoke to him. She was a real pain in the ass. Always wanting more money. It was the only thing the girls wanted. Money spoke. Nothing else.

He smiled and nodded his head towards her. She replied with a look of disdain and turned back to the girls saying something or other. They all giggled and chattered away in their own language.

Mike didn't care what they were talking about. He'd never know anyway. He'd learned to speak the language when he first arrived. What a waste of time that had been! Whenever he spoke in the local tongue they just lapsed into a different dialect. They never spoke the proper language in front of him.

To understand them was impossible. There were about five different versions of their language and the girls could mix them all up to form new versions. Bar-girl speak, he called it. He'd given up trying and only spoke English now.

He turned back to the bar. At least they were working. Half the time they didn't bother to turn up. No reason given. Just didn't come to work. He'd given up asking why.

Tam had seen the look Mike had given her. The one just before he smiled. It was a look of distaste. She'd seen it before on the faces of the farangs who stayed too long. She turned away.

'Old fool,' she said, to the other girls.

They laughed at her nerve and chattered away amongst themselves. They were young and knew nothing. She was their leader. They did what she said.

None of the farangs were any better than Mike. Drunk fools who tried to understand the life of a bar girl. How could they understand? The big farang, Barry, was off again. Loud mouthed and vulgar. They were all the same.

Tam was fed up. She'd been working this bar for three years now and had reached the limit of her boredom threshold. It was better to move on after a few years. The regulars got fed up with the same woman and the money reduced as much as their interest. She had slept with all of them. Big Barry wasn't, that was for sure.

Two young farangs were walking towards the bar with their eyes bulging. Their white skin betrayed the fact that they were new to the country.

'Hello. Welcome.' The girls called in English.

They all spoke English to the farangs. Everyone spoke English. It didn't matter where the farangs came from. Tam had even learned enough to understand the conversation at the bar behind her, but she wouldn't tell Mike that.

In fact, most of the girls could speak a little English. They learned very quickly. Big Barry was wrong about that, but then, Big Barry was wrong about most things.

They could love alright. Tam herself had once loved a man so much it hurt her to think about him. Yes, they could love. They just didn't want to love a fat old drunk farang that shouted too much. What was the matter with these stupid farangs anyway? It was easy to understand the girls. Really easy. Just give us all your money and piss off back to your own country. Simple.

The two young farangs didn't stop. The girls tried everything, but they just laughed, smiled and walked on. There were too many bars, too many girls. Young farangs, especially good-looking young farangs, could always get a good deal. And the best looking girls.

Mike would be disappointed not to get another few customers into the bar, but who cared? She wouldn't stay there much longer. The old man didn't pay enough, that was the problem. She'd only ever come here for the money. In the early days she'd earned a small fortune compared to what she could earn at home.

After her boyfriend had left her alone with their baby, she had tried hard to get decent work. She was the eldest of three siblings and it was down to her to pay for the life her parents had given her. As the eldest, it fell upon her to take care of her parents, her brother and sister and, of course, her own baby. There had been only one way to earn that kind of money, and it wasn't from working in the local market.

Eight years, and three bars later, she had sent enough money home for the family to live a good life. The problem was that, as good as their lives became, they always wanted more. The new clothes would wear out. The motorbikes would need replacing. The house needed constant work. It never stopped. She could never stop. She had put her brother and sister through good schools. Paid every bill. Her son was doing well even though she seldom saw him. Yes, they all had good lives. Paid for by her.

Tam looked to the future and saw nothing. Only today. Think only about today. Maybe her luck would get better. Maybe it wouldn't. She'd make an offering at the shrine. Maybe the spirits would look upon her favorably.

Another farang walked towards them. Old. Alone. She could deal with him. She moved forward. She smiled.

'Hello. Where you from?' she asked, taking his arm and leading him towards the other drunks.

Mike smoked another cigarette. Drank another whiskey. He drank more profit than he made. Already his small army pension was subsidizing the rent. He wouldn't be able to keep going much longer. The girls screwed him whenever they could. Tam was a real bitch. She had forced him into paying the girls more than the other bars and, over the years, she had replaced the old girls with her friends. He already paid for their accommodation and she forced him into paying them a more than fair wage.

The problem was that if he didn't have any girls he wouldn't have any customers. It was as simple as that. No money, no honey was the local saying. For the bar owners it worked the other way as well. No honey, no money. No girls, no customers.

When he'd first bought the bar he'd enjoyed the wheeling and dealing. He'd enjoyed the challenge of building up a business in this hot and humid country. He'd worked hard and fallen for the smiles. For a while it had all been good. The girls were friendly enough, worked well with the tourists, and gave them what they wanted. The bar had earned good money just from the bar fines.

After a few years however, the girls became wise. And greedy. It wasn't just the girls either. The local police had asked for more protection money each month. He was paying three times what he had paid in the beginning. Three times as much money. About a third of the protection.

In the last year he had needed their response three times. Tourists who had drunk too much. Fighting had broken out. Three separate occasions he had called them. Once, they had turned up, and that was two hours late. They told him he'd have to pay the driver for his 'fast response'. He didn't bother calling them anymore. Now, when a fight broke out, he just left it up to the girls to sort out. Tam was good with an empty beer bottle. She seldom missed. The only time he saw the police these days was when they called for their monthly handout. All the bars had to pay them. One or two had tried to get away without paying, but they hadn't lasted long. First the girls had left. Then the local men had turned up. Drinking as much as they could without bothering to pay. There was nothing the farang owners could do. Who could they call? All the time they drank, the young men smiled. Even the police smiled as they took his money. The land of smiles. Oh yes, they all smiled.

Still, tonight wasn't looking too bad. Tam had brought in another lamb to the slaughter. She laughed and flirted with him. When she put on her act she was quite good. A bit old in the tooth now, but sill pretty good. The poor bastard had already been talked into ringing the bell twice. A short for everyone, including the girls. Another few like him and he would make a profit.

Tam would keep the farang in the bar as long as she could. Every drink he bought her, every time he rang the bell, she got a percentage. When he was too drunk to care, she'd whisper in his ear that she wanted him. Wanted him so bad. He'd pay the bar fine and she'd get a percentage of that as well. All the girls worked that way. Fleece the farangs. Get their money.

Mike sometimes wished he'd been born a woman. When he thought of how hard he had to work to get what these girls could make in a single night, it made him jealous. Not only did he pay them, not only did they get their rooms free, not only did they get a percentage of the drinks and the bar fines, they also got paid directly by the farang for whatever service they were prepared to offer.

He knew he was being unfair. He knew it wasn't that simple. The girls didn't like what they did. It was just another way to earn money. Money that they probably had to send home anyway. He knew they didn't keep much for themselves. Sometimes their boyfriends took what they earned. Occasionally, husbands.

There weren't too many married women working the bars, but he knew one or two. Their husbands were right bastards. He'd never understand the local mentality. Never. Not now, anyway. He'd given up trying.

The evening wore on. A few more new tourists were encouraged to have a beer or two by the remaining girls. Tam left with the now very drunk old farang she had brought in. She had stopped just long enough to collect her drink and fine earnings from the cashier. The smile had disappeared as she counted the notes. She hadn't said goodnight to Mike. Just walked out with her two-legged, portable, ATM machine.

Two a.m. rolled around and the bar closed. Mike couldn't afford to pay the extra money the police demanded to allow him to stay open past closing time. Anyway, the girls had gone. Off to the nearest club, he guessed. That was where they went when they hadn't picked up a farang they liked in the bar.

The regulars finished their drinks, paid their bills and wandered off into the night. There were bars that stayed open. They could find more places to drink.

The cashier, a nice little girl called Pan, tallied up the evenings takings. Not a lot after all. Never mind, there was always tomorrow. He nodded to Pan as she left. She didn't say goodnight either, but at least she gave him a smile. Out of pity, he suspected.

That was what the farangs didn't understand. The smiles weren't just smiles. They were used as communication. Of course they smiled to express happiness. Who didn't? But they also smiled to acknowledge inferior persons. The wai, the formal greeting, was only used for people with an equal or greater standing in life. The smile was used for children and lesser human beings. Like farangs. The locals thought it extremely funny. The farangs just didn't get the joke.

Mike sat at the bar and lit another cigarette. He couldn't remember the last time anyone had given him a wai. Why should they? He only deserved a smile. He'd close and lock the sliding steel doors in a minute. Another cigarette first. Maybe another whiskey as well. He looked around the bar.

Once it had been his pride and joy. He had built it up and made it into a good business. All the locals had worked well for him in those days. He'd had money to spend. He paid for their services. Plumbers, electricians, builders. Everyone. When he'd first opened, all the girls came running. Good lookers as well. They knew that a new bar attracted more customers. And it was in a good position. Right on the corner of the beach road and the main entertainment centre. Where the lady boys strutted their stuff.

He'd had a lady boy working in his bar for a while. That had been a few years back. What a disaster that had been. She, he, whatever, had been worse than the girls. Never stopped complaining. It had been so difficult to get rid of her, him, as well. In the end Mike had to pay a friend of his, who owned one of the really big clubs, to offer her, him, whatever, a job. Cost the bar a lot of money that little experience did.

He gazed around the bar through bleary eyes. A right mess now. All the furnishings were old. Half the lights didn't work. Only two out of the five urinals still flushed. He didn't know the state of the female toilets. Never went in there. Never mind, all in the past now. Tomorrow was another day. He knew there wouldn't be too many more tomorrows and hoped he'd be able to raise enough money for a flight back to England. The trouble was that there was nothing for him there, either.

Thirty five years in the army. Joined at eighteen. Man and boy. It gave him his pension. Nothing more. Even that was being taxed. Sixty five years old and nothing to show for his life other than a run down bar and a chesty cough. Too many cigarettes.

He lit another. One more before closing the bar. He'd have to clean the place up in the morning. He always did. Couldn't afford a cleaner any more. Another whiskey and then off to bed.

The small upstairs room wasn't perfect. It wasn't even good. In fact it was bloody horrible. No air conditioning. Not even a real bed. Just a mattress on the floor. It would do though. All he needed to do was sleep. He didn't need to entertain these days. Couldn't afford it. He smiled to himself. He gulped the last of his whiskey, poured another to take to bed, and turned away from the bar to head for the doors. When he looked up he saw her.

She was just standing in the doorway looking around the bar. Her eyes skirted over him quickly. They didn't need to linger. He looked like every other tired old farang.

He walked a few paces toward her, meaning to say 'hello', but stopped before he got too far. There was something about her. Something about the way she stood. She had the same long, black and straight hair the other girls had. She wore a pair of denim jeans and a white t-shirt. Same as a lot of the other girls. Her skin was lighter. A shade of light coffee or maybe honey. Her eyes were dark brown. Nothing strange about that. All the girls had dark brown eyes. There was something else. Mike concentrated. Maybe he'd drunk too many whiskies. The girl didn't say anything. She just carried on looking. As though she were summing up. Thinking. Planning in her mind.

Mike continued to look at her. She didn't seem to mind. She was beautiful that was for sure. Very beautiful. Even his old bones could see that. Long legs, slim waist, great looking breasts. She was stunning. But that wasn't it. There was something about her. An air of confidence. A maturity beyond her years. Mind you, he didn't have a clue how old she was. She looked about twenty-two, maybe a little older. He couldn't be sure. Then it hit him. He suddenly saw what was different about her.

He took another couple of steps. She was similar to all the other girls. Dressed the way they dressed. Same eyes. Same hair. Everything the same except for one big difference. This was no girl. When Mike looked at her what he saw was a woman. A woman with a mind of her own.

As he approached she looked at him again. Straight into his eyes. No shyness. No coyness. No smile. She looked deep into his eyes. Assessing the man she saw walking toward her. He hesitated. Unsure. He'd seen it all. Knew it all. But he'd never seen anyone like this woman before. She was so confident. So sure of herself. He stopped again.

She blinked and, as her eyes flicked open, she smiled. She had decided. The smile was honest and open. She wasn't laughing. Not at him. She was smiling. The first genuine smile he had seen for a long, long time.

'Hello,' she said, in perfect English. 'You must be Mike.'

She didn't offer her hand, just stood there, looking at him. The smile had broken his spell. Now she looked like any other girl. Beautiful, yes, but not unlike any of the other girls he had seen. She looked younger when she smiled. Twenty, maybe even nineteen.

'Er, yes. I'm Mike.' He stammered. The first time in his life he had ever stammered. He coughed into his fist. 'Can I help you? We're closed I'm afraid.'

'Yes. You can't pay the police,' she said. 'We need to talk, Mike.'

*****

Mike had closed the main doors and was back sitting at the bar listening. The woman sat beside him had introduced herself as Siswan and she had a proposition for him. Mike hadn't lit a cigarette for almost twenty minutes. He didn't think she'd like that. He hadn't touched the whiskey in front of him either. He didn't know why, but her voice, and what she was saying, had him hooked.

'So, that's what I have in mind, Mike. What do you think?' she finished.

'Why me? Why this bar?' he asked.

'It's in a good position,' she told him.

'Yes, but why me? You could take this place over in a few weeks. I know how it works.'

'That's true, Mike. I could. But to do that I would have to involve local help.'

'And?'

'I don't want to work with the locals.'

'Why not?'

'Mike, what do you need from life? A better room? Another pack of cigarettes? A bottle of whiskey?' She looked at him. 'You don't need anything more.'

'Well, I don't know about that. I'm not dead yet, you know,' he answered. My god, she knows more about me than I know about myself, he thought. He couldn't think of anything else he needed from life. 'Maybe I'd like some new clothes.' It was the only thing he could come up with. She had him mesmerized.

'Yes, well, that's not a bad idea,' she laughed, as she looked at his worn t-shirt and shorts. 'The thing is, Mike, is that you don't need, or want, very much. If I enlist the help of locals they'll try to take everything. They want the money, you see?'

She had other reasons for not working with her own people, but she wasn't about to explain all that to Mike. He seemed an amiable enough guy. She would be able to get along with him. It wouldn't be for too long.

'How do I know that you won't just rip me off anyway?' he asked.

'Mike. Be realistic. What on earth do you have to lose?' She looked into his eyes again.

This woman was offering him hope. A little hope in the land of guiles. He didn't have anything to lose. Another few weeks and it would all be over anyway.

'I've already got girls working here.' He told her.

'No, Mike. You don't. You have five girls who sit on their backsides. One of them, Tam, is fleecing you for as much as she can get before she moves on. You have four others who sometimes don't even bother to turn up. You have a cashier, called Pan, who is dipping the till for thirty percent of everything you take and you can't afford a cleaner. You don't have anyone actually working.' She wasn't smiling.

Pan? Dipping the till? He thought she was a nice girl. A girl who didn't want to go with farangs and so struggled on her monthly wage. Christ. Thirty percent?

'On top of all that, Mike, you pay too much as a monthly wage, give away fifty percent of lady drinks and bar fines and pay twice as much for the girls' accommodation as you need to,' Siswan informed him.

'But, I thought we agreed ten percent? The rooms are hard to get. I don't know.' He tailed off. He knew they were fleecing him. He just hadn't realized by how much.

'Yes, Mike. You don't watch anymore. You just sit and drink the last of the profits. You trust the smiles. You know so much and yet you still fall for the smiles,' she said.

'What can I do?' He looked as though the final plank had fallen from the bottom of his world. He was hanging in mid air.

'You agree to my proposal. You trust me,' she said, throwing him the only line he'd ever get the chance to grab.

'Okay. As you said, what have I got to lose?' Fifty percent of something was a lot better than all of sod all.

'Nothing, Mike, but everything to gain.' She held out her hand.

He looked into her face. She wasn't smiling. She was stunningly beautiful. He'd never met anyone like her before. If only he'd been thirty years younger. He took her hand. Shook it. She had a good grip. There was a scar on her arm. It ran from her wrist almost to the underside of her elbow. It looked angry. He wondered how she'd got it.

'Thanks, Mike,' she said, letting his hand go. 'One last thing.'

'Yes?' he said. He was in a bit of a daze.

'If you ever so much as put a finger on me without my permission I'll cut it off. Okay?'

He started to smile but, as he looked into her eyes, stopped. She meant it. He didn't doubt for one second that she meant it. Maybe he'd got it wrong. Maybe she was a lot older than he thought. He didn't know.

'And I'll need a key for the doors,' she added.

'Uh, yes. Okay,' he said, and passed her the key from his pocket. He had another upstairs. Somewhere.

'Well, that's that settled then.' She stood. 'I'll see you tomorrow evening at six. Goodnight, Mike.'

'Just one other thing, er, Miss Siswan.'

'Just Siswan will do, Mike.'

'Er, right. Just one thing. You are old enough to work in a bar, aren't you?'
Mike was having his doubts about his estimates. This woman was confident, sure of herself and clever, but he couldn't help wondering. There was something weird going on.

She opened her purse, took out her ID card and gave it to him.

'Ah, okay. Twenty one. Yes, I thought so. Had to be sure, you know,' he said, looking at the date of birth on her card.

'Don't be stupid, Mike,' she said, taking the card back and putting it into her purse again. 'It's a fake.'

He just looked. Oh my god, he thought, what the hell am I getting into?

'Don't worry. It's a very good fake.' She smiled. A genuine smile. 'Goodnight,' she said again, and left the bar.

He heard her locking the doors with the key he'd given her.

Mike just sat there. He didn't reach for the whiskey. He didn't light a cigarette. He just sat there. What the hell had just happened, he asked himself? He didn't know what the girls were going to say. He didn't know what the regulars would say. Bloody hell, he didn't know what to say himself! He just sat there looking around at the old bar.

If she was as good as her word, and he didn't think for a moment that she wouldn't be, this place was going to see a few changes, that was for sure. He could hear the bass from the nightclub a few doors up. They were doing good business. They could afford to pay the cops. He wondered to himself. Maybe, just maybe, in a few months, he'd be able to afford to pay them as well. He smiled to himself. The land of smiles, eh? At least when Siswan had smiled he hadn't seen the guile. Maybe she was telling the truth?

Ah, well, better get the old body up the stairs. Another day tomorrow. A hell of a day by the sound of it. He climbed off the barstool. He'd seen it all. Heard it all. A smile in the land of guiles.

'Well, bugger me,' he laughed to himself. He just realized that she'd actually said 'goodnight' to him. He walked to the stairs leading to his squalid room. The untouched glass of whiskey sat on the bar.

*****

Tam eventually turned up at ten the following night. The farang from the night before had had more strength than she had guessed, and it had been almost six in the morning by the time she got to sleep.

Must have been on Viagra, she thought. She hated whoever had invented the drug. Kept them going all night. Still, she'd made quite a bit from him and, if he wasn't too tired, he said he would be back for more tonight. In a way she hoped the old fool wouldn't come again. She was too tired to go through another night like that. Still, the money was good. She could always pick up some lubricating jelly from the local store.
The other girls sat outside in their normal places. Well, three of them were. Looked like Jom was going to be late. If she turned up at all.

'Where's Jom?' she asked.

'She's got a farang. From the club last night,' one of them told her.

Oh, well. Good for her. They all had more of a chance at picking up farangs at the club than they did in this dump. The bar was old, needed a facelift. Never got any new customers. If it wasn't for her, the place would have been closed down months ago.

She didn't care anymore. She wouldn't be staying too much longer. Another bar had just opened in the next street. A friend of hers was going to get one of the other girls into some kind of trouble and then get Tam in to take her place. Probably tell the farang owner that the girl had been stealing. It was easy. All the girls made places for their friends. That reminded her to get her cut from Pan. The little bitch was holding out on her.

Couldn't do anything like that in the locally owned bars though. The owners knew every trick in the book and weren't soft when it came to dealing with the girls. She had a friend who had been cut so badly she'd never be able to work again. Not with farangs anyway. The locals would still pay. A pittance mind, but it was better than nothing.

Tam looked around the bar. Mike was sat in his usual place. A few of the regulars were there. Who was that? A new girl. Sat on the stool next to Mike. Who the bloody hell was she? No new girl could just walk in without going through her. She turned back to the three bored girls sat in their chairs.

'Who's that?' she asked, pointing toward the bar.

'Don't know. She was there when we arrived.'

Tam looked back at the bar. The girl was talking, laughing. With a small shake of her head her hair shimmered in the lights of the bar. The stupid farangs were all gazing at her. Open mouthed half of them. Big Barry wasn't even talking. What the hell was going on, she thought to herself? The bloody farangs were all spellbound.

Mike sat in his normal place and watched the faces of his regulars. He couldn't believe what was happening. Siswan spoke to them all in perfect English. Within a few seconds she had learned all their names and used them when she spoke. It made it more personal, more intimate, somehow. She gave each one her attention and looked them in the eyes. She smiled. Open, warm-hearted smiles, that drew all of them in. Even Big Barry. The man hadn't said a word for the last hour.

'So, Tim, what do you do over here?' Siswan asked.

'Oh, I just came here to meet a girl like you, darling.' Tim smiled.

Forever the smoothie, our Tim, Mike thought. How would she deal with him?

'Oh, that's a lovely thing to say, Tim. Thank you so much,' Siswan answered, looking the old lech in the eye.

Mike couldn't believe it. Tim blushed. The old trout actually blushed. My god, this woman had something. Something every man would want.

He was really enjoying himself. He hadn't had a drop of whiskey and, every time he wanted a cigarette, he excused himself and went outside to smoke it. He hadn't had many of those, to tell the truth. He didn't want to miss Siswan in action. She was wonderful. Every time she took a sip from her glass the regulars drank from theirs. Every time she finished her drink someone would order another round. And that wasn't all either.

Pan, who he was so disappointed with, sat there with a red-faced scowl and was obviously in a bad mood. Siswan had spoken quietly to her when she'd arrived and, every time a drink was ordered, Siswan took the bar chit and checked it against the duplicate. No fudging the figures anymore. Not for Pan, anyway. And it wasn't that Siswan made a big deal out of it either. She just smiled, held out her hand, a quick glance, another smile, back to the regulars. They didn't even notice.

Now she was finishing her drink. She didn't drink fast. Not so fast that anything became too obvious. She just took a sip every now and then. Between speaking. Between smiles. She made it look so natural. But it wasn't.

The regulars had already spent twice as much as they normally would, and, this was the good bit, none of them minded. They all knew they were spending more, they just didn't care. She was leading them all by the nose and they knew it. They all actually knew what was happening and it didn't matter.

She entertained them. She didn't fleece them. Oh, yes she was taking their money, no problem there. She was making them spend like they never had before. What was so good, so incredible, was that they didn't mind. Not in the least. She was even telling them.

'Oh, gentleman. I feel terrible,' she said. 'Here I am wittering on about nothing and you are all buying me drinks. It must be my turn to buy a round?'

'No. Not at all. My turn.' Big Barry spoke up. 'Haven't enjoyed myself this much in years.' He added, downing his whiskey and ordering a round for everyone.

The other thing Siswan had done when she had first arrived that evening was to make Mike take down the bell.

'No free drinks, Mike,' she had told him. 'If the girls can't earn their own, they go without.'

He hadn't argued. What was the point. It hadn't been working his way for years. He had to trust her.

'Another thing,' she said, as he climbed down from the bar. 'No matter what I order, no matter who orders for me, I only ever drink orange juice. I only ever use the same glass and never let anyone else open the carton. Only you or me. Okay?'

'Oh, yes. Sure thing. Er, why Siswan?' he asked her.

'Mike, you are going to have to think for yourself, you know,' she had admonished him. 'I don't want my drinks spiked. Surely you've heard of that?'

'Oh, yes, right. That won't happen. The regulars are good guys. Good enough, anyway.'

'Not the customers, Mike. The girls.'

Mike didn't fully understand. He thought the girls all stuck together. After seeing Pan's face however, he knew that wasn't going to be the case anymore.

He brought himself back to the present. Big Barry was telling everyone a story from his childhood. It wasn't that funny but everyone laughed when Siswan did.

'Barry. You and I need to talk more. Under that big chest of yours I believe there beats a heart of gold.' She smiled at the big man.

Mike saw her take a quick glance around the bar. She swiveled on her stool to look at the entrance.

'Ah, excuse me please? There's someone who I need to have a quick word with. I won't be long. Have a drink on me whilst I'm gone.' She smiled and slid off the stool.

'Wouldn't hear of it,' Tim called out. 'Another round, young Pan. My tab.'

Mike just couldn't believe it. Mind you, he thought, there's going to be trouble now. He watched as Siswan moved across the floor to where Tam stood, waiting.

Tam looked at the girl coming toward her. Twenty? Maybe twenty-one? She wasn't too sure. Difficult to tell with some of these new girls.

Probably only eighteen. Done up like a tart. Except that this one wasn't.

She didn't wear any makeup at all as far as Tam could tell. Didn't wear the same clothes either. Black, tailored trousers, white, short sleeved blouse. Nothing fancy. Nothing flash. Looked good. Who the bloody hell was she? Didn't matter who she was though. She wasn't going to have just any girl off the street walking into her bar without so much as a wai.

'Hello, Tam.' Siswan gave her the formal greeting. Hands raised as if in prayer. A slight bow of the head. A wai.

Tam didn't offer one back. She began to smile. The normal response to a lesser person. She didn't get very far though. The girl spoke again.

'I wai to you as an equal, Tam,' she said. 'If you smile back at me, I'll cut your cheeks open to your ears and you'll smile for evermore.'

Tam's mouth opened as though to speak. She looked at the girl whose eyes flicked down momentarily. Tam looked down. Saw the small blade she held in her hand. Out of sight of the men at the bar. A wicked looking blade. Evil. She looked back up in shock. Where the hell had that come from? The girl didn't smile. She didn't move a muscle.

'Who are you?' Tam managed to say.

'I'm the person who is replacing you.' Siswan told her.

The other girls were watching. They expected Tam to do something. They hadn't seen the knife either. Couldn't clearly make out what was being said. Any second now, they thought. Tam was bound to slap her. Tam was a good fighter, that's why they all did as she said.

'But you can't just expect me to walk out,' Tam said.

If she just turned away now she would lose face in front of the other girls. She wouldn't be able to command any respect in the future. She'd have to move away. Another town. She wasn't going to take this girl on though. She could tell when someone meant what they were saying. She didn't fancy her chances. Not one little bit. She only ever fought when she knew she would win. What could she do?

As though reading her thoughts, Siswan turned her arm slightly. The one holding the knife. Tam could clearly see the scar running most of the way up her forearm.

'Please. I can't just walk.'

She looked up into a face that showed nothing. No emotion. Siswan just looked at her.

'Yes, you can. You wai to me now. Turn around. Walk out and don't come back,' she said, with a voice like ice.

The three girls, sat on their chairs, couldn't believe their eyes. Tam gave a low wai, turned, and walked past them without saying a word. She was finished. There would be no other bars, not in this town. Not as a leader. Within hours, every girl in every bar would know what had happened.

They looked at one another and then looked up. The new girl was walking toward them. She was smiling. Smiling at the inferior girls.

Chapter 3

Siswan checked out the girls as she walked towards them. They were all half turned in their chairs. Two wearing black mini-skirts. One in shorts. Low cut tops. Too much makeup. Normal bar girls all looking at her. Looks of shock. Mouths slightly open. A worried look in their eyes. Good, she thought, they should be worried.

'Hello girls,' she said and smiled at them. 'Mind if I join you?'

One of them, Apple, stood and gave her a wai. She didn't wai back. The other two, Tak and Lon, remained seated and just looked.

'No. Better idea. You join me,' Siswan said. Without waiting for a reply, she turned and walked back past the bar to the far end of the room.

'Won't be long,' she smiled at the men sat at the bar. 'Just having a very quick meeting.' It was a genuine smile.

'No problem, Siswan. I'll keep them entertained,' Mike laughed.

The regulars groaned in good humour. Mike was going to be a good partner, she thought. He still had enough common sense. He may even have some enthusiasm left. She smiled again.

'Oh, gentlemen. I am so sorry!'

They all laughed. Mike laughed with them. He had a sense of humour as well.

When she reached the far end of the room she sat down on one of the chairs. It was a gloomy spot. Half the electric lights had failed. Just as well, she thought, makes the dirt harder to see. No one came this far into the bar any more.

The girls slowly followed and sat down in the chairs near her. Tak and Lon still acted sullen. Apple was the only one who seemed the least bit interested in what was happening.

'Anyone want to leave?' Siswan asked, politely enough.

None of the girls moved. Tak and Lon knew enough to wait until all the cards were on the table. They'd seen takeovers before. Apple was just interested. She would be the easy one to convert.

Siswan took a coin out of her pocket. She put in on the table in front of the girls. They all looked at it.

'If I had ten of these and I gave you fifty percent, how many would you have?' she asked.

'Five,' Apple replied quickly.

'And if I had a hundred and gave you ten percent, how many would you have?'

'Ten.' Apple was the quickest again.

'So, is ten percent of a hundred better than fifty percent of ten?'

'Er, yes. That's obvious,' Lon replied this time.

'How much did you send home last month?' Siswan asked her.

'Six thousand,' Lon said.

'And were your family pleased?'

'No. They never are.'

'Would they be pleased if you sent them ten thousand?'

'I doubt it,' Lon answered.

'Then don't,' Siswan said.

The three girls looked at her incredulously. If they earned ten thousand they'd have to send it home. That was why they were here.

'If they aren't going to be happy with ten thousand, only send them the six they are used to. Keep the rest for yourselves,' Siswan said.

'What rest?' Tak said. 'I only sent five. That was all I earned.'

'Soon you are going to be earning a lot more,' Siswan told them. 'If you are prepared to work hard.'

'But why should we believe you?' Lon asked. 'I mean, if we earn good money, you'll want some of it. Tam always did.'

Siswan looked the young girl in the eyes. Nineteen, she guessed. Hardly any education. Sent to earn money for the family. A family that was too bloody lazy to take care of itself. A pretty girl as well.

'Lon, I have no interest in what you earn. I won't take anything from you if you work hard,' she told her.

Lon looked at her. All three of them looked at her. She wasn't smiling. She looked as though she meant it. Meant every word.

'Okay. Suppose we do what you want. How much can we earn?' Tak asked.

'Oh, in a good month, I'll be expecting you to earn twenty, maybe twenty five thousand,' Siswan replied.

'And what do we have to do?' Apple was interested. In fact, she was very interested! She'd only earned three thousand last month and her boyfriend had taken that.

'Right now you go home. All of you go home. Get a good night's rest and meet me back here at nine tomorrow morning,' Siswan said.

'What? Just go home?' Lon asked.

'Yes,' Siswan told her.

Out of the three, Apple was going to be the easiest. Tak and Lon might make it. If they didn't rebel. If Tam's way of doing things hadn't corrupted them too much. Siswan waited for them to understand.

'We just go?' Tak said.

'Yes. Go home,' Siswan told them. 'And I do mean go home. If you go off to another bar, or club, I'll know. I'm giving you a night off. Sleep. Believe me you are going to need the rest.'

'Okay,' Apple smiled and stood. She could do with a good night's sleep. She wasn't going to argue.

The other two followed her example. Their faces betrayed the fact that they thought the idea ridiculous. Tak gave Lon a knowing look. The club down the road would just be getting busy.

'One other thing girls,' Siswan stood as well. She was a good two inches taller than any of them. 'You will always wai to me. I will never tell you again.'

The three girls were caught off guard. Apple was the first to offer the formal farewell. Tak and Lon followed quickly after. The look in Siswan's eyes told them they'd better.

'Mike is your boss. He deserves kindness and respect from you. You will always show him both,' Siswan said.

The three girls looked at her again. They had never offered Mike anything other than contempt. Tam had told them he was just a farang fool that deserved nothing more than to be fleeced.

'You all have a lot to learn.' Siswan told them. 'Tak, I saw the look you gave to Lon. You all think you are clever but you're not. You are just stupid peasant girls who never think about tomorrow. Apple, you are no better. You let a lazy man take all your money even though he is having sex with someone else. Now, you can all believe me, or you can think I'm lying, but I tell you this, if you cross me, if you make me lose face, I'll make sure you never work with farang again.'

Siswan had spoken quietly, calmly. She hadn't raised her voice much above a whisper. She looked slowly across the faces of the three girls stood in front of her. She had their attention now. Their full, undivided, attention.

'I gave you your chance to leave. You decided to stay. Show your respect. Always,' She told them. 'If Jom wants her job make sure she's with you tomorrow morning.'

Mike hadn't understood a word of what was said at the far end of the bar. He reckoned Siswan had been laying down some ground rules. Couldn't be sure. It was all bar-girl speak. Anyway, it looked like it was over now. The girls were all standing. He hoped they'd get back to work. The regulars were drinking like fish, but it would still be good to get some fresh blood in.

The conversation at the bar had picked up again and Mike tuned in to what was being said. Barry was having his say. Something about how to please a girl. Oh right. Like any of them knew how to do that. Out of the corner of his eye he saw the three girls wai to Siswan. Blimey, he thought, that's a turn up. They hadn't done that to Tam and she was their leader. Had been, he reminded himself. Something told him she wouldn't be coming back.

Tim ordered yet another round of drinks. They were in good moods. Even John, who normally kept so quiet had joined in the conversation.

'I loved a girl once,' he said, to nobody in particular.

'Really John?' Barry asked. 'Who was that then?'

'Lovely girl she was,' John reminisced. 'Had a tattoo on her bum.'

'What did it say?' Tim asked.

'No entry,' John said.

The rest of them burst out laughing. Big Barry spluttered whiskey all over the bar.

'Bloody hell, John,' he shouted, after coughing his airways clear. 'I thought you were being serious.'

'I was,' John said. He went back to his beer and his memories. He wasn't laughing.

'Yes. Well, er. Thanks for that moment, John. Good of you to share that with us,' Tim said, still grinning.

Mike held his hand out to Pan. She looked up at him with a puzzled expression. He smiled. She passed him the bar chit for the drinks Tim had ordered. Mike checked it and passed it back. She looked sullen. Siswan was walking back towards him. The three girls followed in her wake.

'Well done, Mike. We'll make a bar owner out of you yet,' she whispered in his ear. 'The girls are going home now.'

'What for?' Mike asked.

'Oh. They're just tired. They need to get some sleep.'

The look in her eyes told him that was all there was to say on the subject. She had already turned away before he could argue.

'Oh dear, Barry,' she laughed. 'You seem to have made a bit of a mess haven't you. You really ought to be able to find your mouth by now, you know.'

Siswan took a cloth and mopped up the drink Barry had spluttered over the bar.

'Pan?' Siswan spoke in the local tongue. 'Always keep the bar clean. There's a good girl'

Mike watched her eyes. They didn't smile even though her mouth did. He wasn't sure what she'd said to Pan, but he guessed. Things are changing around here, he thought. But why send the girls home? He didn't understand that. Surely they were needed? Oh well. Best not to argue. He started to turn his attention back to the regulars.

'Goodnight, Mike,' Apple said, offering him a very polite wai.

He was startled. What the hell was this? They hadn't said 'goodnight' to him before, let alone given him a wai. My god, now Tak and Lon were doing the same. He slipped off his stool. Started to raise his hands in response.

'A smile will do, Mike,' Siswan interrupted him. 'Just a smile.'

He smiled at the three girls. They all took a quick glance at Siswan. They all nodded their heads to her as though in acquiescence. Bloody hell, Mike thought, this was a right turn up, and no mistake.

'Goodnight girls,' he said.

The three of them filed out. He looked to Siswan. Wanted to ask her what was happening. He couldn't. She was busy with the regulars again. She had her arm resting gently across John's shoulders.

'I'm sure she was a lovely girl, John,' she was saying.

My god, Mike thought yet again, she hadn't missed a trick. Not a word. Even whilst she had been talking to the girls she'd kept an ear on the bar. Bloody hell.

It was two-thirty in the morning. The bar had closed. The regulars had gone home. Pan had gone home. Siswan and Mike sat at the bar adding up the evenings takings. Mike hadn't believed the first count so they were going through the chits again.

'But that's almost as much as we were taking when the bar was doing well,' he said, when the totals agreed for the second time.

'Yes. Not a lot is it?' Siswan told him.

'It's a hell of a lot compared with normal, Siswan.'

'Mike, it's chicken feed.' She looked at him. 'A bar like this, in this position, should be making twenty times this amount. On a bad night.'

'Yes. But even so.' He tailed off. Twenty times? That would be a bloody fortune.

'I'm glad you are so easily pleased,' she laughed. 'That's why I chose you.'

'Does this mean I could buy a new pair of shorts?' he laughed with her. It was easy to laugh with her.

'I'd prefer you to get trousers, Mike,' she told him. 'And a new shirt.'

'Right you are. I'll pop out tomorrow afternoon,' he agreed.

'The girls will be here in six hours. We're going shopping. You can come,' she said.

'Eh, what for?' he asked.

'For new uniforms,' she told him, with a smile.

'Hang on, Siswan,' he said. 'I know we did well tonight, but we didn't do that well.'

'It's alright, Mike. I'll pay and, when the bar makes enough, it will pay me back.' Her voice suggested that there would be no doubt about that. 'The cleaners will be here at eleven.'

'What cleaners?' he asked.

'Cleaners, Mike. You know. People who come in and clean. It's not that hard to understand,' Siswan told him.

'Oh. Right. Well, I'd best get to bed then. Looks like it's going to be a busy day tomorrow.'

'Today, Mike. It's going to be a busy day, today.'

'Oh, yes. Today.'

'I'll see you later, then. I'll lock up.' She stood before him and gave him a wai. She waited.

Oh, bloody hell, he thought. What do I do? If I wai, will she tell me off? If I don't, will that be wrong? What if I smile? Hang on, Mike thought. He knew what to do. He'd known for a long time. A smile is used for children and lesser persons. It's used to acknowledge people with a lower standing in life. People you don't need to show respect. He stood and gave her the most polite wai he could.

'Well done, Mike. We'll get along just fine. Goodnight,' she said and smiled at him before turning away.

'Goodnight, Siswan,' he said, watching her leave.

Time for a whiskey, he thought. No better not. Maybe a cigarette? No. Best just get some sleep. He turned towards the stairs at the back of the bar. For the first time in a long time there was a smile on his face. Life was certainly going to get busy.

*****

Over the course of the next six weeks Siswan made changes. Lots of them. The bar was cleaned. Top to bottom. The lights were fixed. Some replaced. The toilets were repaired. The place shone like a new bar.

That was the least of it. The girls were given a makeover the like of which Mike had never seen before. They all wore identical uniforms. Short skirts, not too short mind, and skimpy tops that revealed their stomachs rather than their breasts. High heeled, open-toed sandals that made them taller, more elegant. They looked sexy. Incredibly sexy.

Siswan taught them how to apply just the right amount of make-up. It looked as though they weren't wearing any. Their long black hair shone in the new lighting. They looked good. And it wasn't just their looks she had changed. It was their attitude. They acted differently. For one thing, they were more respectful. More friendly.

'You can all speak English,' Siswan told them. 'So don't be afraid to talk.'

'But what do we say?' Jom asked.

Siswan had dealt with Jom in exactly same way as the others. The girl had turned up on the morning they all went shopping. Lon and Tak hadn't gone to a club either. Just to bed.

'Tell them stories. Funny stories about your life. About your family. Don't make the stories too long or they'll get bored. Listen to what they have to say. Enjoy their company. Don't just pretend, learn to really enjoy,' Siswan had told them.

'But they talk bad and just try for a free grope,' Tak said.

Siswan had been patient. She'd told them how to deal with a farang that swore too much. How to move away whenever a hand strayed too far.

'Tell them. Be direct. Farangs don't mind being told. They aren't the same as local men. They don't get angry. Just tell them that they can look as much as they want, but to touch will cost them money. Laugh as you tell them,' Siswan said.

She had demonstrated exactly want she meant. She had taken the loudest, most drunk and foul mouthed farang and, within minutes, had him acting like a little school boy.

'You see?' she said later to the girls. 'It's not up to them how they behave. It's up to you.'

'But what if we can't control them? What if they go too far?'

'Then you come to me or Mike,' she said. 'If ever you get into trouble, if ever you are unsure, you come to me or Mike. About anything.'

The girls felt better. They felt as though Siswan was working with them. Was one of them. Willing to help. She was a hard boss, that was for sure. She wouldn't allow anything underhand. No one was allowed to take advantage, but when they worked hard, did as she expected, she took care of them. Was fair to them.

She had cut their drink and bar fine commissions to ten percent. She wouldn't allow anyone to dip their hand in the till. Wouldn't let them sit in the chairs outside. They had to be inside. Looking after the customers. Checking that their glasses were full, without being obvious about it.

She showed them how to smile, how to laugh with the regulars. Even though they heard the same story twenty times, it didn't matter. Laugh and say the right thing, always. She taught them respect for the customer.

'The customer is always right,' she told them. 'Even when he's wrong, he's still right.'

Slowly the girls began to learn. Apple picked it up the quickest, just as Siswan had thought. Slowly though, they all got it. The bar began to attract new customers.

As farangs walked past, they could hear the laughter coming from within. There were no girls outside trying to tempt them. There didn't need to be. When they looked through the doors they could see smart, sexy girls all chatting and having fun with the customers. It looked like a good place to be. The girls really looked as though they were enjoying themselves, rather than just pretending. Even Pan was coming out of her shell. She was being bought so many drinks and earning so many tips, she was making more than when she'd been stealing from the till.

New customers came and stayed. Became regulars. Tourists would come every night of their two week holiday. They liked the place. It was full of laughter and fun.

'Don't ask the farangs to go with you,' Siswan taught the girls. 'Make sure it's their idea.'

'But what if they don't ask?' Tak said.

'Oh, they will. As soon as they realize that you don't care one way or the other, they'll ask. Men are easy. You'll see.'

And she'd been right. The less interest the girls showed, the more interest the men had. Even the regular regulars were finding themselves going home with a girl on their arm every now and then.

'Don't just aim for the good looking farangs. The chances are they will have had lots of girls and may be a health risk. Their money isn't any better than an old or ugly one, either.' Siswan taught them. 'Remember to look after the regulars. They're the ones who deserve better treatment.'

She never missed a trick. She made certain that a farang wasn't left alone for too long. She circulated, spoke to everyone. Made sure no one was lonely. Before long the bar was packed every night. Twenty times the takings turned into thirty times. Still she wanted more.

'Mike, we need two more girls,' she told him at the end of a busy night. 'I'll look out for a couple tomorrow.'

'Oh, right you are,' Mike said.

He didn't know why she bothered to ask him. She was running the place. In charge of it all. He did his best, of course. Tried to come up with new ideas. Tried to keep up with her, but she was miles ahead of him. She never seemed to sleep. Always the first to arrive. She worked tirelessly. He was too old for all this now. She was leaving him behind.

The funny thing was that Siswan did keep asking him. She included him in everything she did. He knew she could walk all over him, but she didn't. At the end of every night she went over the books with him. Showed him exactly what had been earned. Clearly showed him the profits, the outgoings, the expenses. She had halved how much he was paying for the girls accommodation. She had found them a much nicer place closer to the bar at half the price of the other rooms. The girls were over the moon. They each had their own small room as well as a large lounge where they could watch TV or just sit and talk. The landlord gave them no trouble at all and even sent a woman around to clean the place once a week.

The bar was not only paying for itself it was making a handsome profit. More than Mike had ever earned before.

'We need your room, Mike,' Siswan told him one day.

'My room?' He looked worried.

Maybe this was the final push. When she got him out and took over completely. He didn't know why she kept him there.

'Yes. To make the food,' she smiled.

'Food?'

'We can make a lot of money from food, Mike.' She sat him down at the bar and went over her new idea. 'We don't do anything too fancy. Just bar snacks, but we make them very tasty and good value.'

He just looked at her. It was a good idea and would keep everyone drinking instead of leaving to find a restaurant. But what about him? What about his room?

'We talked about this before, Mike,' she said.

'Did we?'

'Yes. The very first night we met.'

'Oh. Yes. I expect so.'

'Yes. We discussed what you needed. Whiskey. Cigarettes. A better room. Remember? You added that you wanted some new clothes.'

'But I'm hardly drinking. Don't smoke so much either,' he muttered.

'That's good, Mike. You were only killing yourself, anyway.' She looked at him and smiled. 'I've found you a really nice place. Care to take a look?'

Mike moved into his new apartment two days later. It was a fantastic place. A big lounge, large bedroom, bathroom, kitchen and, best of all, a balcony that afforded him a view right down to the beach.

'So, what do you think?' Siswan asked him, as they looked out at the vista below.

'It's amazing!' he replied. 'It'll cost an arm and a leg though.'

'No. Not very much.'

When she had shown him the rental agreement he could hardly believe his eyes. He would have paid four times that amount.

'I figure we'll be able to make that much on food in less than a week. The rest will be profit,' she told him.

She was right as well. She brought in a short order cook who could knock up bar meals like there was no tomorrow. And they were good. Big servings to suit the farangs. The cook, a local woman named Rican, had been operating her own little stall for the last few years. She was delighted with her new job. She earned more money and no longer had to pay for a licence. Mike took to her friendly attitude immediately and, more often than not, would eat all his meals in his own bar. Rican fussed over him. He liked it.

Siswan brought in two more girls. Young ones who had just arrived in the resort. She hadn't wanted girls who had worked for too long.

'Easier to teach, Mike,' she told him.

She put both of them into the care of Apple and explained what she wanted.

'They aren't to go with anyone until they are ready,' she said to her. 'Don't force them into doing anything that they aren't willing to do.'

'Okay, Miss Siswan.'

Apple and the other girls all called her 'Miss Siswan' now. She hadn't told them to, they just did. Out of respect.

Apple, Tak and Lon were all earning good money. Apple had taken eighteen thousand home in her wage packet that month.

'Thank you, Miss Siswan.'

She had beamed when she saw the breakdown. Ten percent of the money they were now making was a lot better than the fifty percent she earned before.

'Are you still with your boyfriend?' Siswan asked her.

'I've told him to go, but he won't listen.' He was the only bane in her life now. 'He comes to the house and just takes any money I have.'

Siswan sighed. She knew all about this kind of thing. Sometimes men just wouldn't listen. They had to be taught.

'Okay. I'll see what I can do,' she told Apple. 'Write down his full name and address.'

A week later, she asked Mike if it would be all right for her to deal with the police when they called for their monthly protection money.

'Yes. Why not?' Mike had agreed. He had no reason not to agree. She was dealing with everything. He just couldn't understand why she asked him anymore. He wasn't complaining. He just didn't know.

When the police did call, they were surprised to find themselves dealing with a young local woman. The two officers, in their skin tight brown uniforms were leaning nonchalantly against the bar as she approached them. They were both drinking the beers Pan had given them upon their arrival. They both smiled at Siswan and she made a low wai to them in reply. They just smiled once more. A lesser person. No need to wai back. Didn't deserve respect.

'Thank you for calling,' Siswan said.

'Where's the farang?' the senior of the two asked her. A sergeant.

'Oh, he is far too busy to deal with you two today,' Siswan said. 'He asked me to speak with you instead.'

That caught their attention. She saw the sudden look of surprise cross the sergeant's face.

'So,' she said, innocently enough. 'What do you want?'

Both of them stood more upright. Became more tense in their attitude. What was she talking about? This bar girl? Who was she to speak to them like this? She must know what they wanted. They came every month. Pay up or move out.

'Protection costs more now,' the sergeant said, with a smile.

'What protection are you talking about?' Siswan carried on looking into his eyes.

'Police protection. You know what I'm talking about.' He was getting a little annoyed. But it wouldn't do to lose face. Not in front of his colleague. Not in front of this woman.

'We don't get any protection from you,' Siswan stated.

'Everyone gets protection,' he said, emphatically.

'How much does it cost?' she asked.

'Five thousand.' That would teach her. They had only been taking three before. They knew this bar couldn't afford too much more.

'No,' Siswan said.

He couldn't believe what she had said. He looked at her. She looked a little different than the other girls. More beautiful, sure, but there was something else. Something hard about her. She acted older than she looked. More confident. As though this was something she did every day.

'I will speak with the farang,' he told her.

'No. You will speak with me,' she answered.

'I tell you. Five thousand!' He was angry now.

'That is a stupid price for what I want.' She remained calm.

He was just about to storm out. He'd make her pay for this outrage. How dare she speak to him this way. Wait, what had she said? He stopped. Wait, think. What had she just said? He was puzzled.

'What do you want?' he asked, cautiously.

'Several things,' she said. 'Firstly, when you come into this bar I do not want you in uniform. It makes the girls nervous.'

Yes, but not you though, he thought to himself. It doesn't make you nervous at all. He decided to listen. There might be something in what she had to say.

'Go on,' he said, calmer now.

'If we call you, we want you here quickly. Let's say five minutes maximum. Any later and we'll deduct the amount we pay. We want a written agreement that you will not charge extra for a fast response.'

She knew exactly what she wanted. She laid it out like a list.

'We will need another agreement that the cost of protection will not increase for another year and then only by a maximum of five percent.'

He nodded. He couldn't help himself. There was something about the way she spoke. The way she looked at him. He wasn't talking to a bar girl. He knew that now.

'If we do need your help, we expect you to be courteous. Don't come in here with your macho attitude.'

He began to take a real interest. This woman was no fool. She knew exactly what she wanted. This was the same arrangement they had with the big bars. The ones that could afford to pay for the best protection.

'We want a late night extension. Four o'clock. We won't want to work any later than that.'

It sounded as though she had finished. She was just looking at him to make sure he had understood everything she had said.

'And how much are you willing to pay?' the sergeant asked, testing her.

He'd already worked it all out. She was asking for everything. Even some of the really busy bars didn't get a five minute response. He was interested though. Not so much with the deal, more interested in her. He looked at her properly. Not a bar girl. Definitely. Maybe a five minutes response would be okay. How much, though? That was the important bit. He knew that level of protection would be ten thousand a month. Nothing less.

'Twenty thousand a month,' she said.

He looked at her. About to laugh. That was twice what the other bars were paying. In the end he didn't laugh. He just listened as she spoke again.

'That's twice what the other bars are paying. We want twice the service. You send a man down here every two hours. No uniform. He just glances through the door. Makes sure everything is all right and leaves. He doesn't come in unless there's a problem.'

He nodded. What else could he do? This woman was no bar girl, he thought, again. She was clever. Beautiful, and clever.

'For that money we'll take good care of you,' he told her. 'What is your name please?'

'Siswan,' she told him.

'Well, Siswan, my name is Mirak. I think we'll get along just fine,' he smiled. A genuine smile.

'Thank you, Mirak,' she smiled back. 'There is a favour I need to ask you.'

'No problem. Ask away.'

He was hooked. Captivated. He knew it, so did she. Siswan handed him the piece of paper Apple had given her. A name. An address.

'One of our girls is very upset,' she told him.

Nothing more needed to be said. A visit would be arranged. A talk. Perhaps more if the words weren't enough.

'Very well. It will be taken care of,' Mirak said, slipping the paper into his pocket. 'Now, a question of money?'

When all the agreements had been signed, when all the paperwork was in place, Siswan handed over nineteen thousand and some change.

'We agreed twenty?' Mirak said, counting the money.

'Yes. Of course,' she smiled at him. 'But you have to pay for your beers, gentlemen. We aren't a charity, you know.'

'But your cashier gave them to us. We didn't ask,' Mirak was smiling.

'But you accepted them, Mirak. Nothing in this life is for free,' Siswan said in reply.

Mirak looked into her face. He laughed. He'd never met anyone like her before. Standing straight he made a formal wai to her. As an equal. His colleague joined him. This woman deserved respect.

'Thank you, Mirak,' she said.

He smiled, turned and left the bar. As he walked he shook his head as though to clear it.

Siswan told Mike everything that had happened with the police. He just listened and nodded as she explained what she had arranged. When she told him how much it cost he was shocked to say the least.

'How much!' It wasn't a question.

'Mike, twenty thousand is nothing. We'll be making that much in just a few hours. Trust me,' she told him.

It worked out really well. Every now and then they would spot the plainclothes police officer taking a quick look to ensure everything was well. He did as he was told and never entered the bar unless needed. The police never bothered them, helped them out when they needed it and gave them the very best service. Apple never heard from her ex-boyfriend again and the bar stayed open until four every morning. Siswan knew she had done the right thing. The bar was gaining respect. She was gaining respect. That was what mattered.

It was making money as well. Big money. More money than Mike had ever earned before. Every night the place heaved with customers. The girls were working hard, had their pick of the farangs, and never looked happier. Apple was the first of them to hit twenty five thousand in a month. Tak wasn't too far behind.

'I don't believe it!' she said early one evening when they were all sat eating. 'Miss Siswan, you were right! Peter is all over me now!'

Peter was a new regular. He'd been in almost every night for the last month. He couldn't take his eyes off Tak. Wanted her to stop working in the bar.

'What happened?' Lon asked.

'I liked him. When I first saw him I liked him. He didn't swear and was very polite,' Tak said, excitedly. 'So, I remembered what Miss Siswan said, and ignored him.'

'Ignored him?' One of the newer girls didn't get it.

'Yes. The more I ignored him the more interested he became!' Tak told them all. 'Finally, when I thought he couldn't take any more, I spoke to him.'

'What did you say?'

'I said, "hello, I haven't seen you in here before, are you on holiday?" and then smiled. Now he wants me to go to Germany with him!'

'Are you going?' Apple asked.

'I don't know. What do you think, Miss Siswan?' Tak asked her. All the girls waited for her answer.

'You must do what you think is right, Tak. You came here to sell your body to make money. It is not a good thing to do in this country. Any country. It is not a good way to live. If you think Peter can offer you a good life you should take it,' she told them.

'But what about my family? I have to take care of them.' Tak asked.

'Why?' Siswan was suddenly very serious. 'Why do any of you have to take care of your families? What have they done for you? You didn't ask to be born. You didn't ask them to bring you into this world. Why do you owe them anything? They are just people. People you happen to be related to. You owe them nothing.'

The girls looked at her. They saw anger in her eyes. What she said was contrary to everything they believed, everything they had been taught. They had to look after their families, didn't they? They had been brought up to believe that. It was their duty. The only way to make merit for their souls. They had to do it. Had to.

'You work hard. Make good money.' She looked into their faces. 'And then you give it all away. What will you do when the farangs no longer want you? What will you do when you are old?'

The girls never thought about being old. Today was important. Not tomorrow. They didn't understand this way of thinking. Work, make money, send it home. That was all they were used to. Apple was the first to break the silence that followed.

'What about you, Miss Siswan? What will you do when you are old?'

'I won't be working in a bar, Apple'

Siswan looked at their faces. What she had said had upset them. She could see that. Maybe their lives were different. Maybe they hadn't been through what she had been through. They were like children. Little girls who were playing at living. She couldn't believe how naive they were.

It had only been a few months since she had met them. How quickly would they allow someone else to take over when she left? Miss Siswan they called her. Out of respect. Respect for what? How much money they were now making? Because she earned respect? Deserved it? Good god, if only they knew the life she had been through. How much respect would they show her then? Miss Siswan. A title reserved for older women. Women who commanded respect. Would they call her that if they knew? If they knew that she had just passed her eighteenth birthday?

She had been seventeen years old when she walked into Mike's bar. A seventeen year old girl that had seen too much. Learned too much. Knew too much.

Respect? She could hardly bear to look at her own reflection in a mirror. How many of these girls would ever feel like that? She hoped none of them would ever need to go through what she had gone through. She wouldn't have wished that upon anyone. Not anyone. Without realizing it, her fingers stroked the angry scar on her arm.

Chapter 4

When Siswan had walked away from her childhood five years before, she didn't have a clue as to where she was going or what she was going to do. She just knew she had to get away.

Even as she walked along the dusty road clutching her small bundle of belongs, she could hear the voice of her mother. The condemnation. The spite. Their relationship was over. The mother despised the daughter.

Siswan walked towards her future with her head held high. She would not allow the events of the last year to crush her body or her spirit. She didn't know where she was going, but anywhere had to be better than her village. It had to be better. She would make sure it was.

The small amount of money she had made Bak give her wouldn't last for long. She would need to earn more and she knew of only one way to make money. Men. They were the answer. They had the power. The money. They were the ones in control. Please them or starve. She'd rather starve. That was the one thing she had learned really well.

It was almost dark by the time she made the town. The noise of the traffic, the lights, the thousands of people all hurrying to get somewhere, unnerved her. She felt lost. Alone. Small.

Only once had she ever been there before. When she was very young her mother had brought her in on the bus. That had been different. She had held her mother's hand and been amazed by all the sights and sounds she saw. The big cars, trucks and motorbikes all roaring their way around the streets. The tall buildings that made her neck ache as she tried to see all the way to the top. The excitement of seeing all those people coming and going had made her dizzy.

Now though, it was different. Now she was brushing shoulders with those people, as they bustled to and fro, and the contact made her feel even more alone. So many people that she didn't know.

When she had walked in her village she had known everyone. Every face she saw she knew. Even on Buddha days, when the whole village gathered together to visit the temple, she knew every face. Recognized every person. Some to talk to, others just to say hello to, some to be afraid of. It didn't matter how many people turned up, and sometimes there seemed like hundreds, she knew everyone.

In this town there were thousands of people. Tens of thousands. She knew none of them. Not one face stood out from the crowds for her. Not one. She was alone. For the first time in her life, she was truly alone.

Walking aimlessly down through the crowded streets she felt tired. Her legs ached from their long walk. She was hot, sticky and dirty. She wanted a shower. Something to eat. A good night's sleep in her little bed. It was that last thought that saved her.

The thought of her little, safe and comfortable bed, saved her from giving up. Saved her from crying and being afraid. Stopped her from being the little frightened girl that she almost allowed herself to become.

That little bed. Where she would lie and listen to her father. Hear his drunken rants. Hear the sound of her mother crying. Waiting anxiously, hoping that Bak wouldn't come to her. No. The thought of that bed filled her with revulsion. Her mother had condemned her. There would be no more tears.

With a shrug of resolve, she hefted her small bundle of clothes over her shoulder and, more determined than ever, continued her walk into the centre of the town. Whatever happened now, whatever happened in the future, she was going to be the one in control.

She looked into the shop windows as she walked. So many beautiful things. Clothes. Jewelry. Ornaments. Of every size, shape and colour. The sights made her realize how shabby she must look. Her worn jeans, faded t-shirt, old sandals. Her hair was dirty and hung across her face. Her skin felt as though it were caked in dirt. She felt unclean. Inside and out.

It was dark by the time she arrived at the park in the centre of the town. The garish street lights made the shadows look real. More alive than the objects that made them. There were still people about. Motorbikes zipped past her, their drivers, sometimes their passengers, cast her a glance. No smiles. No signs of recognition.

She sat down on the grass bank that enclosed the central lake of the park and watched as people walked by. So many people. Out for an evening stroll. Some with partners. Some alone. They all walked by.

She bent down towards the water. Scooped some in her hands and rinsed her face and arms. A couple walking by, paused to watch, then walked on, laughing. Siswan didn't mind. At least they had seen her. Made a comment concerning her existence. She had begun to think that perhaps she had become invisible. She rinsed the water through her hair. Pulled her fingers through it. Tried for a semblance of normality.

She collected her thoughts. She needed to eat and sleep somewhere. The small street cafes over the road may be able to help. There must be something she could do to earn a bed for the night.

Crossing the road, she looked along the row of small eating areas. They were nothing more than rattan mats spread out over the pavement. The customers sat cross-legged on cushions as they ate the meals prepared on small charcoal grilles. Siswan wandered up to the first and stood looking at the meats being slowly cooked by an old woman.

'Yes?' The old woman was looking at her expectantly.

'Hello.' Siswan gave her a wai. The old woman smiled in reply.

'Do you want to eat?' she asked.

'Can I work for you?' Siswan asked, in all innocence.

The old woman cackled. She revealed black stumps of teeth and a yellow coated tongue.

'Why?' she asked.

'I have nowhere to go. I need a bed, somewhere to shower. Food,' Siswan told her.

'So do I,' the old woman cackled again. 'No. No work here.'

Siswan left her and wandered down the road to the next. The story was the same. No work. No bed. No food. She tried every cafe along that road and then the next. Nothing. No work. No help. No pity offered and none expected.

By the time she got back to the park, the street cafes were closing. There were less people about. The old woman with the black teeth was collecting her cushions. She looked crooked, old and frail as she bent to pick them up and load them into the trailer attached to her old motorbike. Siswan wandered over and started to roll up the rattan mats.

'I told you before. No work. Not here,' the old woman told her.

'I know. I heard you. I'm only helping you, that's all,' Siswan replied.

'So you think I'll take pity on you, is that it?'

'No. I'm just helping. You don't have to talk.' Siswan bent and rolled another mat.

'I won't, you know,' the old woman said, as she took the mats. 'I've already told you.'

Siswan didn't reply. She just collected the rest of the mats, stored them in the old trailer, and then wandered back across the street to the park.

She guessed she could sleep there for the night. It didn't look like it was going to rain. She heard the old woman start the motorbike behind her. Heard it pull away from the kerb.

'Here.' The shout came from behind her.

Siswan turned. The old woman had driven across the road and was sat on her bike holding one of the mats out.

'Make sure you bring it back tomorrow.'

'I will. Thank you.' Siswan said, and took the proffered mat.

It was the first act of kindness she had seen since leaving home. She was grateful for the mat. She gave a wai to the old woman who, after looking at her a moment longer, drove off down the road.

That night, Siswan lay on the rattan mat in the park. She had made her bed under the branches of a big old blossom tree that stood to one side of the small lake. She used her small bundle of clothes as a pillow. In her hand she held the small knife. The blade was very sharp and she made sure she didn't cut herself in her sleep.

She spent a total of eight nights sleeping in the park before having to move on. Eight nights alone in the dark. She had been disturbed only once. A brown rat, one of the dozens that came out at night to scavenge for food, ventured too close. Siswan had cut it almost in half and thrown its bloody carcass far out into the waters of the lake. A rat was nothing compared to a scorpion.

During the days she wandered from one business to the next, looking for work. She discovered a large restaurant that threw out food at the end of the day and she managed to get enough from the big green bins to keep her going.

As she drove off the dogs that threatened to bite her, she remembered how easy it had been to get food in her village. A short stroll into the fields and you could eat your fill of fresh vegetables and fruit. This wasn't her village. Nothing grew around here. Just buildings. Concrete buildings.

Every night she helped the old woman roll up her mats and every night she was rewarded with the loan of one to sleep on.

Apart from the fact that she couldn't wash properly, Siswan felt she was doing okay. Alone in the world, with nowhere to go and nothing to do, she struggled on. Her mind was unchanged. It was better than the village. Better than hearing her mother cry.

It was on the ninth night that her luck changed. She washed, as usual, in the waters of the small lake. She ran her fingers through her hair and, out of sight of the road, washed and changed her clothes as best she could.

As she rolled out the mat under the branches of the big blossom tree she heard voices coming toward her. Laughter. Shouts. A group of boys came into view as they crossed the small footbridge that led into the park. Siswan rolled up the mat quietly and ducked behind the tree. She didn't want to be seen alone. Not at night. Not by men.

The four boys walked the small path that led towards her. She ducked back into the shadow of the tree and they moved past without seeing her. They were loud. Excited. One of them carried a plastic bag. Siswan heard the chink of glass on glass as they walked further away.

She didn't stay where she was. When they had drunk their beers they would wander back this way, she thought. She would skirt around them and head over to the far side. She'd be safe there.

As she walked around the edge of the lake she could hear their shouts and laughter as they consumed the beer. Young boys seeking some fun. That was okay. She could avoid them. She would never understand how men thought fun could only be found in alcohol, but it didn't matter. As long as she kept out of their way, she'd be alright.

Finding a spot on the other side of the park was easy. She rolled out her mat under another tree that had branches falling almost to the ground. Inside their canopy it was like a small room. Hardly noticeable from the path or the road, she lay her head down on her small bundle and fell asleep clutching her knife.

Hardly an hour passed before she was shaken awake. Rough hands were grabbing her shoulders. The smell of whiskey was the first thing she noticed. Still half asleep she thought of Bak. He was there. Waking her up. Touching her.

She moved instinctively. The knife moved like a blur in the dark. The blade caught what little light reached under the canopy of branches. A yell. Almost a scream. Then silence. Except for heavy breathing. She pulled herself awake. Into a sitting position. Ready to stand and run.

'You'll pay for that.' A voice. Slurred. Old. The smell of whiskey.

She felt sudden pain in her arm. He had lashed out at her face and she had raised her arm instinctively, in expectation of the blow. She fought to get to her feet. To run.

Hands grabbed at her. Caught her by the hair. Pulled her down. Another pain, this time in the face. He had hit her. She tasted the blood from inside her nose as it ran down her throat. She was stunned. Shocked by the sudden violence that interrupted her sleep. Couldn't think. She needed more time, but was offered none.

She lashed out once more with the knife. Missed. Her arm flailed against nothing. It was held. A strong grip. She couldn't bring the knife back into play. She tried to kick, to pull away, but the grip was too strong.

She felt the small knife being wrenched out of her hand. Felt another flash of pain as he struck her again, across the cheek this time. She stopped fighting. Stopped struggling. The pain raced across her vision. Her head span and reeled in the dark. Hands pulled at her clothes. She heard the raw sound of the cloth being ripped. Her t-shirt was torn apart. Hands touching. Feeling. Rubbing against her bare flesh. The front of her jeans were pulled open. The smell of whiskey. Overpowering. She fought for clarity. She could still taste the blood. Her mind struggled to hold onto something. Something real. Tried to concentrate. Her head span. She stopped it. The pain still throbbed in her face. She blocked it out. Her vision was blurred. She blinked it clear. What was happening to her was wrong. It would be her fault. She knew it would all be her fault. It didn't matter. What was happening was still wrong. Her mother had condemned her. She could hear her voice.

A calmness overtook her. A curtain fell on the pain. The panic left her. She concentrated. The child within her could no longer be heard. This had to stop. It had to stop now.

'No!' She shouted and thrust her knees up as hard as she could. It worked. She felt the contact. Heard the sudden intake of air. The groan as he slipped from above her to the side.

She reacted at once. She rolled away from him, onto her front. Clambered to her knees. To her feet. Ran forward, away from where he lay. Through the low branches as they tried to prevent her escape. Tangled in her hair. She pulled free. Fought to get away. A hand grabbed her ankle. Pulled her back. She fell. Turning onto her back she lashed out with the other foot. Kicking and yelling as loud as she could. She felt a contact again. Kicked once more. Heard the gasp of wind. Kicked again. She would not allow this to happen. She didn't deserve it. No matter what her mother said, she didn't deserve any of it.

She leant forward. She felt with her hands. With her fingers. She wanted to feel his face. To check where he was. She wanted to scratch. Dig her fingers into his eyes. To fight back. To remove his sting. Take away his venom.

A shock of pain ripped into her forearm. The knife. He had used her knife. She pulled back quickly. The blade cut into her, dragged its way down through the flesh of her arm. She felt the hot searing pain as it made its way to her wrist. No! She didn't deserve this!

She kicked again. Felt her heel crunch into his face. His nose. She heard his bones break. The yell of pain. The sudden release. He had pulled away. The knife was no longer in her arm. Her legs were free. The hot blood ran down to her hand. Sticky. Wet.
She turned, stood and ran. She ran through the branches, across the path. She didn't chose a direction. She hadn't the time.

The blood flowed freely from her arm. She glanced down at it. Saw the blood pumping out. She felt faint. The cut ran all the way down her forearm. From the inside of her elbow to the inside of her wrist. She could see inside her own arm. It made her dizzy. Made her feel faint. Light headed. She had to get help.

She ran straight into the group of boys returning from their midnight drinking excursion. Too tired and weak to do anything about it she fell at their feet. Fell upon their mercy. Put herself under their control.

*****

She came to in a bed. A bed with white sheets. White walls surrounded the bed. White light made her eyes hurt. She felt vertiginous. Thirsty. A man. In a white coat.

'How do you feel?' he asked.

His voice was neither kind nor unkind. He just asked the question. She felt she could have said anything. It wouldn't have mattered much to him.

'Thirsty,' she said.

Her voice sounded far away from her. She fought for clarity. She looked at her arm. A white bandage ran from her elbow to her wrist. A needle and tube protruded from the other.

'Yes. That's normal,' the man said. A doctor.

She concentrated. He would have said the same thing whatever she had answered. It was a voice without emotion. A voice of authority.

'The police want to speak with you,' he told her.

'What about?' she asked.

'That is not my concern,' he answered, and left the room.

Siswan lay back onto the pillow. She wanted to sleep. She felt tired. Weary. She closed her eyes. Dozed off. She didn't hear the door open.

'What happened?' another voice asked. Equally without emotion.

She opened her eyes. Looked up. A policeman. Brown, skin tight uniform. Gun on his hip. She was reminded of the policeman in the village. She and her friends had been scared of him. Siswan was too tired to feel frightened now.

'I was attacked,' she said.

'What were you doing in the park?'

'Sleeping.'

'Why were you sleeping in the park?'

Why was he asking her that? Was it wrong to sleep in the park? Who cared about that? Why not ask about the man who attacked her? Was this all going to be her fault? Were they going to tell her off? Arrest her?

'Why?' she asked.

'Yes. Why were you sleeping in the park?' he asked, again.

'Because I wanted to,' she answered. 'Because I couldn't sleep anywhere else.'

'Where are you from?'

'A village.'

'What village?'

She gave him the name of a village she had heard about before. It was miles from her own.

'And how did you come to be sleeping in the park?' He didn't stop asking the same question.

'I came into the town this afternoon,' she said, wearily. 'I missed the bus home. I was going to get the morning bus home tomorrow.'

'Don't you know it's dangerous to sleep in the park?'

'I do now. I didn't before.'

'There are a lot of drunks who sleep there at night. How old are you?'

'Sixteen,' she lied, quickly.

He seemed to accept the lie. Didn't say anything about it.

'What is your name?'

'Bee,' she lied, again.

'Were you raped, Bee?' he asked. Again there was no emotion in his voice.

'No. I fought him off.'

'We caught the man who attacked you,' he told her.

She opened her eyes fully. Tried to lift her head off the pillow.

'Who was he?' She wanted to know. Wanted to know everything about him.

'Just an old drunk. He claimed you were in his bed. Where he slept at night. He said you attacked him when he tried to wake you up.'

'He ripped my clothes.' It was all she could think of to say.

Had the old man only been trying to get his bed back? Had she attacked him first?

'He has a nasty cut on his hand and a broken nose,' the policeman said.

'He cut my arm,' she said.

'He says that you did that as he was trying to give you back your knife. Was it your knife, Bee?'

'No. I didn't have a knife,' she said.

'So, it was his knife then?'

'I don't know.'

She felt young again. Like a little girl. This was going to end up being her fault. But she had smelt the whiskey. Felt his breath on her. His hands had rubbed against her. Yes, but did you deserve it, she asked herself silently? Had the old man only wanted her to move out of his sleeping place? She felt confused. Close to tears. No, she would not cry.

'I'll tell you what happened as far as we know, Bee. Then you can fill in the details, okay?' he said.

'I'll try,' she answered.

The police had received an anonymous phone call from a young man who sounded as though he'd been drinking. He told them that there was a girl in the park who had been cut. She was bleeding a lot.

When the police arrived at the park there had been no sign of the young man. The police guessed that he was an underage drinker, out with some friends, and had run off rather than face the police.

When they checked the area he had mentioned, the police had come across Siswan lying face down and unconscious. They called a medic from the local hospital who attended to her arm to stop the bleeding.

Whilst that was going on, the police checked around the perimeter of the park. It wasn't too difficult to follow the trail of blood back to an old tree. Looking under the branches they found the old man snoring on a rattan mat. He had a cloth tied around a cut on his hand and his nose had been freshly broken. There was a pair of girls' sandals beside him.

When they had him awake and coherent, he told them he had been attacked by a teenaged girl with a knife. He had found her in his bed and had asked her to move. She turned on him, cut his hand, broke his nose and ran away. The police had taken him, along with the girl, to the town hospital. He was now asleep a few doors down the hallway.

'That's about all we know, Bee,' he finished.

'I didn't know it was his bed,' she said.

'Yes. But it was. All this could have just been an argument over who slept where.'

'But he ripped at my clothes.'

'He says he didn't. He says you must have ripped them clambering through the low branches of the tree.'

'But that's not true!'

'How do we know what's true, Bee? We weren't there.'

Siswan let herself relax back onto the pillow. There was no point in arguing. No point in fighting. Everything that happened was going to be her fault. She could tell by the voice of the policeman. They were always right. Even some drunk in the park. Always the men.

'I'll let you get some rest now, Bee. We'll talk again in the morning.'

He rose from the chair and walked out. She could see him turning right through the glass viewing panel in the door.

More questions in the morning. By which time they will have checked her village. Found out she had lied about that. Found out she had lied about her name. Her age. If she had lied about all that then the old man must be telling the truth. The girl was just a liar.

She knew she wouldn't be able to wait until the morning. She knew there would be more trouble. More than she deserved. Had she attacked for no reason? She didn't know now. Wasn't sure of herself. As she lay there, half awake, half asleep, she remembered the swishing stick. The sharp pain. The sting. Tomorrow the stick would be longer, harder, more brutal. And it wouldn't break.

Struggling against her own body she forced herself awake. She had to leave. Had to get away. She checked the room. Blinked in the bright white light of the overhead fluorescent tubes.

Her small bundle of clothes were on a chair in the far corner. She could see where the old drunk had ripped a strip off the sheet. Presumably to make his bandage. Her torn t-shirt hung over the back of the chair. Her jeans and sandals were on the floor. The rattan mat the old woman had loaned her wasn't there. Neither was her knife.

Checking her body she found she was dressed in a white nightgown. She felt cleaner. Maybe they had washed her as she slept. She didn't know. Under the white bandage that covered her right arm she felt a throbbing pain. It pulsed as though there was something alive inside the sterile wrapping. Not exactly agony. An itching sensation. She wanted to scratch it.

In her other arm there was a needle. Attached to the needle was a tube. The tube led up to a plastic bag half full of blood hanging from a metal stand. A plaster held the needle in place. She needed to get up. Needed to get away. Her head sank back onto the pillow.

She fought against the need to sleep. Just rest for a few minutes, she thought. Just rest a while. Give the policeman time to leave. Give her body the time to regain a little strength. Just a few minutes. She closed her eyes.

When she opened them again, the garish white light had been replaced with a faint glow from the corridor beyond the door. The glass viewing panel seemed to hang in the dark. She had slept and cursed herself for being so stupid. She glanced up at the bag of blood. It was almost empty. She had to go. Had to get away.

She lifted a corner of the plaster holding the needle. It pulled at her skin as she peeled it back. A small bruise marked the entry point of the needle. She pulled it out. Dark, red blood, almost black in the dim light, dripped onto the white linen. Left a stain.

She climbed out of the bed quietly. She didn't know where to go. Just away. She slipped off the gown and pulled on her jeans. Opening the bundle she found another tee shirt. She left the torn one hanging on the chair. She didn't want it. Didn't want the memory.

She tied the bundle, stooped to pick up her sandals. Bare foot she went to the glass panel. A corridor. The policeman had turned right. Was that the way out? She opened the door a fraction. Looked out. The corridor ran to the right until it reached double swing doors at the far end. To the left it turned left again. It seemed to lead deeper into the building. She would head right.

Slowly and carefully, she slipped through the doorway. Holding her breath against making any sound, she moved along the corridor keeping her shoulder against the wall. Her arm throbbed. Pounded. She could feel the pulse as though her heart was concealed under the gauze of the bandage.

When she reached the double swing doors she looked through one of the glass panels. A counter on the right. A nurse sat behind the desk. She was reading a book. No. A magazine.

Siswan waited. Knowing she would be caught. She wouldn't be able to get past the nurse. She thought of going back to her room. Accepting her fate. Tomorrow there would be trouble. Today, she corrected herself. She guessed that it must be the early hours of the morning by now.

The nurse glanced up from her magazine. Had she seen her? Had she spotted her looking through the glass? She almost turned to run. Almost went back the way she had come. But something held her still. The nurse hadn't looked at the double doors. She had looked at the computer screen sat in front of her.

Dressed in white trousers and white jacket, the nurse stood and walked out from behind the counter. She turned right. Away from where Siswan watched. She walked past a few doors down the corridor and stepped through one on the left hand side. Now, Siswan told herself. Now. Go now!

She pushed through the doors and quietly made her way down the corridor beyond. Past the counter. No one there. A beeping noise coming from the computer. The sound matched the throb of her arm. Like a heart beat.

She moved along the corridor as quickly as she dared. Here was the room the nurse had entered. She glanced through the glass panel. The big lights were on in the room. The nurse was bent over an old man. He looked frail. Weak. A yellow pallor to his skin. His nose was black and bruised. A bandage on his hand. The drunk. The drunk from the park. Weak and frail.

Siswan ducked down and continued down the corridor. She went through two more sets of double doors. Down a flight of stairs. Along one corridor that led nowhere. Backtracked. Tried another. Saw a way out. Took it. Ran away from the hospital.

All the time she had been thinking. Old. Frail. Weak. He didn't look well enough to attack her. Had she been wrong? Had he just wanted to sleep? The questions ran through her mind again and again. Had she been wrong? Had she attacked him? She ran. Away from the town. Away from the doubt in her mind. What had she done? The thought wailed in her mind. Screamed at her. What had she done?

*****

When Siswan stopped running she had passed the outskirts of the town. She was back in the countryside. The sun had broken the horizon and the fields around her sang with the noise of crickets. The main highway she followed stretched away into the distance and the trucks that passed, buffeted the air against her. Her face and hair were covered in the dust they threw up. She felt alone and tired. Her arm throbbed under the bandage.

She was a young girl in a strange place. She needed help. She imagined all the good things that could happen to her. Maybe a kind old woman would stop and take her home where she could wash and change. Maybe the kind old woman would give her something to eat. Take care of her. Look after her as though she were her own daughter. Perhaps the old woman had lost a daughter and Siswan could be that girl's replacement? The kind old woman would treat her well and, in return, Siswan would grow to love her and take care of her as she grew older.

She shook her head clear of such fantasies. That wasn't how it worked, she told herself. In the real world she had to take care of herself. There was no one else. Just her.

Another truck roared past and she closed her eyes to the grit and dust the huge wheels threw up. The truck braked. Stopped ahead of her. A head appeared out of the passenger window. A young man.

'Where are you going?' he asked, as Siswan drew near.

'Why?' she asked.

'We'll give you a lift if you want,' the young man said.

'Where are you going?' she asked.

She didn't have a clue where she was going. She could hardly just say 'away'. It wouldn't make sense and might even arouse suspicion.

'We're heading all the way to the coast. You wouldn't want to go that far!' he laughed.

'Yes. That's where I'm heading,' she told him.

She didn't know what the coast was, but it sounded far away. That was what she wanted. To be far away. Far away from everything.

'Come on then. Jump in.'

The young man jumped down from the cab and held the door for her. She clambered up and found an older man sat behind the wheel. Two men. One young, one older. She immediately felt nervous. Before she had a chance to change her mind, the younger of the two climbed up beside her and slammed the door. With a crunch of gears, the truck set off towards the far horizon.

'What's your name?' the young man asked her.

'Bee,' she said. The lie came easily.

'I'm Tad and he's Song. He doesn't talk much, but he's a good driver,' Tad informed her.

Siswan glanced at the driver. Dark brown skin, black hair, big hands. A hard looking man who just stared at the road ahead of him.

'So, Bee. What are you doing out here all alone?' Tad asked her.

She was wary. The question could be just curiosity, but it could also hide a threat. All alone. She tried to give a confident air. Someone who knew what they were doing. Someone older.

'I've been visiting my Uncle. Now I'm heading home,' she said.

'What's wrong with your arm?'

'I cut it in the fields. Harvesting. You know.'

'Looks like a bad cut. Many stitches?' Tad asked.

She didn't know what he meant. She knew about stitches though. She'd practiced with her mother. Sewing little patterns onto small squares of cloth. They sold well in the tourist towns, her mother had told her. Had they stitched her arm? Could they do that? She guessed at the number needed to sew back the cut she had seen in her arm.

'Seventeen. I think,' she said.

'Wow. That's a lot! What do you think, Song?'

Song didn't say anything. Just kept driving. The only sign that he had even heard the question was the slight raising of one side of his mouth. As though to say he didn't know. Didn't care.

The rest of the day was spent in the cab of the truck. When it pulled in to refuel, Siswan used the service station to wash. Other than that, the three of them just sat and watched the road unroll ahead of them. Song didn't say much, but Tad kept up a flow of conversation regardless. He was a mine of information. Some useful, some useless.

He told her about the big town on the coast. The one the farangs visited to spend their money.

'They come from all over the world, Bee,' he told her. 'They have lots of money and spend it on beer and women.'

'How do they spend it on women?' Siswan asked.

'They give the girls money to spend time with them. The girls go with them. Spend two weeks with them sometimes. Earn a lot of money. My girlfriend got one farang to give her enough to buy me a motorbike,' Tad smiled at the thought.

Siswan didn't ask anymore. The thought of Bak and his motorbike, the way he had earned it, crept into her mind. She tried to shut it out, but the memories were too fresh. Too easily remembered.

'She says she's going to earn enough for us to buy a house,' Tad continued. 'She's a good girl. Takes good care of me.'

Song snorted. They both looked at him and, for the first time, he spoke.

'A good girl? Sleeping with farangs for money?' he laughed. A short laugh that summed up his feelings towards Tad and his girlfriend.

'You won't be laughing when it happens,' Tad said. 'You'll see.'

Song didn't say anything else and neither did Tad for a while. The three of them watched the road, each lost in their own thoughts.

For Siswan, the road seemed like her future. It stretched out before her as far as she could see. She didn't know where it was taking her and, for the moment at least, she didn't much care. The road lay before her. She was traveling along it. That was good enough for now.

Finally, after almost twelve hours, they approached the outskirts of a big town. The traffic built up once more and Song had to sound the horn several times as he tried to jockey for position amongst the cars, motorbikes and other trucks.

Tad pointed out several farangs walking along the pavements as they drove past.

'There's one!' He pointed, excitedly. 'And another.'

Siswan got a good look at the white skinned foreigners. A man and a woman were bartering with a street trader as the truck slowly rolled by. Through the open window she could make out the strange language they were using.

'That's English, Bee,' Tad explained. 'All the farangs speak English. Even if they don't come from England. English is the most important language in the world.'

'Do you speak it, then?' Siswan asked him.

'No. What do I want to speak it for?' he asked, as a reply.

Song snorted once more. A derisory sound that told them what he thought of the idea of speaking the English language.

Siswan stared at the farangs. According to Tad they were rich. According to Tad they were also stupid and gave their money to girls. All the girls had to do was to pretend to love them.

'But how can you pretend love?' Siswan asked.

'My girlfriend, Bom, just tells them she loves them. They believe her,' Tad answered.

After passing through the busy streets, Song eventually pulled in to a small opening that led into a builders yard. Bringing the truck to a stop, he opened the door and jumped down from the cab. Tad and Siswan followed.

'That's it, Bee,' Tad told her. 'This is as far as we go.'

'Thank you for the lift,' Siswan told him.

'Where are you going now?' Tad asked.

'Oh, I can walk from here. It's only a few more streets,' she said.

'Maybe we'll see you around then,' Tad said, with a smile and a wave.

Siswan looked around the small yard as Tad began unlocking the rear doors of the truck. There were building materials piled high in every corner. A small office stood to one side and, through a side window, she could see Song showing some paperwork to a girl sat inside. There was nothing else for her to do but to stroll back out the way they had entered. She shrugged her bundle over her shoulder and walked towards the small gateway they had driven through.

'Wait.' The call came just as she was about to leave the yard.

She turned to see Song walking purposefully towards her. His stocky frame moved in a crisp, mechanical way, as he approached. Like someone marching rather than walking. He stopped in front of her and looked into her eyes. For a moment he didn't speak. Just looked at her.

When, finally, he spoke she was shocked. For almost twelve hours he hadn't said more than a few words, but he'd obviously been listening.

'I don't know who you are or where you're from,' he said. 'But I know you're running away from something.'

Before she could answer he continued.

'I don't want to know anything. I know enough. But there are things you need to know.'

She stopped thinking about what to say next. She opened her mind to what he had to say. For some reason, her mind told her, what Song was about to tell her would be important.

'Don't pay any attention to him,' Song said, with a nod towards Tad. 'He's young and doesn't know much. His girlfriend is stupid as well.' It was the most she had heard him speak. He continued, 'The farang do have money, but they aren't stupid. If you work with them be careful. We hate to lose face and get angry when it happens. The farang are the same. They take longer to find their anger, but when they do, they are much worse than us. They are bigger and stronger as well. If you work with them learn to understand them first. Learn their ways. You are young, I can tell, but your youth gives you more time. If you want to make money, do it slowly.'

He stopped speaking. Looked into her eyes again. Nodded to himself and began to turn away. He stopped, turned back to her.

'There's a house three streets down that will help you. It is not a nice place, but they have beds and food.' He pointed in the direction she should take. 'In two or three weeks you will need to get those stitches out of your arm. You'll need to wash and clean the bandage every day.' He seemed to have finished.

'Why do you help?' Siswan couldn't prevent the words spilling from her lips.

She'd decided to keep quiet. To tell him nothing. The words just came of their own accord.

'I had a daughter once.' He turned and marched back to help Tad offload the truck. He didn't look back.

Siswan walked out of the yard and into the street. She took the directions Song had given her. The crowds thronged around her. A farang, a big white man wearing shorts that were too short, barged into her. Said something to her. Smiled. Held his hands open as though to show no ill feeling. She smiled back at him and he nodded and moved around her. Her first contact with a farang.

She walked down the busy pavement with Song's words echoing in her mind. Learn their ways, he had said. Learn the ways of the farang.

Chapter 5

Siswan dragged her thoughts back to the present. She looked at the faces of the girls sat around the table. Stopped rubbing at the scar on her arm.

'It's up to you what you do,' she said, quietly. 'Your lives are yours. You have to live them the best way you know how.'

She looked at their faces again. Just girls. Living a life they hadn't expected to live. Enjoying the time they spent together. Playing at living. She remembered the times she had played with her cousins. She and Ped had been the closest.

'Come on girls. Time for work,' she told them, and began to collect the dishes together.

They wouldn't let her finish. It wasn't her place to tidy up after them. They would do it. She deserved more respect. She was their leader. Their boss.

'Miss Siswan?' Apple asked, as the others went about their relative tasks.

'Yes, Apple.'

'I only sent ten thousand home last month.'

Apple was asking for approval. A confirmation that what she had done was all right. To be given retribution.

'What did you do with the rest?' Siswan asked.

'I opened a bank account and saved it.' Her voice sounded guilty. As though she had done wrong.

'You gave your family more than you have given them before, Apple. They'll be pleased,' Siswan told her. 'And you have enough saved to send them more if there's no work in the future.'

'Yes. That's what I thought,' Apple said, pleased that she'd done the right thing.

'How are the new girls coming on?' Siswan asked.

'They're doing well. Jen wants to go with a farang. Bell is beginning to talk to them,' Apple reported.

'Okay. Don't rush them. Give them time to learn. Another couple of weeks for Jen I think.'

'Okay, Miss Siswan. I'll tell her.' Apple gave a wai and went to help the other girls get the bar ready.

Siswan looked about the place. It was beginning to look good. They needed to replace some of the old bar stools, but otherwise, it wasn't looking too bad. She saw Mike come through the main doors and went over to talk to him. She had a few ideas she wanted to ask him about.

'No way!' Mike retorted after she had explained. 'That'll cost a fortune!'

'No it won't, Mike. You know it won't. Why are you against it?' she asked, calmly.

'I just am, that's all. The girls already have a day off each week. No one gives the girls two days!' His voice sounded almost petulant.

'Yes. We'd be the first,' she explained. 'The girls will have more time to enjoy themselves and still get a good rest.'

'But I pay them to work,' Mike stated.

She noticed the word 'I' and not the 'we' he had been using up until then. She knew now why he was so against the idea. She could understand him. He'd worked for so long on his own, making his own decisions, that now he felt a little lost. As though the carpet was being pulled out from under his feet. She had taken over. Had put in place all her ideas. Worst of all, those ideas were working. The bar was making a fortune. She guessed he must be feeling left out. Perhaps a little annoyed that he hadn't been able to do it without her help.

'Okay, Mike. Perhaps it is a stupid idea,' she conceded. 'Maybe the girls don't look tired. Maybe they won't get bored.'

'Oh, I know what you're saying, Siswan. Yes, the girls could do with an extra day, I agree. But it will be expensive, that's all I'm saying.' He was already giving in.

She looked at his face. He didn't look back. Just stared ahead of him. He needed something. Something to convince him that everything was all right. He needed placating. She put her hand on his arm. Pressed slightly so that she knew he felt her touch. He was like a little boy. Even at Mike's age, men were still like little boys. Afraid. Alone. Frightened of things they didn't understand.

'I like you, Mike,' she said to him.

His eyes turned to meet hers. She continued to look. Didn't turn away. She concentrated on him. Tried to make him feel her honesty.

'There are lots of bars struggling out there.' She nodded towards the street. 'I chose this one because of you.'

'Because I'm a soft touch, you mean.' His voice was quieter but no less petulant.

'No. Because you are kind, Mike,' she told him. 'You behave like a gentleman. Even when the girls were ripping you off, you behaved like a gentleman.'

'That's just because I was too soft to do anything about it.' He was coming around. Flattered by her compliment.

'Mike. You don't swear. You don't try to touch the girls. You are the last of a dying breed. A true gentleman.' She smiled.

'I'll agree with the dying bit.' He smiled back. Couldn't stop himself. 'But I'm no gentleman, Siswan. I run what amounts to a brothel. I make money from girls selling themselves to strangers.'

'You don't force them to do it,' Siswan said.

'Be that as it may, I'm still giving them a place to work. An outlet from which they can operate. I'm no better than a pimp really.' He spoke quietly now. As though he had a conscience. Felt guilty.

'That sort of thing happens all over the world, Mike. How many women are used to portray sex for a product that has nothing to do with sex?' she asked. 'Just watch the television commercials, Mike. Look at the billboards, the magazines. Pimps are everywhere. Even women are pimping off the bodies of other women.'

'It doesn't make it right, Siswan,' he said.

'No, Mike. It isn't right. None of this is right.' She indicated the bar. 'What happens here is that we open it up. Make it obvious. Girls are for sale in this part of the world just as they are in every other part of the world. We don't pretend it doesn't exist though. We don't hide it away. '

'I suppose we don't have actual pimps as such.' He was beginning to think.

'Only people like you and me, Mike.' She smiled once more.

'You're not a pimp, Siswan. You work harder than any of the girls,' he told her.

'Do I, Mike?' She raised an eyebrow. 'Have you ever seen me go with a farang?'

'Well, er, no. Not now you come to mention it.' He turned more towards her.

'No. And yet I make more money than all the girls put together,' she told him. 'I'm the biggest pimp you ever met, Mike.'

'Yes, you are,' he smiled. 'I don't get it. Why are you doing all this? I thought maybe you were looking for a farang husband. Someone to take care of you.'

'No, Mike.' She laughed. 'I don't need anyone to take care of me.'

'Everyone needs someone, Siswan. Everyone,' he told her.

'No Mike. I don't need anyone. Not to take care of me anyway,' she said. 'Maybe I just like taking care of you.'

'It feels that way, you know. It feels like I'm just a doddering old hindrance to you,' he said.

'Well, you're not. I like you. I told you that before.' She laughed. Held his arm a little tighter. 'You are like a father to me.'

He looked deep into her eyes. Yes, and you're the daughter I wish I had, he thought to himself. There was no point in arguing. Fathers never won when it came to arguing with their daughters.

'Okay. Up to you. Give the girls the extra day if you want.' He was smiling as he said it. She could twist him around her finger. They both knew it. She kissed him on the cheek. Squeezed his arm.

'Thank you, Papa,' she laughed. 'You'll see I'm right in the end.'

When the girls found out about the extra day they were over the moon. It meant they could get their laundry done. Do all the mundane things they needed to do and still have a night out to enjoy themselves. The second day meant they would get enough sleep to feel refreshed when they got back to work.

'It's a great idea!' Lon exclaimed.

'We'll be able to go to the cinema,' Tak said.

They were all enthusiastic. Even Jen and Bell, who hadn't been there long enough to make the same money as the others, were excited by the thought of two days off.

'We'll be taking on two more girls to cover the time,' Siswan told them. 'You'll all have to help them fit in.'

'No problem, Miss Siswan,' Apple said.

Apple had done a good job with Jen and Bell. Hadn't rushed them. Taught them how to smile. How to win over the men. How to enjoy a farang conversation. She'd even shown them how to deal with the drunk farangs. Just as Miss Siswan had taught her.

'Okay. Now, I need to teach you some new things,' Siswan told them all. 'It's how to deal with farang women.'

'We don't get many of them in here,' Apple said.

'We're getting more and more turn up. Sometimes with their boyfriends or husbands, sometimes in pairs or groups. This bar is earning respect. People are saying it's the best bar in town,' Siswan explained.

She went on to tell them how to entertain farang women.

'If they are with their boyfriend, speak to them first. Farang women are treated as equals by their men. Not like our men. The women have as much freedom as the men.'

'What, you mean they can buy boys?' Tak laughed.

'Yes. If they want to. It's up to them. Not many do, but there are some,' Siswan said.

Tak stopped laughing. They all started to pay attention. Women who could buy boys? It wasn't something they understood.

'Give them more respect and a higher wai than you give to their male partners,' Siswan said. 'Make sure you speak directly to them. Smile at them. Make them feel welcome. That way they won't see you as a threat to their men.'

She went on to explain that farang women often came in pairs or groups. They drank. Sometimes got more drunk than the men. They were loud and enjoyed themselves.

'But that's not right,' Lon said.

'Why not?' Siswan asked her.

'Well, women shouldn't behave like that.'

'Who says?'

'It's just not done, that's all.'

'It's not done where?' Siswan pushed against their beliefs.

'Well. We can't do that. Not if we're not working.'

'So, it's okay to be drunk and loud when you're working, is it?'

'It's a part of the job., isn't it?' Lon was tailing off. She didn't like being the focus of Miss Siswan's attention.

'You don't know enough,' Siswan said to all of them. 'You know your lives. Your upbringing. You aren't dealing with locals. You're dealing with people who have been taught that it's okay to enjoy themselves.'

'What if they want to buy a girl?' Tak asked.

'Fancy going with a farang woman, do you, Tak?' Siswan smiled.

Tak went red. She hadn't meant that exactly. She had just wanted to know where she stood when dealing with them. Now everyone was laughing at her.

'I know why you asked,' Siswan told her. 'Again, it's up to you. I don't know what your tendencies are, but if a farang woman asks, and you want to try it, why not? It can't be as bad as going with some of the men. But, and I mean this, I don't want this bar becoming a gay bar, so use your discretion.'

The first of the customers entered the bar behind her. A group of four men. Two of them had their farang girlfriends with them. The girls looked defensive. As though they weren't sure about going into a bar with all these sexy local women.

'See?' Siswan said to the girls. 'Off you go, and remember, the women are just as important as the men. Maybe even more so.'

She watched as the girls dispersed. Apple and Tak made straight for the women. They each offered their highest wai. The two farang women looked a little unsure. One of them tried a wai in reply. Almost got it right. Not quite. Apple showed them to a table. Held the arm of one of the women. Smiled beautifully. Talked directly to her. Made her feel more important than the men. Tak took the orders and went off to get the drinks.

Siswan watched as Apple chatted away quite animatedly to the two farang women. Before long they were chatting back. Feeling at ease. Laughing. When Tak returned she gave the drinks to the women before the men. Unheard off in her own culture. Men first. Always the men first.

Siswan wanted farang women to come to the bar. She knew it would attract even more men. Farang men always went where the best looking girls were. It was a fact of life. They would be even more inclined to drink in a bar that catered for Western women as well as locals. More to look at.

The girls were learning. Learning to understand the ways of the farang. They were becoming more like professional entertainers than bar girls. Almost like the Japanese Geisha girls of old. Less clothing though.

Siswan gave Apple and Tak a smile and a nod as she walked past to greet the next customers. The bar was going to be busy that night. Very busy.

It was a little after one in the morning when the fight broke out. Two male farangs sat at the bar started it. Mike had heard their earlier conversation and had been a little concerned but, after they had continued arguing without resorting to violence, he hadn't been overly worried.

He'd heard the same argument before. It was over one of the girls. It was always over a girl. A few too many to drink. A disagreement. A row. Either it escalated into a scuffle, or it just died down without any trouble. All quite normal in the land of guile.

In all the time Mike had been there, he had only seen one or two really serious fights and those had been dealt with by the police. A quick beating with the nightsticks, a night in the cells, a fine for causing trouble. The police dealt quickly and sternly with troublemakers.

These two seemed to be happy just arguing. He left them to it and concentrated on the customers to his right. A nice couple who wanted to know about life as an expat. He was trying to make it sound interesting. It wasn't that easy. How did he make sitting in a bar every night interesting? The two men continued their argument in the background.

'All I'm saying is she's my girl. That's all.'

'How can she be your girl? She's a hooker.'

'Yeah, but while I'm here she's mine.'

'Half an hour ago you said you wanted another!'

'Yeah, well I've changed my mind.'

'Okay. I don't want her, anyway.'

'So why were you talking to her then?'

'I was just saying hello.'

'How do I know that. You were talking their lingo.'

'Bloody hell, Jim. She said hello to me first. What am I supposed to do, ignore her?'

'You know she was with me last night,' Jim argued.

'Yes, I know. But I didn't know you wanted her again tonight. You said you didn't.'

'What I'm saying is, if she was with me last night, a friend, a proper friend, wouldn't go with her the following night.'

'I'm not going to go with her. I just said hello. I've already told you I don't go with the girls.'

'Don't tell me you never go with a girl, Phil. What are you, gay?'

Phil was getting exasperated. He'd been in the country for a year working on a book. Jim was someone he knew from back home who had latched onto him as though he were an old friend.

To be honest he didn't like the guy that much. Now he was being accused of trying to take some girl the guy had bought the night before.

When he had first arrived he had indulged once or twice himself. He knew the score. First timers were always amazed by the promiscuity of the bar girls. Couldn't resist really. But he'd learned. Learned a bit of the language as well. Now he was happy to enjoy a few drinks with them, get to know one or two quite well. In fact, he had a few friends now. People who he liked. Not like this jerk who seemed to fall in love with every girl he bought. He even expected them to love him in return.

'Jim, I'm trying to explain. I like the girls. I don't buy them anymore. There's nothing wrong with being polite,' he said, sounding more than a little exasperated.

'Yeah, but why speak the lingo in front of me? I don't know what you're saying to her, do I?' Jim was getting even more animated. His finger was pointing at Phil's chest.

'But why would you want to know? What's it got to do with you?' Phil was getting fed up with this. The conversation just went around in circles.

'Because she's my girl.'

'Why is she working here tonight, then?'

'That's her job.'

'Exactly. So someone could walk in and bar fine her right now.'

'No. She's waiting for me. I can see that. So should you.'

'All she's waiting for, Jim, is for someone to pay her bar fine. Anyone.'

Jim didn't understand Phil. He'd come over to see him and now the bastard was trying to take away his girl. He talked to all of them in their own language. When they laughed he was sure they were laughing at him. He'd seen the smile he gave his girl. What did he go and smile at her for, if he didn't want her? He knew what was going on here. He'd seen guys like Phil before. Always interested in some other man's woman. Couldn't pull their own.

'You're just jealous,' he told Phil.

'Jealous that you bought a hooker, Jim? How on earth do you work that one out?'

'Because I saw her first and now you wish you had.'

'No. I don't wish I'd seen her first, Jim. I saw her last week, before you got here, and the week before, and I didn't buy her then either. Just said hello, same as tonight.' Phil was getting truly bored with the conversation.

'She told me she liked me a lot,' Jim said, emphatically. As though that were the end of it.

'So, what are you going to do about it?' Phil asked, taking another pull from his beer.

'What do you mean?' Jim asked in return.

'Well, if you like her so much, and she likes you, are you going to let her carry on selling her body in a bar?'

'I can't do anything about that, can I?' Jim raised his voice.

'Yes, you can. You could pay her enough money each month to take care of her, her child, her mother, father and the rest of the family.'

'I haven't got that kind of money,' Jim blurted out.

'How do you know, you didn't even ask how much it would cost?' Phil said.

'Don't act bloody superior with me, Phil. I notice you don't have a bloody girlfriend.'

'My choice, Jim. But, really, how can you think of her as a girlfriend, someone who you expect to like you, when you leave her working in a bar?' Phil asked.

'I haven't got enough money for a long standing girlfriend, right? But when I buy one I expect to be treated proper. And I treat them proper in return,' Jim stated.

'Yeah, right,' Phil said. 'And you think buying a girl is a proper way to treat them?'

'She said she liked me,' Jim repeated himself. 'Said she liked me a lot because I'm always smiling.'

'They all do, Jim. It's a part of the game,' Phil told him. He was truly fed up with this conversation. 'So, do you want to stay here or go elsewhere?' he asked, trying to change the topic.

'I'm staying here. I told you.' Jim was slurring slightly.

'Okay. Well, in that case, I'm going to nip down and see Dave. The first bar we went to, remember?'

'Yeah, you do that, Phil. Whilst you're at it, why don't you just fuck off?' Jim was raising his voice.

Phil couldn't be bothered any more. The idiot would be going home in two days. He was glad. With a shrug he started to slide off the barstool. He called for his bill in the local language. The young girl behind the counter smiled to let him know she had heard.

'There you go again!' Jim shouted. 'Trying to pull the cashier now!'

'What the hell is the matter with you, Jim?' Phil asked. 'Why are you shouting? You're a bloody embarrassment.'

Jim suddenly picked up his bottle of beer and threw the contents at Phil. Beer splashed over the bar as well as a few other customers. Not much actually landed on Phil.

'You really are pathetic, Jim,' Phil laughed and then stopped as Jim swung the bottle towards his head.

All hell broke lose in a matter of seconds. When Jim swung the bottle, Phil moved to one side and bumped into another farang who, in turn, spilt his beer all over his girlfriend. She took a few steps back and barged into Lon who was serving drinks to a table full of customers. The tray Lon held flipped up and spilt glass and contents all over the table. The first farang swung a blow at Jim and caught him on the side of the head, just above his ear.

As Jim fell backwards he knocked into Big Barry who, without stopping to think, launched a blow towards the first farang. Phil ducked away from the fight and barged into another group who had just arrived at the bar.

Within seconds, girls were screaming, people were trying to get out of the way and several farangs were stepping into the fray with intent. Glasses and bottles started to fly.

'Call the police.' Siswan told Apple.

There was no point in trying to stop the fight themselves. Siswan had seen enough bar fights to know when things had gone beyond reasoning. She watched as the first bar stool was broken across Big Barry's back. They would definitely have to buy more now.

The rest of the girls moved towards where Siswan stood safely out of range of the rampaging farangs. Mike edged his way around the perimeter to join them.

'Bloody hell, Siswan,' he laughed. 'Haven't had a night like this for years!'

'When you farangs get going there's no stopping you is there?' she smiled back.

There was no need to be upset by the brawl. No real damage was being done. The girls, including Pan, had all managed to get clear. Big Barry was enjoying himself. John, normally so quiet, was whooping out loud as he belted another head with an ashtray. Even the farang girls joined in. Two of them were giving Jim a real hammering.

It was Mirak who turned up a couple of minutes later. He was wearing civilian clothes even though the two constables with him were in full uniform. They both had their nightsticks out.

Instead of charging in and breaking a few sculls however, Mirak held them back and spoke to Siswan.

'Hello, Siswan,' he said. 'How would you like us to deal with this?'

'With the minimum of fuss, Mirak,' she said. 'Please use discretion.'

'Okay. No problem,' he said to her. 'Good to see you again.'

Without waiting for a reply, he walked back to his constables. Said a few words. The three of them moved into the fray. The constables refrained from using their nightsticks, but made sure no one interfered with the passage of their boss. One or two farangs felt themselves being shoved unceremoniously aside. When they reached the centre, Mirak took a police whistle from his pocket and blew an ear piercing blast that stopped everyone in their tracks.

'We can do this two ways,' he said in perfect English. 'The easy way or, better still, my way.' He shot a grin to Siswan.

She watched as he placated the farang customers. Was surprised how easily he calmed everyone down. He even cracked a joke or two to put everyone at their ease. He inspected one or two sculls and, having found Jim with a nasty gash across his forehead, instructed his constables to escort him to the hospital. Finally, when calm had once again descended and the customers returned to drinking and talking about what had happened, he returned to where Siswan stood with Mike and the girls.

'No trouble, Siswan. They seem quite happy,' he said.

'You handled that very well, Mirak. Thank you,' she replied.

'Some are easier than others to deal with.' He grinned.

He gave a nod towards Mike and even went as far as to offer him a genuine smile. Siswan was impressed. Here was a man who appeared so confident in his manner. A man who had obviously learned the ways of the farang. Mike nodded in reply before he and the girls went back to work, leaving the police sergeant and Siswan alone.

'Thank you again, Mirak,' she said, not really knowing what else to say.

'Your bar is doing very well, Siswan. I'm very impressed,' he told her as he looked around.

'It's not my bar, Mirak. I just work here.'

'Well, before you came it was ready to close down.'

'It just needed a little help, that's all.'

'Do you work every day?' he asked, looking into her eyes.

'Yes.' She cut him off.

She didn't want any complications. Not now. Now that everything was starting to go right in her life. Especially the type of complications a local man could bring. Especially, a local policeman.

'I was wondering if, perhaps, you would like to meet up for a coffee one day?' he asked her.

His voice sounded slightly unsure. As though he wasn't used to asking that type of question.

'No. Thank you, but no,' she replied.

'Oh, okay.' He sounded disappointed. 'Well, maybe we'll meet again under better circumstances.'

'Probably when you come for your money.' Siswan couldn't help the cutting remark. Couldn't prevent herself from testing him. To see how he reacted. To her surprise, he laughed.

'Yes. Probably,' he said. 'Mind you, I think you got your money's worth this month.'

'I was impressed by the way you handled it.' She softened a little.

'Thank you. That makes us both impressed by each other. Something in common, Siswan.' He grinned. Such an infectious grin.

'I'd better be getting back to work,' she told him, without moving.

'Yes. Me too.' He didn't move either.

'Look,' he started.

'I just,' she began.

They both laughed. Siswan couldn't help but like the man. All of her experience told her not to like him. Not to trust him. To leave well enough alone. But there was something in his confident and easy manner that attracted her.

'You first,' she said.

'No. No, ladies first. I insist.'

'Okay. I was just going to say that I don't need any complications in my life at the moment.

I'm busy and I'm happy, okay?' She looked into his eyes.

'That's fair enough, Siswan. I don't want to be a complication to you,' he said, seriously. 'I only proposed a coffee, not marriage.'

She tried really hard. Told herself that it wouldn't be any good. Mentally kicked herself to bring her mind back to the business in hand. She didn't have time for this. Didn't have the inclination. She didn't need anyone. She reminded herself that the only person she could trust, the only person she could truly rely upon, was herself.

No, she wouldn't fall for this man with his infectious smile and confident, yet boyish, charms. No. Definitely not.

'Well, I could meet you tomorrow at eleven.' She couldn't believe the treachery of her own voice. 'Just for a coffee,' she quickly added.

He smiled. Not only did his mouth smile, his eyes did as well. His whole face lit up. She just couldn't prevent herself from smiling with him.

'That's great,' he said. 'Meet you at the coffee bar up the road?'

'Yes. Alright,' she told him. 'I have to go back to work now.'

'Thank you, Siswan,' he said, and gave her a wai. 'See you tomorrow.'

She gave a wai of her own and turned back to the bar. She felt hot. Her face was flushed. What the hell was she doing? This wasn't a part of her plan. She shook her mind free. Back to work. There were one or two customers still looking a little shocked. She didn't want to lose their custom. She smiled and moved towards them.

*****

When Siswan left the bar in the early hours of the morning she walked up the main road to the bank. She used the twenty-four-hour deposit drawer and banked just over sixty thousand. Not bad for one evening. The bar was doing really well. After deducting overheads, her and Mike were splitting almost a million a month between them. Her personal bank account stood at nearly three million. Not bad for a girl who had started out with absolutely nothing.

It wasn't enough though. Not yet. She reckoned on another two years, maybe three. By then she would have enough. She knew the local attitude of only thinking about today because tomorrow may never come was stupid. What if tomorrow did come? She was planning for hers.

She hailed a motorbike taxi and gave directions to her room. There was no need to use anything other than a motorbike taxi. They were cheap and she wasn't out to impress anyone.

As she stepped into her small room on the third floor of the apartment block she kicked off her shoes. It wasn't polite to wear shoes into one's own home. Even a home as simply furnished as hers. A single room that contained a bed, a chair and table, a wardrobe and a basic dresser with a mirror. She didn't need anything else and it was extremely cheap.

She took off her clothes and went to the bathroom to shower. Pouring cold water from the large bucket stood in the corner, she washed her body and hair. Drying herself with a white towel she moved across the small room and sat at the dresser. She looked at her reflection in the mirror.

'You fool,' she said to herself.

She didn't know why she had agreed to meet Mirak for a coffee. It was most annoying. The last thing she needed was a man in her life. She used the towel to dry her wet hair. She couldn't help but think about him. His smile. The way his face lit up. His confident manner. The way he had controlled the farangs fighting in the bar. So confident and yet not so much that he became arrogant. It was most infuriating that she couldn't yet find anything not to like about him.

She shook her head and allowed her hair to fall across her shoulders. She took a note pad and pen from the small drawer in front of her. A quick line to Ped.

Siswan had kept her promise to her cousin and sent her money each month to take care of her parents. She realized she was a hypocrite. Always telling the girls that their families didn't deserve any help and yet here she was, sending money home. Just like a bar girl.

Ped had written back a few times thanking her and telling her how her parents were doing. Her father was very ill. Her mother not quite so bad. Siswan guessed her father would not be too long for this world. She hoped he would return as a dog. A dog that would be beaten every day by a cruel master.

The note she wrote this time told Ped to buy a mobile telephone and she included her own telephone number. It would be easier than writing. She wrote out a cheque for twelve thousand and, together with the note, she sealed the envelope. She stood it on its edge by the mirror to remind her to post it before meeting Mirak.

She looked at her image once more. An image she still found difficult to face. No one else saw what she saw. They only saw what was on the surface. A woman. A woman with a pretty face and a pleasant smile. They didn't see what she saw. The hurt. The pain. The revulsion of what she had been made to do and the things she had made herself do. The condemnation from her own mother.

She turned away and made for her small bed. She switched on the ceiling fan. The breeze it produced was hardly cool, but the noise was strangely soothing. She lowered herself to the bed and switched off the light.

Lying in the dark, with the sound of the fan circling above her, she allowed her thoughts to wander. The bar was doing very well. Mike was a good partner and allowed her the freedom she needed to operate. The fight earlier in the evening had been a little unexpected, but it had soon been resolved. By Mirak, of all people. He was her only concern.

The charming and confident Mirak had gotten past her defence. She couldn't understand how it had happened. She sighed in the dark. It had been her own fault. She was the one who had accepted the offer of coffee. Why? She didn't know. Didn't understand her own actions. Why hadn't she just left it? Let the conversation end? She hadn't though.

She had deliberately told herself not to accept his invitation. Had turned him down. Had stopped him asking again. And then, when everything was settled, she had suggested meeting tomorrow morning. This morning, she corrected herself. In a few hours time. She couldn't believe it.

'You fool,' she berated herself, again.

She didn't need anyone. Didn't want anyone. Yet here she was, telling Mike he was like a father to her and arranging to meet Mirak for a coffee. What was happening to her?

It was true about Mike though. He was like the father she had always dreamed of having. Not like a real father at all. He was mild mannered. Polite. Kind in his own way. And, most importantly, he had a conscience. He even felt guilty over the way he lived his life. She wished he was her father. He wouldn't have beaten her mother. She knew that about him. He wouldn't beat a woman.

Now Mirak. First Mike and now Mirak. What on earth did she think she was doing? She determined that when they met she would be polite, refuse another date and leave him in no doubt that he wasn't needed. Wasn't wanted. Wasn't welcome. She didn't need anyone other than herself.

With a shrug and an almost angry pull at the thin sheet that covered her, Siswan turned onto her side and closed her eyes tight. Better to think of something else. Better to go to sleep and deal with Mirak when she awoke. There was little point in thinking about it now. She allowed her mind to drift to other matters.

She would need to order more bar stools. Would need to make sure that the bar was cleaned from top to bottom again. She'd check with the cleaners after she'd had some sleep. After she'd met with Mirak, she told herself.

She was going around in circles! Everything seemed to be leading back to him. To his smile. The way his eyes lit up. His confident and easy manner.

'Oh stop it!' she said aloud in the dark.

She concentrated on something else. Anything else. Something that would take his image away from the front of her mind. She remembered the workhouse. The first real bed she had since leaving the village. She couldn't call the hospital bed a real bed. It wasn't as though she had really slept in it. Not like the workhouse bed. She'd slept in that one sure enough. Slept from exhaustion. A dreamless sleep that did little to ease the aches and pains in her tired body. Not for the first few weeks anyway.

Chapter 6

When Siswan eventually found the house that Song had mentioned, she was tired and dizzy from dodging the people that strolled along the busy pavements. So many people. Farangs wandered along looking into the local stalls that sold everything their owners could think of to entice the rich foreigners to spend money. More locals rushed back and forth calling to the white skinned westerners.

'Massage?'

'Tuk-Tuk?'

'Watch, very cheap watch?'

'Suit? You want good suit?'

She couldn't take it all in. There was too much to understand. So much she didn't know. Restaurants and cafes lined the streets. Coffee shops, bars, ice cream parlours. She didn't have a clue. Couldn't comprehend what was going on. She had never seen anything like it.

Arriving at the front of the house, she looked up at its worn façade. Paint peeled off the wooden frames of the windows. The concrete exterior looked worn and dirty. It was in a back street. Away from the throngs of holiday makers that wandered the main road.

The steps leading up to the front door were almost covered in pairs of old, worn, rubber flip flops. She slid her feet out of her own and left them on the bottom step. Her feet were dirty. She felt ashamed. The rest of her body felt just as stained.

She walked up the steps and into the darkened foyer. An old wooden desk stood off to one side with an equally old woman sat behind it. On the desk was a book. Its binding was worn and faded, but Siswan could make out that it had once been red. The old woman eyed her as she approached.

'Hello,' Siswan said, and gave a wai.

'What's your name?' the old woman croaked.

There was no other welcome. No wai. Not even a smile. Siswan considered herself too lowly to complain. It didn't matter anyway. This was her last hope. She needed a bed, a shower, something to eat.

'Bee,' she said.

'Identity card?' The old woman raised an eyebrow.

'I don't have one,' Siswan answered, in all honesty.

'Where are you from?'

Siswan lied again, giving the old woman the name of a village they had passed through on their way to the coast.

'You will have to share. Sign here.' The old woman turned the worn book towards her and opened the pages to the most recent. 'You can write, can't you?'

'Yes. I can write. And read,' Siswan told her as she inserted her false name on the first free line.

'Most of you can't,' the old woman said, as she turned the book towards her and checked what Siswan had written.

Siswan didn't answer or make a comment. There didn't seem to be any need. The old woman didn't appear to care.

'What's the matter with your arm?'

'I cut it working in the fields,' Siswan told her.

She didn't ask any further questions. She'd seen enough girls walk in here with bandages or scars. They all said they cut themselves working in the fields.

'Room eleven.' She nodded towards the back of the foyer where Siswan could make out a flight of stairs. 'Back here at seven tomorrow morning to start work.'

'What will I be doing?' Siswan asked.

'Laundry,' the old woman told her.

Siswan started towards the stairs. Her small bundle of clothes seemed heavy as they swung from her arm. Before she reached the first step she stopped and turned.

'What is your name?' she asked the back of the old woman.

'Ma.' She didn't turn. Just said the word.

'Thank you, Ma,' Siswan said and, once again, made for the stairs.

The room was small. There was a single, dim light bulb hanging by a twisted wire from the ceiling. There was no window. The walls were bare concrete. No paint. No colour. The air hung heavy and smelled musty. Two beds, one on each side of the room, contained single, foam-filled mattresses. Nothing else. No sheets. No pillows.

There was a rail along one wall. Two t-shirts and a pair of worn shorts hung from it. To the left an opening, that had once been filled with a door, led to a small bathroom. A hole in the floor, surrounded by a white porcelain rim, sufficed as the toilet. A large black dustbin, filled with water, contained a small plastic yellow bowl. The combination served as a shower and toilet cistern. It was enough.

Siswan chose the bed nearest the door. Opened her bundle on it. Hung up her shirts and spare shorts on the rail beside the existing clothing. She stripped off and stepped into the bathroom. Washed herself from head to feet. The cold water made her feel more awake. Cooler. She found what remained of a bar of soap on the floor beside the large bucket. She used it to wash herself and her hair. It felt good to get clean again.

She removed the grubby bandage from her arm and looked, for the first time, at the scar that ran down to her wrist. Black stitches held the wound closed. The flesh on either side looked red and swollen. She counted eighteen stitches.

After carefully washing her arm, and making sure she rinsed it thoroughly with the cold water, she washed the bandage and hung it over the rail. The thin gauze wouldn't take long to dry in this heat, she decided.

She dried herself, using one of her spare shirts. She was very careful to dry the stitches in her arm. Then she washed the shirt and the other clothes she had been wearing. She hung the wet items in the bathroom to drip dry.

By the time she had finished her laundry, the bandage was dry enough to replace. She wound it, as best she could, around her arm and tied it off at the wrist. It would do to protect the wound from dirt.

Finally, when she felt that she was ready for the following day, she pulled a clean shirt over her head to act as a nightgown and allowed herself to collapse onto the single bare mattress of her chosen bed. Within minutes she was fast asleep.

It seemed only a short time before she was shaken rudely awake. She was still too tired to do anything about it. A hand shook her shoulder, a voice spoke.

'You're in my bed.'

Siswan rolled over and looked into the face of an older girl. Her thoughts returned to the old man in the park. He had said much the same thing. The eyes staring at her were cold and hard. There was no kindness within them.

'I said, you're in my bed!' the girl shouted at her.

'I'm sorry,' Siswan mumbled sleepily. 'I didn't know.'

She struggled to her feet and crossed the small space to fall onto the other bed. It sagged badly in the middle and she realized why the girl had been so insistent that she move. She rolled about trying to get comfortable. In the end, despite the awkward position the bed forced her to take up, she fell asleep once more.

When she awoke in the early hours of the morning, her body ached from her uncomfortable sleeping position. She stretched her limbs as best she could before trying to sit up. She didn't know what time it was, but guessed it was early. She was so used to waking early that she would have surprised herself more than anyone to have overslept.

She slowly crossed to turn on the small light. Her body still felt stiff and her back hurt as she walked the few paces. She turned on the light and saw, for the first time, her roommates' prostrate body lying prone on her bed. She lay naked and didn't move. The only sign that she was even alive was the slight raising of her chest as she breathed.

Siswan took a few seconds to look at the girl. She didn't look quite so old as she had the previous night. Maybe sixteen or seventeen. Her breasts were fully developed and hung slightly to either side of her body. The dark patch of her pubic hair formed a tangled triangle as it descended between her legs. She carried more weight than Siswan. Slightly chubby, Siswan thought.

The girl's long black hair was strewn around her head and framed her face as she lay on the old mattress. One hand lay across her stomach and Siswan noted the broken fingernails and weather beaten skin. Her hands looked as though they worked hard.

Suddenly, the girl moved. A turn of her body. A small groan. The light no doubt disturbing her slumber. Siswan moved at once. She didn't want to be caught staring at the girl. She moved towards the bathroom. She would take another shower, get dressed and go downstairs to see what the day would bring.

When she entered the bathroom she found that all her clothes had been taken down from their various hanging places and thrown onto the floor next to the toilet hole. With a silent sigh she started to pick them up, only to notice the strong smell of urine emanating from them. Siswan stopped picking the clothes up. Why would a girl she didn't know do something like that? What kind of girl, what kind of person, would be so unkind? An anger began to swell inside her. She had felt this anger before. The time she had finally dealt with Bak. Now she felt it again. A slow anger. An anger that could be used.

She picked up a shirt from the top of the pile. Twisted it until it wouldn't turn anymore. Folded it, and twisted again. When she finished she held a hardened club of cloth that was soaked in urine. She returned to the small bedroom.

The girl had turned fully onto her stomach. Her bare buttocks rose into the air. Siswan could make out small, pale stretch marks on her skin. Without thinking too much about what she was doing she allowed the anger within her to well up. Allowed it to control her actions. Her feelings. She brought the homemade club down as hard as she possibly could across the girl's buttocks.

There was a moment of hesitation. A moment before what had happened penetrated the mind of the sleeping girl. A second or two passed before the intense pain she felt made her fully awake. During that time Siswan watched in compassionless fascination as the stretch marks on the girl's bottom disappeared beneath the redness that rose from deep within the skin.

With a suddenness that made Siswan take a step back the girl awoke, turned and screamed all in one go. She twitched off the bed as though her backside was on fire.

Within moments she understood what had happened and looked at Siswan with evil intent written in her eyes. She started quickly. So quickly it almost took Siswan by surprise. The girl's arms reached out towards her and her fingers sought to scratch. Siswan moved too fast.

Even as the hands came together to claw their way through her skin, she ducked beneath them. Moving to the side, she swung the club once more. This time she caught the girl across the ribs. She heard the gasp of air escape the girl's lungs. Even as she started to turn, Siswan hit her again. This time across her shoulder. The girl was nowhere near as fast as a scorpion. Not so dangerous either. She fought like a girl. Tried again to scratch Siswan. To grab her hair. To slap her. A cat fighter.

Siswan was no match for her opponent. With ease she twisted away from her clawing hands. Slipped beneath her open handed slaps. She hit her again and again with the coiled shirt until, with a suddenness that matched the beginning, the fight was over.

The girl slipped to the floor and hung her head in defeat. Siswan had beaten her. She sat down on the edge of her bed and looked at the girl. Waited for the sobs to stop.

'What's your name?' she asked her finally, when the girl was quiet.

'Noy,' the girl answered, quietly.

'Mine is Bee. Pleased to meet you, Noy,' Siswan said, with a smile.

Noy looked up. Her hair covered half her face. She brushed it away with the back of her hand. She sniffed loudly and rubbed the tears away from her eyes. She looked into the smiling face of Siswan and couldn't help but smile back.

'Pleased to meet you too, Bee,' she said, and held out her hand.

They shook hands and laughed. Siswan helped her up. Noy stood only an inch or two taller than her.

'Sorry about the clothes,' Noy said. 'I had a bad day yesterday,' she added, as an excuse.

'Sorry about the bruises,' Siswan said.

Noy looked down. The red welts across her shoulder and chest were already beginning to turn blue. The one across her backside was almost black. She twisted as far as she could to see it.

'I won't be able to sit down for a while, that's for sure,' she said, as she craned her neck.

'No. I don't expect you will,' Siswan agreed.

Noy stopped inspecting her body and turned to face Siswan properly.

'How old are you, Bee?' she asked.

'Sixteen,' Siswan told her, without hesitation.

'A year younger than me. Where are you from? What are you doing in this dump?'

Siswan gave her the name of the village she had given to Ma. Told her she was here because of a family dispute. Nothing else.

'What happened to your arm?'

'I cut it working in the fields.'

'Oh, really?' Noy couldn't be sure if the girl was telling the truth, or not. It was difficult to tell.

'No. Not really,' Siswan said, looking Noy in the eyes.

For the next three weeks Siswan worked in the laundry washing sheets and towels from hotels, tablecloths from restaurants and everyday clothing from farangs. The never ending piles of dirty clothes were brought to the back of the house by trucks, carts and even piled high on the back of motorbikes.

The back yard contained a large shed made from corrugated steel sheets that, during the height of the day, became unbearably hot. Together with ten or so girls, she loaded the big copper vats, stirred the clothes by hand with wooden poles whilst the water boiled, lifted the heavy bundles into the concrete trough that ran down one side of the shed, and rinsed it all under the cold water from the continuously running taps.

Once rinsed, the clothing had to be hung out on the multitude of clothes lines to dry in the sun. If, as it did on many occasions, it rained, the girls all had to stop what they were doing and run to bring it in before it was ruined.

When the clothes were dry they had to be ironed, using old, worn-out electric irons that sometimes got hot, sometimes didn't. Once ironed, the clothing had to be folded and bagged ready for the return trip to the customers. The hardest part was trying to keep track of what belonged to whom. Customers often complained that some item or another had gone missing.

It was long, hot and hard work that wore Siswan out each day. Every evening she had just enough energy to wash her own clothing, clean the bandage on her arm, shower and then collapse onto her uncomfortable bed to sleep a dreamless sleep. Her fingernails began to break at the edges and her hands became worn and sore from the caustic washing powders.

Hardly any of the girls spoke as they worked. They were too tired. Had nothing to say. They just got on with their given work and fell into their beds at night. Ma allowed each girl a small breakfast of rice and, usually, dried fish. Sometimes pork if she could get it cheap enough. Lunch consisted of more rice, some vegetables served with hot spices and, if they were lucky, maybe some chicken or chicken broth. Most of the time Siswan felt hungry.

She quickly learned that it did no good to complain. Ma wasn't even the owner of the place. She just worked there for a man who lived further up country.

He came down once whilst Siswan was there. A small man, with a small moustache. He looked like a weasel. He didn't stay long. Just looked into the shed one day and inspected some of the finished laundry. Siswan had heard him tell Ma that he expected her to use less soap. It was expensive, he said. Get the girls to stir more. That was cheaper.

During those first weeks some girls left and new ones arrived to take their places. There seemed to be a steady stream of girls all willing to work for the price of two meals, a shower and a bed. Siswan found it hard to believe that other girls were in the same position as she was. She thought she was alone. The only one.

At the end of almost four weeks, Ma informed her that she had earned a day off. Noy had the same day. One day off in almost four weeks. It didn't seem all that fair to Siswan, but she looked forward to the following morning. Nothing to do for a whole day.

Her and Noy had become friends. Not close friends. Not in the true sense of the word, but close enough to believe that there was a connection. A common bond perhaps. Noy had taught her to go through the pockets of the clothing just in case a farang had left some money in them.

'Always check, Bee. One girl, last month I think it was, found two thousand. She doesn't work here anymore.'

Siswan checked every pocket she came across, but never found anything. The fact was that the room cleaners who collected the laundry in the hotels did the same thing. The delivery drivers who collected the bundles from the hotels also checked. The girls who unpacked the trucks and motorbikes had a look. By the time the pockets finally arrived in Siswan's hands, they had been picked clean. She checked anyway. Someone may have missed something.

She never truly believed that she would find anything of value. It was a dream the girls shared. Feel inside a pocket. Find a wad of notes. A fortune. Leave the workhouse, find a handsome man. Live happily ever after. A shared fantasy in which they all took part.

When the work was finished, Siswan and Noy went back to their room to plan for the following day.

Siswan made straight for the bathroom to wash the stench of laundry from her skin and hair. She removed the plastic bag she wrapped around her arm each day to keep her bandage dry and slowly unwound the bandage itself. During the last few days her arm had started to itch and the redness surrounding the scar had grown more vivid. Small blisters of puss gathered around the stitches themselves.

'This doesn't look too good,' she said to Noy, as she walked back into the bedroom.

The words were wasted. Noy was already fast asleep, having crashed onto her bed the moment they had entered the room. Siswan had never been able to do that. She couldn't sleep without having first taken the time to clean herself and her clothing. In fact, now that her body was getting used to the laundry work, she found she didn't need much sleep at all.

She sat down on the edge of her bed and examined the black stitching more closely. It seemed as though the thread was getting thinner just as it left, or entered, her skin. As though it was being eaten away by the puss. When she plucked at the first one, it came apart under her fingers. The skin stretched back to a normal position as it became released from the bonds of the thread. The redness under that part of her arm lessened. The knot still protruded from her skin. She pulled it. The broken end of the thread disappeared into her arm and, as she pulled further, came out on the other side of the scar, leaving her arm bare in that one spot.

It had stung as she withdrew the thread, but not too much. Her skin looked better. The small blisters didn't look so swollen. Carefully she pulled and played with all the other stitches until, finally, her arm was bare. The scar ran along the length of her lower arm. It looked a little red and swollen but when she pulled at her skin the wound didn't open. The small pin prick marks made by the stitches made her arm look as though it had a built in zipper. She smiled at the analogy she made.

She returned to the bathroom and washed her arm carefully. She rinsed it thoroughly and, using what was left of her fingernails, she cleaned away the small pussy scabs that surrounded the holes left by the thread. Inspecting her arm afterwards, she decided that it didn't look too bad.

It gave her a tool in fact. People would take her more seriously when they saw it. It made her appear tougher. Harder. Older. She shook Noy awake to show her.

Noy was impressed. Not only by the scar, but also the fact that Siswan had removed the stitches herself.

'Didn't it hurt?' she asked, as she inspected her friend's arm.

'A little. Not much,' Siswan told her. 'What are we going to do tomorrow?'

'Tonight, Bee. You mean what are we going to do tonight!' Noy laughed.

'What do you mean? I'm tired. I need to sleep.' Siswan was confused.

'Get a couple of hours sleep now. I'll wake you up when it's time,' Noy said, before rolling over on her bed.

Siswan did as she was told. She lay down on her bed, tossed around a couple of times to get comfortable, and fell asleep.

When Noy woke her up she yawned and stretched the ache out of her back and shoulders.

'What time is it?' she asked, sleepily.

'Time to get up, get dressed and head for the beach,' Noy told her.

'The beach?'

'Yes.'

'What's a beach?' Siswan asked.

'You don't know what a beach is?' Noy asked, incredulously.

'No. I don't.'

'Where the sea comes in? Sand? People walking, farangs swimming? You don't know?'

'No. I know about walking, swimming and sand, but I don't know what a beach is, okay?' Siswan was a little annoyed by her own lack of knowledge.

'Okay. Okay. I'll show you,' Noy said, quickly. She didn't want her friend to get angry. The bruises had faded, but the memory hadn't.

They both dressed and headed out of the house. Ma was at her usual station behind the old desk as they walked out through the foyer. She didn't say anything. Didn't even acknowledge them.

The two girls headed back down the street towards the main road that Siswan had last walked a month before. They both wore shorts and t-shirts. Their rubber sandals made their characteristic flapping sound as they moved along the pavement.

Siswan became aware of the noise before anything else. The heavy beat of the bass was felt, rather than heard, as they approached the main road. It was dark by the time they arrived and the lights from the bars, restaurants and coffee houses seemed to make everything more real, more alive, than when she had last walked along in the light of day.

People were everywhere. Farangs dressed in casual attire thronged the pavements as they moved from shop to shop and from bar to bar. The street traders plied their goods, services and everything else they could think of, as the rich westerners strolled by.

Siswan started to walk along the pavement in a daze. She had never seen so many people. So much traffic. Motorbikes and tuk-tuks roared past her as they searched for customers amongst the thousands of holidaymakers looking for some fun, some action. The music from the various bars filled her head. She found it hard just concentrating on walking without bumping into people.

'No. This way, Bee.' Noy caught her by the arm and pulled her across the main road.

They had to dodge their way across. The traffic never slowed. Never paused in its search to earn another few coins.

Noy half dragged Siswan along the pavement on the other side of the road. She led her down a set of concrete steps and through a maze of palm trees and foliage until they were far enough away from the road to be able to speak without having to shout.

'Take off your flip flops,' Noy told her, as she bent to pick up her own.

A few more steps and they were on the beach. Siswan could feel the grating coolness of the sand as it rubbed between her toes and scratched at the soles of her feet. It felt good as she walked, her feet sinking into the soft sand with each step.

In the light from the road behind her, Siswan could make out the piles of sun beds that were placed at the top of the beach. They were long, white plastic chairs that looked really comfortable. The piles of blue and green foam mattresses looked far more enticing than the one on her bed in the workhouse.

Noy led her further down towards the inky blackness that lay beyond the sand. Her feet felt the first of the wet sand. She didn't sink so low into it. Found it easier to walk. A cool breeze blew in off the sea into her face. The smell of salt. As her eyes became accustomed to the dim light she saw the white froth of the waves as they fell onto the sand. Stretching away to her left and right she could make out the white waves. The noise as they rushed towards the shore was like nothing she had heard before.

When the wind had made the high stalks of sugar cane rustle back in her village she had loved the sound they made. The waves were even better than that. Each rhythmic crash was like hearing her own heart beating. She ran the last few paces towards the sea.

'Wait, Bee. Don't go in!' Noy called too late.

Siswan felt the cool water on her feet, ankles and knees when she walked out to meet the waves as they rushed towards her. Soon her shorts were soaked. Her t-shirt drenched. Her hair matted and wet. She didn't care. She laughed out loud as wave after wave fought to push her back out of the water. To cast her back upon the dry land where she belonged. The power of the waves threatened to knock her off her feet and the roar they made drowned out the music and traffic from the road behind her.

Finally, when her mouth was filled with the salty taste of the sea and her nose ran from having breathed in too much water, she made for the shore and collapsed onto the sand beside Noy's feet.

'Oh, that was so good!' she laughed. 'I never knew! It's so big!'

'You're mad, Bee. You don't know what's out there waiting to trap you.'

'What do you mean?' She looked up into the face of her friend.

'The sea is full of spirits. Fishermen and sailors who have died out there.' She gestured with her hand. 'There's all sorts of spirits and ghosts.'

'But you said that the farang go swimming,' Siswan said.

'Yes. But the farang aren't like us. They don't know about the spirits. They don't know what could enter their bodies.' Noy sounded slightly exasperated.

Siswan sat on the sand and looked out at the sea. She watched the waves as they came rolling in towards her.

'Maybe they do know,' she said, quietly. 'Maybe they do know and, because they know, they aren't afraid.'

'No, Bee. They can't know. How could they know about ghosts. No one knows,' Noy chided her.

'Well, if no one knows, Noy, it could be that there's nothing to be afraid of?'

'Well. I've heard stories. People have been taken by the spirits and never seen again,' Noy said, emphatically.

'Maybe they just drowned?' Siswan asked, pointedly.

Noy didn't say any more on the subject of the sea. Her attention had been drawn towards the lone farang walking along the edge of the water towards them.

'He looks okay.' She nodded her head for Siswan to follow.

'How do you know? It's dark.' Siswan squinted at the lone figure of the man.

'He's alone and old. That's good enough. Wait here,' Noy said, before starting to walk towards the man.

Siswan watched idly as her friend held a short conversation with the man. After a few moments Noy came trotting back towards her.

'He says yes. You watch out for police or lady boys. If you see anyone coming, whistle or shout, okay?' Noy told her, before turning and running back to the farang.

She took him by the hand, led him back up the beach towards the pile of sun beds they had seen earlier, and ducked out of sight.

Siswan sat on the sand and waited. An awful feeling began to make its way up through her stomach to her brain. She had a feeling she knew what Noy was doing with the farang. She had done it enough times in the sugar cane. She didn't know what to do. Should she leave? Should she stay? It was wrong. What Noy was doing was wrong. What the farang was doing was wrong. Siswan knew that. She knew that with all her heart. It was wrong. Her mother had told her that it was wrong.

Minutes went by. Siswan was still undecided. It suddenly dawned on her where Noy had been the first night she had arrived at the workhouse. What had she said in the morning? She'd had a bad day. That was it. A bad day. What had she meant? It had been bad enough for her to have pushed Siswan out of bed and urinate on her clothes. A bad day. Was this a good day then? Did a bad day mean no farangs to pleasure?

More time went by. Siswan saw another farang walking along the beach in the dim light. A girl walked down from the top of the beach to talk to him. After a few moments they both walked back in the direction she had come. Was this happening everywhere? Were the girls getting paid? Surely this was wrong? Why didn't someone stop it?

Noy and the farang emerged from the pile of sun beds about ten minutes later. The farang continued his stroll along the beach and Noy came running back towards where Siswan waited.

'Two hundred and fifty!' Noy waved the notes in front of Siswan as she sat down beside her. 'You can have the fifty. I told him it would cost that much for you to look out for the police.'

She handed Siswan the fifty. She took it in stunned amazement. That would be the first time she ever accepted money from the prostitution of another girl. It wouldn't be the last.

'What did you do?' Siswan asked.

'Oh, you know. Lady smoke.' Noy made a gesture with her hand and mouth.

Siswan didn't need to know anymore. She knew the gesture. She was amazed by Noy's complete lack of inhibitions. Amazed that she had made two hundred from doing it. No wonder Bak had been able to pay for everything and buy a new motorbike. Albeit on credit.

'Have you ever been caught?' Siswan asked.

'No. Came close once or twice. Sometimes the police patrol the beach. If they find anyone they take all the money from the girl and fine the farang another five hundred. It's the lady boys you have to watch out for though,' Noy told her matter of factly.

'Lady boys?' Siswan didn't know what a lady boy was.

'Yeah. You know. Men who want to be women. They do a show in the main street and then, later, come down to the beach to offer themselves to the farangs.'

'What do they offer?'

'Lady smokes. Like we do. Apparently they are really good at it. Some of the farangs will only go with a lady boy for a lady smoke,' Noy said.

'Oh,' Siswan said, in mild surprise.

'Yes. But we have to watch out for them. It's okay now, whilst they're doing their show, but later, when they come here to work, the girls have to go.'

'Why?' Siswan asked.

'The lady boys will beat or even kill anyone working their beach, Bee. Everyone knows that. Even the police stay away,' Noy explained. 'The beach work at night makes a lot of money. The lady boys aren't worried about picking pockets either.'

'They steal?' Siswan was amazed.

No one she knew actually stole. It was against all the rules of their religion. Mustn't kill or steal. It wasn't good for the soul and you'd never get into heaven.

'They only steal from the farangs, Bee. That doesn't really count, you know.'

'Why not?'

'Well, the farangs are rich. They can afford it. They have too much money anyway. No one really cares about a drunk farang losing a few thousand. What does it matter? He just goes to an ATM machine and gets some more,' Noy laughed. 'They really are stupid.'

'Who? The lady boys or the farangs?' Siswan asked.

'The farangs, of course. They just want sex. They'll pay to get it as well,' Noy said.

Her voice sounded a little unsure. Uncertain of what she had just said. She went quiet.

Siswan didn't speak for a while either. If the farangs were stupid how come they had so much money? It didn't make sense to her. If they were stupid, how could they afford to pay for a holiday to this place? How could they afford to pay for the sex they wanted?

If they are so stupid why is it us living in a workhouse, washing their laundry, whilst they stay in big hotels? She didn't understand. Who, exactly, was being stupid?

'My name isn't Bee,' she said, at last. 'It's Siswan.'

'Mine's Sood,' Noy told her.

'I think we're the stupid ones, Sood.'

'I think you're right,' Sood answered, softly. The earlier excitement in her voice had passed. 'Let's go and buy some whiskey.'

'No. I don't like whiskey.'

They sat on the wet sand and watched the waves roll up to their feet. They both sat in silence until Sood broke it.

'We can't just sit here all night, Siswan.'

'No. I suppose not.' Siswan would have been quite happy to do just that.

'Come on. Let's go.'

'Where?'

'We'll walk along the beach. There might be another farang,' Sood didn't sound so enthusiastic about meeting another westerner.

The two girls walked along the sand. They carried their flip flops and allowed the sea to wash over their feet. Siswan loved the feel of the cool water swirling around her ankles. Her shorts and shirt were still wet but she didn't mind. It was a warm evening and they would soon dry.

They didn't meet any more farangs as they walked and Siswan was pleased that they didn't. She had secretly hoped they wouldn't.

Once they had walked to the far end of the beach they turned and came back along the pavement under the palm trees. The noise of the traffic drowned out the sound of the waves breaking on the shore. The music emanating from the bars on the other side of the road sounded presumptuous and phony compared to the rhythmic beat of the ocean. Man's puny attempt to copy the pure music of nature.

When they reached the point where they had first crossed the busy road, Siswan turned to cross again. Sood stopped her.

'I'm not going to go back just yet, Siswan,' she told her, almost as an apology.

Siswan looked at her friend in the lights cast by the bars and restaurants. Her face looked sad.

'Okay. When you get back don't touch my clothes,' Siswan joked, and took her hand. Held it for a moment. Let Sood know that she understood. That she knew.

'I won't be long. Just another hour or so,' Sood smiled her thanks in reply.

Siswan stood for a moment, watching as her friend crossed the road and wandered along the busy street. Soon she was lost to sight. Enveloped by the tourists.

*****

The following day Siswan awoke alone in the small room. She knew she would. There was no surprise. When she had watched Sood disappear in the crowds the previous night she knew she wouldn't see her again. Something in her manner. The way she had walked away. Siswan allowed herself a pang of regret.

She went to the bathroom and showered. Put on clean clothes. Went downstairs to see what was for breakfast. A few of the other girls were already up and preparing the morning meal. A great pile of clothes had already arrived to be washed. The gas flames under the big copper boilers were already lit and the water was warming. The smell of caustic soda hung in the air.

Siswan walked over to the first of the piles of clothes. She began separating them into various piles that matched their ownership. She sifted quickly through the pockets of the shorts and trousers that she came across. Always the dream. Follow the dream.

As she delved through the pockets of a pair of cargo shorts she felt something in one of the small pockets. The pockets were so small that they weren't intended to actually hold anything. Just for show. A fashion statement. Obviously the owner hadn't realized and had put something in one of them. She pushed her finger deep into the small pocket. Only big enough to carry a pencil, or maybe a small, rolled up piece of paper. No wonder no one had found whatever it was before.

It didn't feel much larger than the seams holding the shorts together. She hooked her finger slightly, caught the bottom of the object. Pulled. A tight roll of paper came out with her finger. Hardly bigger than a cigarette.

'What are you doing here, Bee?' A voice from behind her. Ma's voice.

Siswan quickly fisted the roll of paper. Hid it from view against her palm. She turned towards Ma, dropping the shorts back onto the pile.

'I'm just sorting the clothes,' she said, trying not to sound guilty.

'It's your day off, you stupid girl. Or don't you want a day off?' Ma scorned.

Siswan had forgotten. Completely forgotten. Her mind hadn't been able to comprehend a whole day off, so she had forgotten about it. The concern for Sood, the knowledge that she wouldn't be there in the morning, the events of the previous evening had been enough. A whole day. To do what? Suddenly she knew. She knew exactly what she was going to do with her day off.

'Oh, no. I mean, yes. I just came for some breakfast. It wasn't ready so I started sorting the clothes. Just helping out. Sorry,' she blurted to the portly old woman.

'Stupid girl,' Ma said again, and wandered back to the house.

Siswan quickly pocketed the small roll and went across the yard to see if breakfast was ready. As she turned away, she checked which pile the shorts had come from. It wasn't one of the big hotels. An apartment block, just a short walk from the workhouse, sometimes sent their sheets and guests' clothes to be laundered.

The apartments were for locals who had money or, sometimes, long term farangs who were either retired or working. She guessed the shorts belonged to a farang. They were large. Too large for a local.

After she had eaten, Siswan walked back down the small street to the beach road. It was quiet at that time of the morning. A few people wandered along, mostly locals on their way to work. Some street cleaners were picking up the refuse left from the night before. A few motorbikes whisked their drivers and passengers to wherever they wanted to go.

A dog, a flea bitten old mongrel with a nasty scar running down the side of its face, was sniffing around some dustbins. Hoping for a meal. Preferably meat. It looked up at Siswan as she passed and for a moment they locked eyes. The dog turned away to continue its exploration.

The beach was virtually deserted. A few people were walking along in the sand, but not many. One or two of the piles of sun beds were being laid out ready for the influx of tourists all wanting to laze in the sun. Siswan looked out at the ocean. It was huge. As big as the sky. The waves pounded in against the shore and the sound, as they crashed down, was almost frightening in its intensity. She immediately realized that the previous night she had only ventured a very short way into the water. The waves beyond where she had splashed about were huge. Taller than she stood.

She sat on the sand and looked out to sea in total fascination. Each wave began to rise far out to sea. Then, as it neared the shore, it rose higher and higher, until the very top of the wave fell down onto the base. The water curled downwards and, for a moment, the wave formed a tube. A tunnel of water. Siswan imagined what it would be like inside. Completely surrounded by water! The tunnels, or tubes, didn't last long. The weight of the water above came crashing down to form great walls of white foam that surged towards the shore. Each time a wave rolled in, it became smaller and smaller until, finally, it lapped gently at her feet as she sat on the sand.

She picked one out with her eyes. Far out, beyond the white splashing foam. She followed its progress as it travelled towards her. Rising. Rising higher. Folding. Turning into a tunnel. The roar of sound as it crashed down. The white churning foam as it surged towards the beach. The slowing down. Fading away. Smaller. Smaller. Would it reach her feet? Would it have the strength to wash over the water from the previous wave that was already beginning to flow back to the sea? Come on little wave, she thought, you can do it. She pushed her feet further towards the small wave as it fought to reach her. By now, the huge tunnel of water she had watched earlier was just a small ripple as it eventually nudged against her feet. It had made it.

She felt a sense of loss as it receded down the sand to find its way back to the sea. Within moments it was engulfed by the next wave and she could follow its progress no more.

She felt an affinity with each wave as it tried to climb the sands of the beach to reach her. The waves kept coming. One after another. To Siswan, as she sat watching them, they seemed alive. To be the guardians of the sea. Each one ready to throw anyone who tried to get past them, back onto the shore. To reach the relative calm beyond the waves, you first had to get past their ferocity. Like obstacles blocking your path to a calmer future they stood against you. Had to be overcome.

The sea was just like her life, she thought to herself. If she wanted to get somewhere she was going to have to get past these obstacles. The things that stood in her way. With the sea it was easy to see the problem. The waves were there. One after another. Ready to toss you back. To discard you. Her problems were just like that. To get anywhere she was going to have to fight. To overcome each obstacle that presented itself to her.

She listed the problems in her mind; her own waves. She had no money apart from the fifty Sood had given her. She was too young. She was alone, especially with her friend gone, and she didn't know what she was doing.

She could make money by offering pleasure to men, but she didn't want to do that again. The main problem was not knowing what she was supposed to be doing with her life. She had to decide what it was she wanted. What she could do. Why, when it came right down to it, was she here? Why was she alive? A reason to live. That was what she needed more than anything else.

Suddenly, to her right, there was the sound of police sirens. A wailing banshee of noise that brought her out of her reverie. People were running down towards the sea. Towards the waves. She couldn't see what it was they had seen but there seemed to be much excitement. She stood and started to walk towards the attraction.

By the time she arrived, quite a big crowd had gathered. They all seemed focused on something lying in the shallows. She pushed through the crowds. Tried to see what was causing all the fuss. Couldn't get through.

From the far side of the crowd came the shouts of policemen as they forced their way through the gathering throng. People moved away. Away from the police as they cleared a path for the ambulance crew.

As the crowd moved, a gap opened in front of Siswan. A gap big enough for her to see through. She could see what it was that had attracted all the people.

Suddenly, at that precise moment, Siswan knew exactly why she was there. Why she was alive. Suddenly, like a wave crashing down around her, all her doubts were washed away. The clarity in her mind was stunning in its simplicity.

As Siswan stared down at the dead body of her friend, the answer to her earlier question became obvious. As she took in the pale, water-soaked skin, the dark bruises that marked Sood's face, the cuts on her arms, the deep, vivid red gash that wound its way around her throat, Siswan knew exactly what it was she was going to do. Waves or no waves.

Chapter 7

Siswan awoke at nine in the morning. She told herself that she would have plenty of time to rest when she was older. Now, whilst she was still young, there were things to do. A lot to do.

When she had showered and dressed, she slipped the letter to Ped into her small handbag and left the room. She had enough time to stroll along the beach front before meeting with Mirak. She still loved to watch the sea. To look beyond the waves.

As she walked down towards the beach she thought about her next move. Obviously she would have to run it past Mike, but she didn't think he'd object. Apple was doing really well and, with a little incentive, she was sure the girl would agree to the changes.

A car, drawing near to her, sounded its horn. She looked to see a group of young locals leering at her. They waved and called out as they drove past. Young boys hoping for a reaction. She didn't give one. Just walked on. Young boys, as young as she was, were of no interest to her.

When she reached the beach she kicked off her sandals. Not rubber flip flops any more. She relished the feel of the soft sand as it squeezed between her toes. She never forgot the first time she had seen the sea. It had become a friend to her. A friend she had learned from. Now, as then, the waves came rolling in to the shore. Each one an obstacle to overcome. She smiled as she walked along the water's edge. She was overcoming them. Beating the waves.

She saw two people ahead of her. Sat in the sunshine allowing the shallow waves to wash over them. A man and a woman. Young. About twenty, maybe twenty-one. The woman wore a small black bikini, as so often chosen by the farang visitors. The man, a pair of boxer swim shorts.

The two lovers lay back, holding hands, fingers caressing one another. The water gently lapped at their bodies. A sensual touch on their naked skin. The caress of the water; like a lover's kiss. The hot sun warmed their upturned faces. They turned to one another. Said something that Siswan couldn't hear. A smile from the woman. A special moment they enjoyed together. With one another. For one another.

She walked past, careful not to disturb them. Could she do that with Mirak? With any man? She didn't think so. Couldn't see herself being that emotional with another human being.

At the far end of the beach she walked back up to the road, wiped the sand from her feet, and replaced her sandals. Okay, she thought to herself, let's get this over with. She walked back along the road. The same route she had walked so many times before.

When she arrived at the café, Mirak was already there. He sat at an outside table, a cup of coffee in front of him. He was looking the other way when she approached. Expecting her to come from the other direction. The direction of the bar. She took a few seconds to look at him.

He had the light brown skin of all the local men. A touch darker perhaps, unlike her own. Dark hair, cut short. He wasn't fat, but he wasn't skinny either. Well built. Maybe a little swarthy looking. He wore a light green polo shirt and a pair of tan, chino styled trousers. A pair of soft leather, light brown, deck shoes complimented his outfit. He didn't wear any jewelry as far as Siswan could tell and she was pleased about that. So many men seemed to like wearing chunky gold rings or bracelets these days. She didn't like the fashion. It made a statement she didn't care about.

Mirak did wear a watch though. Gold rim, brown leather strap. It looked old. Slightly out of place on his young wrist. Like an old man's watch. All in all he looked good. Smart but casual. His dress imitated his manner. Quietly confident. Nothing flash. She approached the table.

'Am I late?' she said, looking at the half empty cup of coffee.

Mirak stood. Smiled warmly. Even though she had surprised him, he wasn't caught totally off guard.

'No. Not at all,' he said, gesturing to the seat opposite him. 'I was a little early.'

She sat down facing him. Put her handbag on the table. She wasn't sure why she was there. Didn't understand her feelings towards this man.

'Did you manage to get enough sleep?' he asked, as he signaled for the waitress to attend.

'Yes. Enough for me, anyway. I don't sleep that much,' she answered.

'What would you like?' he asked, when the waitress came to their table.

'A glass of water, please. With some ice and lemon.'

Mirak ordered the water and another coffee for himself. He turned in his chair slightly. Pointed himself more towards Siswan. He leant back in his seat. Casual.

'It's a lovely day,' he said.

'Yes. Quite lovely,' she answered.

There was a moment or two of silence. Neither of them could think of anything to say. The waitress bought their drinks. Siswan knew she should say something. Help him out a little.

The fact was that she was out of her element here. She didn't feel in control. Not like in the bar. In the bar she had a goal. A reason to chat, to flirt, to smile and make the customers feel relaxed. Here she didn't know what to say or do. This was real. The bar was all pretense.

'How long have you lived here, Siswan.' Mirak asked, finally.

'About five years now,' she answered. 'And you?'

'I've only been here for a year. I was posted here when I made sergeant.'

'Where were you before?'

'Oh. Up in the north. A small town. No farangs there to deal with,' he said and smiled.

'Do you like the farangs?' she asked.

'Yes. Most of them. They behave differently than us, but I guess I like them,' he told her.

'They certainly are different,' she said.

'I take it you like them, then?' he asked.

'Yes. I like the way they talk about things. Real things. Real feelings. They show their emotions so easily. Most of us tend to bottle things up.'

'That's true,' he said. 'Mind you, they do have a lot more problems than we do.'

'How so?' she asked, interested.

'Well. Their concept of love, for one thing. I mean, we all know what goes on here, right? Girls for sale, that sort of thing. But when a farang buys a girl he expects so much more than just a night of sex. He really wants the girl to like him.'

Siswan nodded her agreement. She'd seen the same thing many times. The male tourists certainly did expect something more than just sex. The girls had some interesting stories to tell.

'You'd be amazed at some of the things we get called out for,' Mirak continued. 'Farangs who take their money back if the girl doesn't show him enough affection. Men who get angry when they find out the girl they bought has a boyfriend or husband. All sorts of problems that the farang finds hard to deal with.' He paused for a moment. 'They just don't want to accept that all the girls want is their money. They seem to think there should be some kind of emotional feeling attached to the sex.'

'What about you, Mirak? Do you think sex is all there is?' She couldn't help asking.

'Of course not. But there is a big difference between falling in love with someone and buying someone for a night,' he said.

'That's true. Buying someone is so much simpler, don't you think?' She sipped her water as she looked at him.

'I wouldn't know, Siswan,' he said.

'You've never been in love?' she asked.

'I've never bought a girl,' he answered, with a smile.

She didn't know whether to believe him or not. Most of the local men she knew were always buying girls. The girls who couldn't get a farang. They were cheap and the local men didn't care about such mundane things as emotion. All they wanted, all they expected, was sex. Sex for money. The cheaper the better. She didn't think Mirak would be interested in that. He didn't look the type. Maybe he was telling the truth.

'That's an interesting watch, Mirak,' she said, changing the subject completely.

He brought his wrist up. Looked at the watch, turned his arm to show the strap. Held it out towards her.

'It was my father's,' he said.

'I thought it looked old,' she said, as she looked closely at the faded face and slightly marked gold case.

'It was his father's before him,' Mirak went on. 'I suppose it's like a family heirloom, in a way. Passed down from father to son.'

'When did your father give it to you?' she asked.

'Just before he died,' he answered, pulling his arm back.

'Oh. I'm sorry.' Siswan looked quickly into his face to see if she had offended him.

'That's okay,' he told her, with a smile. 'He died when I was quite young. A tumour, apparently. I didn't know him all that well.'

'Even so. It was wrong of me to pry.' Siswan was pleased he wasn't offended.

She wasn't too sure why she was concerned. What did it matter what he thought? She felt confused. Her head was telling her one thing but, her heart seemed to be telling her something completely different. This was no good. She would have to get away. Give herself time to think. To examine her feelings. Mirak reached across the small table and placed his hand on hers.

'Actually, Siswan. I would like it if you wanted to know more about me,' he said.

She slowly removed her hand from under his. His touch had been soft. Gentle. A shiver had wandered up her arm. Not an unpleasant feeling.

'I have to go, now. I'm sorry,' she said, rising from her chair.

'I'm sorry. Did I offend you?' He stood.

'No. No, not at all. It's just that I have things to do. I have to meet the cleaners. I have to order new bar stools. No. It isn't you.' She spoke quickly, almost added 'it's me' but managed to stop herself.

'Well, would you mind if I walked you to the bar? It's only a short distance. I'm sure I can stop myself from offending you again,' he said.

'Very well. If you want to,' Siswan told him.

Whilst she waited for Mirak to pay the bill, Siswan tried to pull herself together. She just didn't know what was happening. Her heart was beating faster. Her face felt hot. She tried to slow her breathing. Tried to control her feelings. Control her body.

'Right, shall we go?' Mirak asked, turning to her after paying the waitress.

'Yes. Thank you for the drink,' she said. She was breathing a little easier.

She turned from the café and started to walk along the pavement towards the bar. The tourists and locals made passage awkward and she felt sorry for Mirak as he wound in and around groups of people whilst still trying to stay beside her. Suddenly he reached out. Held her arm.

'Siswan. Would you like to walk along the beach? I always find it far more relaxing,' he asked her.

She was surprised by his suggestion. It was exactly what she would normally have done. She seldom walked on the shop side of the road. It was far too busy and there was never anything she wanted, or needed, to buy.

'Yes.' She smiled at him. 'That's a good idea.'

They made their way across the road and down to the sand. Kicking off their shoes they walked farther down to the waters edge.

'I love the sound the waves make,' Mirak said, as he walked beside her.

'Really?' she asked.

'Yes, it's like music, or maybe a heartbeat. Nature's heart beating out a rhythm.' He was looking out to sea as he spoke.

Siswan looked to her feet. Watched the sparkling drops of water fly into the air as she walked. Mirak was saying exactly what she thought. Could he read her thoughts? No. That was silly. Lots of people must think the same way about the waves. It was just a coincidence.

'Why weren't you in uniform last night?' she asked, to stop him talking about the waves.

'Oh. I'm a detective now,' he said. 'I got promoted. Sort of.'

'So, how come you came to the bar?'

'I was in the station when the call came in. Thought I'd pop along,' he told her.

'That was good of you,' she said.

'I did have another reason, Siswan.'

She didn't say anything. She watched the water splash off her feet again. She didn't want to encourage him and yet, at the same time, she didn't want him to stop. It was most confusing. And infuriating.

'To be honest,' he continued. 'I wanted to see you again after the first time we met. The call was an ideal opportunity.'

'That's nice of you,' she said.

She didn't know what else to say. It was nice of him. It was flattering to have a handsome man offer such attention. The problem was that she didn't know what it was she wanted. She looked at the waves. Another obstacle? She couldn't tell.

'I'm not too sure what to say,' she told him, honestly.

'Well, you could agree to taking a night off work. Perhaps we could go for a meal, or maybe the cinema, or something?' he suggested.

'I don't know, Mirak. I told you before. I really don't want any complications in my life.' She didn't think she believed the words.

'Yes. You did. Then you suggested a coffee. Even though you drank water,' He said and laughed.

'Yes. Yes, I know. I don't know why I did.' She was looking at her feet again.

'Well, maybe you wanted to, really. Perhaps your heart is in conflict with your head?'

'Yes. Maybe you're right.' Of course he was right. 'Could you let me have your phone number? I could ring you. Let you know.'

'Yes. No problem.' He took a card from his wallet and passed it to her. 'I hope you call, Siswan.'

They finished their walk to the bar in comparative silence. Siswan wasn't too sure what to say and Mirak, guessing her feelings, didn't force the conversation. When they arrived outside the main door he took her hand.

'Thank you, Siswan. I enjoyed our time together,' he said.

'I enjoyed it too, Mirak. Thank you.'

She gently removed her hand and turned to open the bar doors. The steel shutters were already up. The cleaners were inside.

'I hope to see you again, Siswan,' Mirak told her, and started to leave.

She turned back just as he started walking away.

'Mirak,' she called. 'I will call you.'

The smile he gave her sent a small shiver through her body. She didn't know what it was about him but, when he smiled like that, her body seemed to take over.

It was about two hours later that she realized she hadn't posted the letter to Ped. She silently berated herself for having forgotten. She would have to go back down to the main road to the post office. Before that she wanted to talk to Mike and Apple. Mike first though.

He had turned up about an hour before and was upstairs with Rican. He had been spending more and more time with the short order cook. Siswan guessed that it wasn't just her cooking that he was interested in. Good for him, she thought. In fact, it was good for both of them.

She knocked on the door that led to the kitchen before entering. She heard the sudden movement, the sound of dishes being moved, before she walked in.

'Hi Mike,' she said and smiled warmly to both him and Rican.

Mike was sat at the small kitchen table. Rican busied herself with some dishes on the worktop they had installed for her. The place was spotless. Rican had been a good choice. A very good choice if Mike's smile was anything to judge her by.

'Oh, Siswan. Just going over some menu items with Rican,' Mike said.

'Yes, I see.' Siswan grinned at the pair of them. It was so obvious. 'Any chance of a quick chat? If you aren't too busy of course?'

She caught Rican smile to herself just before she turned to the sink.

'Oh, yes. Yes, of course,' Mike said, standing.

Once back downstairs they took up their usual positions at the bar. This was where almost all of their business discussions took place.

'There's a bar for sale, Mike,' Siswan said.

'There's quite a few for sale, Siswan. There always is.' Mike looked at her.

'The one I have in mind would need some work.'

'As much as this one did?'

'Probably more.' She laughed.

'How much are we talking about?' he asked.

'To buy it and get it sorted we're talking three million,' she told him.

Mike was quiet for a moment. He seemed to be thinking about something else. As though what she had suggested was irrelevant.

'Siswan. You have enough money to do that on your own. Why are you discussing it with me?' he asked.

'Don't you want to be involved?'

'It's not that. I just don't understand why you would want me to be involved.' He looked into her eyes. 'I'm just an old man. You're young. Why don't you do it alone, or, better still, with someone your own age?'

'I told you before, you're like a father to me,' she smiled.

'Even so. You really don't need me for the next bar, Siswan. Or the one after that.' He smiled as well.

'Yes I do. I can't do it alone. Not a local woman,' she told him.

'What do you mean?'

'A local woman? On her own? Making money? Come on, Mike. The men wouldn't allow that. They'd move in and take the lot within a week!' She became slightly animated.

'They've left you alone here, Siswan. Everyone knows you run the place and they haven't tried to muscle in. What is it you're afraid of?' Mike asked.

'You really don't know how it works do you? Women are second class here, Mike. They are expected to just cook and clean and pleasure their men. They aren't supposed to go out and get rich!'

'And you think having a farang up front stops them?' Mike asked.

'Yes. Of course. You are a man. A farang man at that. You're expected to have money. Expected to be successful at business. Everyone knows that you're the brains behind this bar. Everyone knows that I'm just doing what you tell me to do,' Siswan pointed out.

'Okay, okay. I can understand some of that. I think,' he said.

'It took me a long time to find out how it all works here, Mike. Every successful woman stands behind a man. Farang mostly, sometimes local. The most successful have a farang husband,' she said.

'You want to marry me?' he asked, with a grin.

'Marry my Papa? That's not allowed,' she said, with a grin of her own.

They sat in silence for a while. Siswan gave Mike the time for everything she had said to sink in. Wanted him to understand why she wanted him. Needed him.

'So, I'm nothing more than a front man for you, then?' he asked, eventually.

'That's how it started, Mike,' she told him honestly. 'When I first approached you that was all I wanted.'

'And now?'

'And now, it's different. Now I want you as my friend,' she answered him.

'How do I know that you're not just saying that to get me to cooperate?' He looked at her.

'You don't. I might be doing just that,' she said.

'I guess I'll never know, will I?'

'You can only know yourself, Mike. You can only believe what you want to believe. That's all anyone can do.' She looked him in the eyes. Hoped that he would believe her.

'Okay, Siswan. Is there any point me looking at this bar, or do you just want me to sign the papers?' he asked.

'I'd like you to see it first. You may not like it.' She hugged his arm. 'We can go tomorrow.'

'Who's going to run it?'

'I will. To begin with,' she answered.

'Who's going to run this place?' He didn't think, for one minute that she expected him to do it.

'Apple. At least I hope so. I'll need to speak to her about it,' she said.

'And what will be my role, exactly?'

'Well, apart from getting fat eating all the food Rican is cooking for you.' She laughed. 'We'll need you to move between the bars. Make sure everyone sees you as the boss.'

'Seems fairly simple. I think I'll be able to manage that,' he smiled.

'Which? The bars or getting fat with Rican?' she asked.

'Oh,' he answered, with a grin. 'Both, I reckon.'

After Siswan had spoken with Apple, she remembered she had to post the letter to Ped. Apple had readily agreed, just as Siswan suspected. It meant more money, more responsibility. She would, to all intents and purposes, be the boss of Mike's Bar. The idea had enthralled the girl.

'And if I need you, you'll only be a few doors away, right?' she had asked Siswan at the end of the discussion.

'Yes. A quick phone call and I'll come straight away. Mike will be around as well, so you'll have nothing to worry about. You'll be fine,' Siswan had told her.

She had meant it too. Apple would learn very quickly. The rest of the girls all looked upon her as second in command already. It would be an easy step to make her the boss.

Apple was, by far, the most intelligent of the bar girls. She understood Siswan and often adopted her approach when dealing with the farangs, and the girls.

'Will I be allowed to change my uniform?' she asked.

'Of course. You can't wear the same as the girls. That wouldn't work at all,' Siswan answered, with a smile.

'I'd like to wear a dress. Nothing too fancy. Maybe a little black number, or a blue one. Dark blue.' Apple was lost in her own thoughts.

Siswan left her to it. The responsibility of her new position would sink in eventually. It wouldn't all be about what colour dress to wear.

Now she had to get down to the post office before it closed. She left the bar just as the rest of the girls turned up for work. They all gave her a wai as she walked past them and she smiled to each in return. She had to admit, they were looking good. All smiles and laughter. No wonder the bar was doing so well. It was all about the girls.

When she had first heard about the bar she wanted to buy, she had gone to take a look. The girls there were tired, bored and dressed like tarts. They lacked sparkle. Lacked anything that would attract anything more than the most tight fisted farangs to the bar.

She knew what was needed. There were two girls that had to go this time. Two who shared the leadership over the others. Even Tam hadn't been that stupid. There could only ever be one boss.

The new bar had too many girls anyway. Siswan had counted eight sat outside the doors looking hostile towards potential customers. She couldn't understand them. They needed customers to make money, but resented them for being able to pay.

She'd seen that before. Girls who went with farangs, talked sweet to them, flirted with them so willingly and then, as soon as the farang was out of earshot, told all and sundry about how inadequate he was, how much of a 'cheap charlie' he was and how much she hated being with him.

She smiled at the term 'cheap charlie'. The actual translation was 'ki neow'. It meant that the farang had money, but wouldn't spend it. Some of the farangs were like that. She would be the first to concede that point. But not half as many as the locals. They were the real 'cheap charlies'. The locals spent all their time fleecing the farangs. Some of them, like herself, made a huge amount of money, but they certainly didn't spend it.

The jet ski and speedboat rides were the biggest con of all. During the times when she could walk along the beach, she would sometimes occupy her mind by working out how much the beach boys were making.

She counted how many times a single jet ski was rented out. Averaged it over a day, a week, a month and, finally, a year. Allowed for rainy days. Allowed for the low season, the high season, maintenance, repairs, even the cost of the actual machine itself. Then she counted out how many jet skis there were. The total for the year was staggering. Almost sixteen million a year in clear profit. And that was without taking into account the speedboats, the parascending and the banana rides.

The beach boys were making a fortune and yet they were so tight with their money it made farangs pale into comparison. No, the real cheap charlies were the locals. Take herself as an example. She lived in a small room because it was cheap. Only used motorbike taxis when she had to, and that was mostly at night. She walked everywhere else. Spent as little as possible on clothes, or anything else she considered a luxury, and never bought a drink.

At least she had a reason for saving her money. A reason for wanting to earn more. With the new bar up and running, her and Mike would soon be making a lot. Real money. Serious money. That was what she needed. A lot of it.

When she reached the post office she paid for a registered delivery for Ped's letter. She didn't trust the regular post. Too many letters went missing. Especially letters containing money or cheques. It was a well known fact throughout the country. If there was money involved, the mail went missing.

She walked back to the bar and thought about Ped. Wondered what she was up to. Her letters had only really talked about Siswan's parents, not about her cousin. It would be good to speak with her by telephone. She could find out a lot more.

*****

Over the next few weeks Siswan found herself very busy. As soon as Mike had signed all the papers, and they had passed over the money, the real work began.

She spent the first few days getting the place cleaned. The toilets had been disgusting and she called in building workers to demolish them and erect new ones. She had the place redecorated and new signage put up outside.

She wanted to call the place 'Mike's Too' but he insisted the name be 'Swan's Bar' as a take on her name. She laughed at the idea but went along with it, just the same.

She converted the back of the bar into a pool playing area and installed four tables with proper lighting and scoreboards. The upstairs was converted into a kitchen and she asked Rican to find another cook who was as good as she was.

She had the old bar ripped out and a new wooden one installed with brand new optics and mirrors. She arranged with two breweries to have draught beers installed as well as bottled. A small room at the back sufficed as the cellar and, although it meant the draymen had to cart fresh barrels through the bar each week, she felt sure that her customers would welcome fresh beer straight from the keg.

New fridges had to be obtained and fitted into the rear of the serving area behind the bar and two new tills, complete with electronic software to account for every drink sold, were slotted in where the customers could easily see them.

She left nothing to chance. Even the lampshades she had installed matched the décor. When she finished she looked around the place with pride. It looked good. Welcoming. There was only one thing left to sort out. The bar girls. Without them, the place would never take off. No matter how good it looked.

She knew of a bar that been built just a year before. The owner, a farang, had spent a fortune on the place. It had every conceivable luxury. Silk cushions to lounge on. Amazing cocktails. Spectacular lighting and the longest, most beautiful, marble bar anyone had ever seen. It failed. No one went there because the farang had a local wife who didn't want him to employ bar girls. No honey, no money!

Six months after it had opened, it closed. A local man had eventually bought it, at a fraction of its true value, and turned it into a disco. With lots of girls. It was making a small fortune.

Siswan had deliberately ignored the girls whilst she had been carrying out the renovations.

She still paid them because she wanted to keep them there. Get them talking. The best advertising she could get, and the cheapest, was to have the girls talking.

They would talk to their friends. Their friends would talk to their friends. Soon, everyone would know about the new place. Other girls would be interested. They would come to take a look. When they did, Siswan would be able to pick out the ones she wanted.

A few had already been to take a look. None that Siswan wanted as yet. Friends of the existing girls. She wanted fresh blood. New girls that could be easily moulded. They would come. They always came.

Eventually, when everything was finished and she was ready to open the doors to customers, she had sorted out the girls she wanted to work for her. Only one of the existing girls remained. The rest were dismissed without any argument.

She took them all down to Mike's Bar. When they peered through the doors they saw a bar in full swing. Girls, who looked fresh and sexy, wandered around taking care of customers who, in turn, were laughing and enjoying themselves.

'This is a bar, girls. A real bar,' she said to them. 'The girls get two days off a week, earn anywhere between eighteen to twenty-five thousand a month and, best of all, they really enjoy themselves. Interested?'

There was a general murmur of 'yes' and 'of course' from the six girls stood around her. She noted who said what.

She saw Apple detach herself from a customer and walk towards them. She looked amazing in her brand new, black dress. The hem wasn't too short, but still short enough to be sexy. Siswan could imagine her sitting on a bar stool. She'd have every pair of male eyes fastened on her legs.

'Hello, Miss Siswan,' Apple smiled and gave a wai to her boss. 'What's happening?' she added, nodding towards the girls.

'The girls needed to see a proper bar in action, Apple. What do you think, reckon we can get more customers than you?' Siswan laughed.

Apple turned and looked in at the bar. The place was heaving. Music blared out from the big speakers and farang men and women danced and sang along with the rock and roll tune.

'Well, I don't know, Miss Siswan.' Apple laughed. 'If anyone can beat us it'll be you, but, even so, you're going to have a real fight on your hands. We won't give up easily.'

Siswan smiled and turned to her new entourage. 'Well, what do you think girls? Are you up to the challenge?'

The girls smiled. Yes, they were up for it. Their bar was bigger, newer and had more to offer. Plus, they had Siswan with them. Yes! Damn right they were up for it.

'Okay, Apple. Give us a month to get warmed up and then we'll compare total turnover for the second. The winners get a free makeover and hairdo, okay?' Siswan said.

'Right you are, Miss Siswan. I could do with a visit to a spa!' Apple laughed. 'I'll let the girls know.'

Siswan looked at her with a slightly surprised expression. She very quickly concealed it with a smile.

'Well, girls. You know what's at stake. Lets go and open up, shall we?'

The girls almost ran back to Swan's Bar. They were going to work harder than they had ever worked before. Just before Siswan followed them, she turned to Apple.

'Well done. You played that well,' she smiled. 'I didn't expect you to tell them it included a spa visit though.'

'You did tell me to make it sound real, Miss Siswan.' Apple laughed. 'And anyway, if we win, I fancy a day at a spa. Either way, you'll be paying.'

'Yes, but we agreed that the Swan would win.' Siswan looked at her protégé.

'Oh, did we? I don't remember that. Oops, sorry.' Apple smiled, unconvincingly.

So, Siswan thought to herself, a mutiny in the ranks. Right, if that's the way you want it, that's the way you'll get it, my girl.

'Fair enough, Apple.' She laughed. 'And, as a side bet, a new outfit for you or me as the winner? Paid for by the loser?'

'You're on!' Apple said, and held out her hand to accept the bet.

That evening went well enough. Siswan had a month to get the girls prepared before the real challenge began. She reckoned she would be able to do it. They were young, eager and ready to give it their all.

When her phone rang she expected it to be Apple backing down. Maybe a new outfit had been a little too much for her to expect. It wasn't Apple though. It was Ped.

'I bought the phone,' her cousin said, as soon as Siswan answered.

'It's good to hear your voice. How are you?' Siswan laughed at her cousin's excitement. She hadn't changed much by the sound of it.

'I'm fine. How are you? I got a job!'

The excitement in Ped's voice reminded Siswan of her childhood. Reminded her of the times she and her cousin had played together, talked together. Before her mind started remembering other things, she tried to shut the thoughts down.

'What job?' she asked. 'Did you finish school?'

'Yes, I finished high school and I got a job in the local market. It doesn't pay much, but it's good fun,' Ped told her.

The two girls talked for several minutes about how Ped was, how Siswan was, what they had both been doing. What they were doing now. Siswan didn't tell her too much. Just that she was working as a cashier in a bar. Earning enough to send money home.

'How are my parents?' Siswan asked.

'Your mother is better, Siswan. She has started going to the temple again. Last week she even spent a few hours working with me,' Ped told her.

Siswan felt a sudden pang of loss, of regret, that she wasn't there to see her mother getting better. She would have liked to visit the temple with her. She recalled their last conversation.

'And my father?' she asked.

'He isn't well, Siswan. Not well at all. I'm not sure you would even recognize him now.'

Siswan didn't feel anything when Ped spoke. No pang of loss or regret. Nothing. Her only thought was why he was taking so long to die.

'What about Bak, Ped?' she asked. 'Have you seen him?'

'No. He left the village a few years ago. No one has seen him since.' Her cousin's voice betrayed the fact that she didn't care.

'Did he tell you where he was going?' She didn't know why she asked.

'No. He came around one day. Started threatening me to give him some money. He was drunk. My father told him to leave. That was the last we saw of him,' Ped replied.

'Okay. I'll send you some more money soon. Thank you, Ped. I'm glad I had you to turn to,' Siswan told her.

'You take care of yourself, Siswan. I hope to see you soon.'

'That would be lovely. I'll call you.'

When Siswan hung up she had to sit down. Her head felt light. She felt a little dizzy. She was breathing heavily. That was the first time in five years that she had actually spoken to anyone from her village. Five years since she last spoken to Ped. Years since she had mentioned Bak's name.

Memories came flooding into her mind. Memories she didn't want. She had tried so hard to forget everything, but now they returned and threatened to engulf her. She could never forget. She had hardened herself against feeling sorry for herself. Kept herself busy all the time so that she wouldn't be able to wallow in her own self pity.

She had managed very well for the last five years. Managed to avoid the memories that lurked in her mind. Managed to block most of them out. Every time she faltered, every time the past tried to make itself known, she had managed to clear her mind through hard work. By keeping herself busy and her mind occupied.

Now the thoughts of what Bak had done to her, what he had forced her to do in the cane fields, came charging towards the front of her mind. A huge wave of emotion swept over her. A wave so big it seemed she would never be able to overcome it. It threatened to engulf her.

She sat there, hoping for an end to the thoughts, fighting to overcome the feelings of remorse. Trying to cling to the present. The present that she had made for herself. She had chosen her own destiny. The long road had led her here. To this now. This moment. She had overcome every obstacle in her path, but she hadn't expected this.

The telephone had seemed such a good idea. So easy. So much simpler than writing letters and trusting to the post. But she hadn't expected this reaction.

Ped's voice, just as she remembered it, opened up doors in her mind that she thought she had locked forever. Now she realized, understood for the first time, the past was always there. She could never run away from it. It was a part of her. Made her what she was. Where would she be now, if it hadn't been for her past?

She had to accept these feelings. To learn from them. Allow them to sweep through her mind. There was no point in trying to block them out. That would be like refusing the use of her arms, or legs. The thoughts were a part of who she was, a part of her very being.

Her breathing slowed. The dizziness receded.

That was how to deal with the memories. Allow them their freedom. Face them as they played out the past. Let them come, let them run through her mind. And then, when she accepted them for what they were, learned from them, allowed them to show her everything they contained, she could forget them. Like a movie at a cinema. She had to watch it all before she could forget it and move on.

Chapter 8

After the police had removed Sood's body from the beach, Siswan had walked away. She had been shocked at the sight of her friend. Shocked by the wounds inflicted upon her body. The gash across her throat had been the worst. It had looked so out of place. A raw red wound across such a soft, smooth neck.

She had been shocked, but not surprised. She had known she wouldn't see her friend again. And she hadn't. Only a lifeless husk that had once contained a soul.

Siswan walked back along the beach. The waves continued their rhythmic song and kept rolling in. They had discarded the body of her friend. Didn't want her. It seemed as if no one had ever wanted her.

The determination in her mind showed in the way Siswan walked along the beach that day. When she reached the far end, she turned and walked back again. Thoughts ran through her young mind as she paced.

To do what she wanted to do was going to take money. A lot of money. She didn't know how much, exactly, but she would find out, she told herself. That was the key. Knowledge. Learn the ways of the farang, Song had told her.

In her mind it was all quite simple. She needed money. The farangs had money. They came here, to her country, to spend it. All she had to do was make them spend it with her. The first thing she needed to find out was what is was they wanted. What they really expected from their holiday in the sun.

She already knew that some came just for sex. What Sood had shown her proved that farang men were no different to the boys in the sugar cane fields. No matter how old they were. She wasn't going down that route.

When she arrived back to where she had started, Siswan walked up the beach to the shade of the palm trees. The sun was high and the temperature had soared. She felt glad that she wasn't working in the laundry. The heat in the steel shed would be almost unbearable.

Sitting herself down against the trunk of a coconut palm, Siswan continued to run her thoughts through her mind. So far she hadn't done so well with her life. She was only thirteen, but knew she looked older. Maybe she could get away with seventeen. Perhaps even eighteen. Her body was changing rapidly. Forming curves in places that had, up until a few months before, been relatively flat.

She guessed that it would be about this time that Bak would have sold her virginity to the highest bidder. She registered, with some horror, that she had been wondering how much he would have made. She had to shut those thoughts out of her mind. It was no good thinking about the past. She was here now. In this place and time. Nothing lay behind her. Only the future was worth thinking about.

She made a silent promise to the memory of Sood that she would fulfill what she was contemplating. All she needed was help with the first step. The first step that would start her off in the direction of her goal.

She watched as the farangs strolled along the beach, lay in the sunshine on the plastic sun beds, roared around the ocean on hired jet skis or, like her, just sat in the shade to watch the day go by.

Wherever she looked they were there. Farangs. Visitors to her country. She wondered why they came. They didn't look that happy. Their faces seldom smiled as they tried to ignore the local traders plying the beach. The ones that did smile, did speak, were soon inundated with traders, all trying to make money from a farang who was buying.

Siswan watched two of them who were sat on sun beds just in front of her. A man and a woman. The man wore a small pair of shorts, the woman, a very small pink bikini. How could they sit there showing off so much of their bodies to the world? Didn't they have any sense of shame?

It would be unheard of to have locals dress the same way. A woman was expected to stay respectably covered. Shorts and a t-shirt were okay, but not what amounted to a pair of panties and a bra! Even the local men wore long shorts down to their knees.

There were very few locals on the beach. Other than the beach boys, who worked the jet skis and speedboats, there were a few who took care of the sun beds. A few who fetched and carried for the farangs whenever they called out for a cool drink.

Of course the local traders, carting their wares around in cooler buckets, or shoulder bags, toured up and down the beach calling to each and every farang they came across. But other than people working, there were no locals lying in the sun. None who were there simply to enjoy the beach. All the locals worked. Making money.

Those that worked in the sun covered themselves from head to foot. Only the beach boys worked with their shirts off. It seemed as though the local women were afraid to expose any part of themselves to the glare of the sun. Afraid that their skin would darken.

Siswan sat and watched the world go by on the beach in front of her. She began to understand just how much she didn't know. Not only about the farang, but also about her own people. She decided that it was time to correct that lack of knowledge. If she was going to keep her promise to Sood, she was going to have to learn an awful lot.

She watched everything. Watched the expressions of the farangs. Noted the sound of their voices. The looks on their faces. She watched them when they went swimming. Watched as they drank, ate, smoked. Everything.

No one noticed the local girl sat in the shade of the big palm tree. No one noticed how she looked and learned. No one noticed her, but she noticed them. She watched them, farangs and locals, and she learned.

When early evening came Siswan decided that, for her first day, she had learned a lot. She had overheard enough conversations to discover that the locals hated the strong sun. They certainly didn't want their skin to go black. It was a bad thing. They envied the white skins of the farangs and couldn't understand why the visitors wanted their skin to be brown.

She learned that some of the farangs grew impatient with all the traders calling out to them. Some even pretended to be asleep behind their dark sunglasses to try and avoid the constant flow of locals selling food, drinks and goods they thought the farangs might buy.

It seemed, to Siswan, that the farangs didn't like the pushy traders. The ones that stood in front of them and continued showing their goods long after the farangs had shaken their heads in refusal.

Siswan learned that it was the traders that didn't push too hard, who didn't infringe upon the visitors, the ones who were polite and smiled as they passed, who sold the most. She learned a lot that day. A lot about the farang and a lot about her own people. The things she had seen fascinated her. She wanted to know more. A lot more.

As she collected her thoughts and prepared to walk back to the workhouse, she saw an old local woman struggling to collect the big sun beds from the beach in front of her. Most of the farangs were busy packing up their stuff to leave the beach and the old woman collected the beds as they became vacant.

Siswan wandered down to help. The old woman looked at her as she bent to pick up the other end of the bed the she was half dragging through the sand, but said nothing.

Siswan helped her back up the beach with all the remaining sun beds and then helped her to pile them, one on top of the other. Finally, when all the beds were piled and all the foam mattresses stored against the pile, the old woman spoke to her.

'All day you've been watching,' she said.

'Yes. Most of it,' Siswan replied.

She made to move away. To walk back up through the palms to the road and the workhouse.

'Want a drink?' the old woman asked, lifting the lid of the big cooler box beside her.

'I don't have any money,' Siswan apologized. The fifty Sood had given her was safely tucked away under the mattress in her room.

'Did I ask for any?'

'No. You didn't. I'm sorry,' Siswan apologized, again. 'Yes. I'd like a drink. Thank you.'

The old woman fished inside the cooler and pulled out a bottle. She held it out to Siswan.

'Not a lot of choice left. The farangs were thirsty today.'

'Thank you,' Siswan said, as she took the bottle.

She unscrewed the top and took a long drink. The contents were cold and made her hiccup when she finished.

'Did you know her?' The woman asked.

'Yes,' Siswan knew who the old woman referred to. 'She was my friend.'

'Bad way to go.' It was a statement.

Siswan sat down beside the cooler and continued to sip her drink. The sun was sliding into the sea and the cool breeze coming off the water felt good. The old woman sat down with her. She took a long pull from a bottle of cold beer. Siswan watched as the contents bubbled inside the bottle.

'Would have given you one, but you're far too young,' the old woman said, when she had finished swallowing.

'How old do I look?' Siswan asked.

'Oh, look. Looks is different from being. You look old enough, I'll give you that.' The old woman looked out to the sea.

'Then how do you know?' Siswan asked her.

'Because you asked,' the old woman answered.

Siswan was confused. She looked at the old woman a little longer and then she too, turned her attention to the sea. They both sat there for a while. The old woman and the young girl. Sat on the sand, looking at the sea. Neither of them spoke. Siswan's mind was full of thoughts. Full of questions, but she didn't speak. Just sat and looked. Finally, when she had finished her beer, the old woman turned to her.

'Well, another day done,' she said.

'Yes. Another one over,' Siswan agreed.

'You sound too old, girl,' the woman told her. 'I'll be here again tomorrow. If you want to help with the beds.'

'I'd like that,' Siswan told her.

She stood, handed the empty bottle back to the old woman, and headed back up the beach to the road. It had been a long day, but she'd learned a lot and maybe, just maybe, she'd found a friend to replace the one she had lost.

When she got back to the workhouse, Ma stopped her before she reached the stairs.

'Police came here today. About the girl who was killed,' she told her. 'They'll be back tomorrow to talk to you. I told them you and her were friends.'

Siswan didn't reply. There didn't seem to be a need. She continued up the stairs to her small room. She couldn't stay there. Not now. If the police came they might want to talk to her about the old man in the park. They might know all about it already.

She berated herself for using the same name in the workhouse as she had given to the policeman in the hospital. The same one she had given to Song and Tad in the truck. How could she have been so stupid? Now they would come and ask her questions. Where did she come from? What was her real name? They would track her movements backwards and she would be caught.

No. Stop it, she thought. That wasn't the way to think. She couldn't just keep running away.

There were thousands of girls called Bee. It was a very common name. That's how it had come to her in the first place. The first name she could think of. There were lots of girls in the workshop as well. Lots of girls who had run away from home. She had to stay. Face them. She had nowhere else to go.

She resolved herself to meet with the police in the morning. Resolved herself to face whatever happened to her. This was another wave she had to overcome. A big wave. She couldn't run away, she was in too deep. She would have to stand and face it.

She removed her clothes and carried them to the bathroom. She started to wash them. Just as she was about to plunge her shorts into the water she remembered the small roll of paper she had found that morning.

She had forgotten all about it. She felt in her pockets. Found it in the back one. Pulled it out. In the dim light she examined what she had found. Started to unroll it. In seconds she saw that it was money. As the small sheets came away, one by one, she opened her eyes wide in real surprise. She lay each note out on the floor in front of her. Five notes. Each one a thousand. Five thousand. More money than she had ever seen before. More than she had ever dreamt of!

She couldn't believe her luck. This was a huge amount of money. To someone who, up until that moment, thought the fifty under her bed was a lot, it was a fortune. She felt the notes. Picked each one up and put them together. Fanned them out in front of her face. Five thousand!

Her excitement soon changed to consternation. The police were coming tomorrow. What if they searched her room? What if they found the money? Would they think she had stolen it? Of course they would. What would a girl in a workhouse be doing with five thousand?

Worse still, it dawned on her, they may think the money had something to do with the death of Sood. They would think she had killed her friend for money.

She dropped the notes on the floor. She suddenly didn't want to touch them. What could she do? Should she go downstairs, tell Ma? No, that wouldn't be any good. Ma would tell the police. Maybe she would keep the money? Either way, Siswan knew that no good would come of telling Ma.

She had to think. She had to calm down. Take control. This was yet another wave. She had to overcome it. One wave at a time. The money first. One thing at a time. She had to put the money somewhere where no one, not even the police, would be able to find it.

She looked around her small room. The two beds. Easy to search. A clothes rail. Not a good hiding place. Concrete walls, concrete floor. No window. Nowhere to hide anything.

She looked into the bathroom. The toilet. A hole in the ground with a porcelain frame that didn't move. A big dustbin half full of water. Too heavy for her to move. The small pail floating in the water. The single tap protruding from the bare wall. Nothing. No holes, no hiding places.

She went back into the bedroom. She was about to give up. About to accept the fact that there was no place to hide anything, when she suddenly recalled what she had thought earlier. The water bucket. Too heavy for her to move.

She went back into the bathroom. The big black plastic dustbin looked back at her with a one-eyed look of pure innocence. She collected the money together. Put it on her bed and went back to the bathroom.

It took her almost half an hour, using the small pail, to empty the dustbin. Finally, when only a small amount of water remained, she could tip it up. She placed the money, together with the fifty she pulled out from under her bed, in a small plastic bag beneath the dustbin. Turning on the tap, she allowed the big bin to fill with fresh water.

When she had finished, and the bin was full, there was no way it could be moved. No way at all. Satisfied with all that she had done, Siswan showered, finished cleaning her clothes and went to bed. She slept soundly in the bed nearest the door. The one with the smooth mattress. Sood would have understood.

Siswan was hanging out freshly washed laundry when the police called the following morning. In fact it was only one policeman. He sauntered into the back yard in his tight brown uniform with Ma at his side.

'Bee?' she called out.

Siswan moved out from behind the big white sheets and walked towards them. She didn't avert her gaze from the policeman's eyes, but instead smiled and offered a wai when she reached him.

'This was her friend,' Ma told him. 'They shared a room.'

The policeman looked her up and down. He didn't say anything in reply to Ma.

'You know that Noy is dead?' he said to Siswan.

'Yes. I saw her body on the beach,' she replied.

'Did she go with the farang a lot?' he asked.

'I don't know. Yesterday was our first day off.'

'You went out together the night before last.' It wasn't a question.

'Yes. We went to the beach. Afterwards, I came back here and she went off alone,' Siswan told him.

'Where did she go?'

'I don't know.'

'Did she say she was going to meet anyone?'

'No.'

The policeman looked her up and down once more. 'What time was it when you came back here?'

Siswan looked up at him. Did he really think she could afford to wear a watch? Did he think a place like this would be considerate enough to put up a clock?

'I'm not sure. About nine, I think. Maybe ten.' She feigned embarrassment.

'It's alright,' he said. 'We know what time she died. You can go back to work now. I may need to speak with you again though.'

She gave a small wai to him and to Ma. Neither of them gave one in return. She turned and walked back to the laundry. She breathed a sigh of relief.

When she returned to her room that evening she found that the police had been there. Someone had, anyway. Sood's shorts and t-shirts were gone from the rail. She wondered if they had searched the place. The dustbin was still full of water so she knew her money was safe. Despite all her concerns the previous night, the wave had turned out to be very small after all. Hardly a ripple.

*****

Siswan spent a little over a year in the workhouse. Just about every day she worked, along with the other girls who came and went, in the heat of the laundry. Every evening, as soon as she'd washed the smell of soap and detergents out of her hair and skin, she would go down to the beach and help the old woman. She spent her days off there, too.

Karn taught Siswan many things. The old woman was a mine of information and the two of them would sit and watch the sun go down talking about the ways of the farangs.

Early in their relationship Karn had given her a gift. Siswan had turned up, as normal, one evening and Karn had handed her a brown bag.

'These will help,' she said, in her matter of fact voice.

Siswan had opened the bag to find a pair of bright yellow rubber gloves. The thick ones, like the women who cleaned the streets wore.

At first, the other girls had laughed when she turned up for work in the laundry wearing them. They thought she was mad to wear the thick rubber gloves in the heat of the shed. After a short time however, they stopped laughing. When the redness faded from Siswan's hands, when her nails strengthened and grew healthy and strong, they had stopped laughing.

Those girls that earned money working on the beach, or those that managed to scrape enough small change together in some other way, soon purchased their own gloves.

Ma had raised an eyebrow at the sight of all the bright yellow and pink gloves, but didn't say anything. The only thing she cared about was that the laundry got done. She didn't care how the girls did it, or what they wore.

A new girl had moved into the small room with Siswan. A small girl who had been too frightened to talk much. Siswan got tired of listening to her cry in her sleep. She tried to comfort her. Tried to tell her that things weren't too bad, that everything would be alright. The girl wouldn't listen. Didn't stop being frightened. Didn't stop crying.

She was gone within a week. Siswan didn't know where she went. No one did. One day she was there, crying and being miserable, the next she was gone. Siswan had felt a small pang of guilt that she hadn't done more to help her.

Another girl had arrived a few days later. She was completely the opposite. So confident. So talkative. She never stopped. Sometimes, especially after a tiring day, Siswan wished she would.

The best times for Siswan were spent sitting with Karn watching the sun go down. The old woman had a philosophical way of looking at life and would come out with some amazing pearls of wisdom.

One evening, after they had piled the sun beds high and were sat drinking their cool beers, she came out with a real gem. She just came out with it all of a sudden. A moment before she spoke, the two of them had been sat in silence.

'When you are young,' she said, staring out to sea, 'you look into the future. When you are old, as old as me, you look into the past. When you're middle aged, however, you spend all your time looking into the mirror.'

Siswan had almost choked as she tried to swallow her beer. Even Karn had to chuckle at Siswan's reaction.

'Where did you get that one?' The young girl finally managed to ask, without choking.

'Something my grandmother used to say when I was young.' Karn still chuckled. 'It's true as well. You'll see.'

Siswan rested her head back against the sun beds. She couldn't think of a better time. Sitting with the old woman, enjoying a cool beer and laughing. What more could she wish for? Her life in the village seemed so far away. So distant.

She knew that it couldn't last forever though. It couldn't even last another year. She had to get on with her life. She had made two promises. A promise to her cousin to send money and a promise to Sood. Both promises that she intended to keep.

She turned to Karn. Looked at the lined skin of the old woman's face. Looked at the wiry hands, the toughness of her forearms. Her life was almost over whilst Siswan's had only just begun.

'I need to learn English,' she said to her.

'That's a good idea,' Karn replied. 'How are you going to do it?'

'I haven't got a clue,' Siswan said, and laughed.

'You've changed a lot since we first met,' Karn told her, with a smile.

'Yes. You've taught me a lot,' Siswan said.

'No. I don't mean what's inside your head. I mean your face. Your attitude. You smile a lot now. Laugh too.' Karn looked at her. 'My old grandmother used to say that melancholy, like hardship and despair, shows in our face, our eyes, even the way we walk. She said that the opposite is also true.'

The two of them sat side by side. Siswan thought about the words Karn's grandmother had spoken. The opposite was also true. She was right. Siswan didn't feel despair anymore. She felt young again. Enthusiastic. She wanted to get moving, to get started. It was time for her to move on. As though Karn had been reading her thoughts she turned to Siswan.

'The bars would be a good place to learn English,' she said, looking at the girl.

'Yes. I guess they would,' Siswan answered.

The truth was that she had already considered working the bars. Not as a bar girl, but perhaps as a cashier. Maybe in one of the day time bars where the girls weren't expected to go with the customers. Only make them drink. Get them ready for the night shift girls to take over. Make their job easier.

'How old do you think I look now, Karn?' she asked.

'You could pass for eighteen now,' The old woman answered, knowingly. 'There is a man I know who may be able to help you. It'll cost you, though.'

'I have some money,' Siswan said.

'It may be expensive. He does a very good job.'

On her next free day Siswan walked down the small street that led to the place Karn's friend worked. It was a copy shop. A place people could go to get photocopies made of their passport, drivers licence or identity card. That wasn't the real purpose of the shop though. The real purpose lay in the small room that the old man showed her after she told him that Karn had sent her.

He had closed the front door of the shop, hung a sign that told customers he would be back later, and led Siswan through a rear corridor to a locked door. Taking a large key from his pocket he opened the door and ushered her through.

She was a little disappointed to find a badly lit stock room full of different kinds of paper and card. A dusty laminating machine stood in a corner next to a small table.

The old man shuffled across the room and turned on a bright work light positioned over the table.

'How old do you want to be?' he asked Siswan.

'Eighteen,' she told him.

'How old are you now?'

'Fourteen.'

'Four years. Yes. I can do four years,' he said, almost to himself.

'How much will it cost?' she asked him.

'Two thousand,' he answered, without a moment's hesitation.

'Alright,' Siswan agreed.

The old man told her to write her name and address down on a piece of card. She had to sign her name inside a rectangular box near the bottom of the card. He handed her what had once been a white blouse.

'What's this for?' she asked.

'You want to be eighteen in an old yellow t-shirt? Put it on.'

Siswan looked for somewhere to change. There didn't seem to be anywhere. She had to agree that her t-shirt didn't do much to make her look any older, but she wasn't about to strip off in front of the old man. She knew that her small bra didn't do enough to hide her breasts any more.

'Don't be shy, girl. I won't look and, even if I did, there's not a lot I can do at my age,' he told her.

In the end, she turned away from him and slipped out of her shirt. She put on the blouse. It smelled musty and stale. The collar was grey with greasy dirt.

'Don't worry. In the light of the flash it looks white enough,' he told her. 'Now, here's some makeup. Don't use too much or else it looks false.'

She took the small plastic box he offered, opened it and examined the various pads, brushes, pencils and powders inside. She didn't have a clue what was what.

'Not worn makeup before?' he asked her.

Without waiting for an answer he took the box and gestured for her to sit on the stool by the table.

Licking the end of a short black pencil he applied a small amount of eyeliner to her eyes. A touch of powder to her cheeks and forehead. Just enough to lessen the shine of her youth.

'You have good skin, girl,' he told her, as he used a small brush to emphasize her mouth a little more.

She could smell his bad breath and stale body odour as he leant over her. She found it difficult to breath and didn't answer.

'The thing with makeup is to apply it so that it doesn't look as though you've got any on. That's the secret. Too many girls just plaster it on without any idea,' he told her, as he worked.

Finally, after a long and lingering examination of her face, he stepped back. Siswan allowed herself a deep breath. He passed her a small mirror.

'What do you think?' he asked.

When Siswan looked in the mirror she was startled by the face that looked back at her. She looked older. A lot older. Her eyes looked larger, the whites brighter. Her mouth looked fuller, less like a girl, more like a woman.

She was shocked at the transformation the old man had made to her face with a few brushes and pencils. And he was right; it didn't look as though she wore makeup. She took another glance in the mirror before handing it back. The woman who glanced back was undoubtedly beautiful.

The old man took a camera from a drawer. It was old and, like everything else, covered in dust and grime.

'Now, hold still. Don't smile. Just look at the camera,' he said.

After taking three photographs, the old man told her to wash her face, change back into her shirt and meet him back in the main shop. He showed her to a small hand basin further down the corridor.

'When will it be ready?' she asked, as she entered the shop.

'Come back in three days,' he told her. 'And bring the money.'

Three days later, Siswan returned to the shop and handed over the money. The old man held out a small plastic card.

'There you go, girl. Four years older.'

Siswan looked at the identity card. It looked a little old, a little grubby. Absolutely perfect in every way. She had seen a few identity cards in her time. Real ones. This one looked no different. No different at all.

'There's something else I'd like you to do for me,' she said.

'What's that? Driver's licence? Marriage certificate? No problem. Price is the same,' he told her.

'No. I don't need anything like that.' She smiled. 'What I want is for you to teach me how to wear makeup.'

The old man laughed. A harsh cackle of a laugh that finished with a coughing fit. Siswan hoped he wasn't going to die on her. Finally, after wiping his mouth with a yellow stained handkerchief, he turned to look at her properly.

'You want an old man to teach you, a lovely young girl, how to wear makeup?' He laughed again, but managed to stop before it turned into a coughing fit.

'Yes,' she answered. 'Why not?'

'Oh, no reason as to why not, girl. No reason at all.'

Siswan watched as he calculated time and expense in his head. Eventually he came up with a figure.

'A thousand,' he told her.

'Five hundred,' she answered, quickly.

'Seven fifty, and I'll let you have the makeup box.'

'Okay, it's a deal.' She smiled.

Over the next week, spending a couple of hours each day, the old man showed her all the tricks about using makeup. She learned how to make her face look narrower, fatter, older and younger. He taught her about eye shadow, lipsticks, powders. What type of brush to use, what type of pencil. How to highlight, darken, emphasize her natural beauty. He showed her how makeup could be used without it being obvious. He taught her the difference between too much and too little.

At the end of the week, Siswan felt confident in her ability to wear a face in public. She tried it out on the last evening. Instead of washing her face clean, as normal, she wandered out wearing the makeup she had applied herself.

Clutching the small box the old man had given her, she walked along the street to the main road. She felt a little conspicuous at first. Her old shorts and faded t-shirt didn't match the radiant beauty her face portrayed.

The looks she received from both locals and farangs were a little intimidating to begin with. Even a few women cast her a second glance.

It was when she overheard a young local man pass a comment to his friend that she became less troubled by her appearance.

'Wow!' Was all he had said, but it was enough for Siswan. She smiled and walked on with her head held just a little higher.

That evening she told Karn she was ready. She had enough money left to rent a small room, buy some new cheap clothes in the market and look for a job in one of the bars.

The old woman had studied Siswan's new identity card for a long time. Finally, as though she were satisfied with what she saw, she handed it back.

'Look for a quiet bar,' Karn told her. 'The customers will want to talk more.'

Siswan told her she was going to leave the workhouse in the morning. There was an apartment block, not too far away from the bar district, that was advertising rooms to let.

'You will have to be careful, Siswan,' Karn told her. 'Watch out for the other girls as well as the men.'

'I will. I'll come back to see you as soon as I get some free time,' Siswan promised.

The two of them sat and watched the sun sink into the sea once more. Siswan felt as though she was watching it for the last time. The last time as a child. She had seen so much and learned so much but, deep down, she was still a child. Armed with her new identity card, that was all about to change. The bars beckoned. That was where she could escape the poverty of her life. That was where she could start to make her dream a reality. The bars with their loud music, bright lights and farang customers. Farangs who had money to spend. She looked forward to meeting them with some trepidation. A little fear, perhaps. Even so, the excitement she felt inside wouldn't go away.

'I'm going to buy a new outfit tomorrow, as well,' she said to Karn.

The old woman looked at her and smiled.

'Something in black, no doubt,' she said.

After a moments hesitation, during which she wondered how the old woman had managed to read her mind, Siswan answered.

'No,' she said, slowly. 'I was thinking of something in white, maybe a dress, or a skirt and blouse.'

'A virgin to the slaughter!' Karn laughed, not unkindly.

'Yes, maybe something in black would be better.' Siswan laughed with her.

'Look, girl,' Karn said, seriously. 'The other girls will cause problems for you. You're young, very beautiful and you have a figure men are going to want.'

'How's that going to cause problems with the girls?'

'They are going to be jealous. You'll get all the attention,' Karn told her.

'But I'm not going to go with the farangs,' Siswan said.

'That won't matter. They'll still see you as a threat. You're going to have to learn quickly, and be on your guard.'

Siswan looked at the old woman. A sudden realization came to her mind.

'You worked the bars before, didn't you,' she said, quietly.

'A long time ago, yes,' Karn told her.

'What was it like?'

'It was different before. The girls all worked together, as a team. The men were different too. Better manners. Now it's harder. Too many girls, not enough customers. It's all about money now,' Karn told her.

'Surely it's always been about the money?' Siswan asked.

'Yes. That's true. But before it was money to buy food. To stay alive. To keep the family in food and clothes,' Karn answered. 'Now it's about cars, motorbikes, the latest telephone, kids education, even houses. Too much for a bar girl to earn.'

Siswan looked out to sea. The waves were still rolling in. As the sun sank behind them, they seemed larger. More powerful.

'Why do people always want more?' Siswan asked, half to herself.

'Because they're told their lives will be better. The latest makeup, the best television, the biggest car. People today rush around trying to get all the things they're told they need and then, once they have it all, they wonder what happened to their lives. Suddenly, after years of earning, they

223

have nothing. Just a pile of junk they didn't know they wanted. Too late then.'

Siswan leant back against the pile of sun beds. The feel of the sand under her legs, the cool breeze coming off the sea. A good friend to talk with. What more could she possibly want? As though in answer to her own question she turned to the old woman.

'I don't want all that stuff,' she said. 'I have another reason for wanting to earn.'

Siswan told Karn of her plans. She told her all about the promise she had made to the memory of her dead friend. She told her why she had left her own village, why she had left the countryside. She told her all about the old man in the park. She told her friend everything.

When Siswan finished talking, Karn said nothing for a while. Just took another swallow of beer and continued looking out to sea. Finally, she spoke.

'If we look hard enough,' she said. 'Open our minds enough. Look real close. Sometimes, just sometimes, we can see ourselves in the faces of others.'

The two of them sat on the beach for another twenty minutes or so. Neither of them spoke. They finished their drinks and sat in silence. Siswan felt an affinity for the old woman who had become her friend. She understood now what Karn had said. She had seen herself in the old woman's face many times.

Chapter 9

Siswan didn't call Mirak for another two weeks. She was busy with Swan's Bar, busy getting everything just right. Apple had turned her incentive idea into a real challenge and the girls from Mike's Bar were taking it seriously. Not only did they want to win a day at a beauty spa, they also invited the challenge itself.

In some ways it was a test of Siswan's leadership. There was no malice involved. None of the girls meant to usurp her status. They just wanted to see how she handled it, how she would win. Not one of the girls, in either of the bars, expected her to lose. Siswan was enjoying the challenge as much as the girls. It kept her mind occupied. Kept her focused.

The only reason she did call Mirak was because she had told him she would. Her workload, and the challenge she was facing, had kept him out of her mind. Kept him at a distance. That was what she wanted, she tried to tell herself.

'I thought you had forgotten all about me,' he joked, when he answered the phone.

'I'm sorry. It's just that I've been so busy.'

'Yes. A new bar,' he told her.

'You know about it, then?' She didn't know why she asked, of course he would know.

Siswan had already dealt with the police for the new bar. She'd got the same deal as Mike's, but for two thousand a month less because it was closer to the police station. The policeman she had dealt with hadn't been as pleasant to look at as Mirak.

'Yes. My friend told me you demanded a discount,' he laughed.

'Well, I didn't demand exactly,' she laughed with him.

That was the problem. It was so easy to laugh with him, even over the phone. There was something about him. About his voice.

'So, are we going to see each other?' he asked.

'Well, I'm still busy. With the new bar. It's not easy,' she felt she was making excuses for herself.

'That's no problem. I could meet you in the bar. That way you wouldn't need to leave work,' he suggested.

'Well, okay.' She couldn't stop herself. 'About nine?'

'Great. See you there.' He sounded pleased.

As soon as she hung up, Siswan knew she'd made a mistake. She was letting him get close. He was disrupting her plans. She had told herself a thousand times that she didn't need anyone, didn't want anyone, and now, here she was, acting like a foolish teenager.

She stopped her train of thought. Smiled to herself. And why shouldn't she? After all, she was just a teenager. She'd almost forgotten.

Mirak turned up at nine and sat at the bar entertaining staff and customers alike with his tales of police work. Siswan enjoyed his company and especially liked the way he smiled at her every so often. She sat and listened, along with everyone else at the bar, as he told a story concerning a farang and his local wife.

'It was when I was stationed in the North,' he told them. 'We didn't get many farangs in those days, but there was one who moved there to be with his wife's family. We received the call at about two in the afternoon.'

As Siswan watched the customers faces it became clear that Mirak had a certain something. He drew people toward him. They liked him. His voice was easy to listen to, his manner relaxed. Comfortable.

'When we arrived, there was a huge argument going on between the farang and several members of his wife's family,' he continued. 'The farang, whose name was Steve as I recall, was most upset.'

Siswan smiled when Mirak glanced her way. She was enjoying listening to him speak. He seemed to be in his element.

'It appeared that, the night before, Steve's wife had told him that the following day her family were coming over to do some fishing in the small lake attached to their land. Steve had thought this a wonderful idea and a great way to get to know the family better.'

He paused to take a sip of the drink in front of him. Siswan noticed that his audience also drank from their own glasses. He was leading them just as she would have done. She had even sipped her own orange juice.

'Anyway, the following morning,' Mirak continued. 'Steve told his wife he was going into town to get a rod and reel. Apparently he had never fished before and was looking forward to learning with her family. His wife, who didn't speak a great deal of English, didn't understand what a rod and reel were, so she just let him get on with it.'

Mirak paused once more. Looked to Siswan and gave her a quick wink.

'You see, Steve had this image of them all sitting on the side of the lake, rods in hand, a few cool beers, getting to know one another,' Mirak told them. 'Off he went, in to town, to find a fishing shop. Meanwhile, his wife's family turned up in the back of a pickup truck.'

Siswan had an idea where the story was going, but didn't say anything to spoil it for the rest of the customers. Even the girls were listening intently as Mirak went on.

'Whilst Steve was equipping himself with the latest carbon fibre extending rod complete with a high tech casting reel, his wife and her family pulled two diesel powered water pumps out of the back of the pickup and started draining the lake.'

He paused to take another drink and to let what he had just said sink in. His timing was just about perfect.

'By the time poor old Steve got back with his fishing gear and a crate of beers, the lake was virtually empty and his wife and her family were wading through the mud picking up all the fish. As you can imagine, Steve wasn't too pleased and started yelling at his wife. Her family joined in on her side and a fight ensued. By the time we got there, the pickup was loaded with fish, Steve had a broken nose and his wife wanted a divorce.'

'What did you do?' one of the girls asked him.

'There wasn't a lot we could do. We arranged a trip to the hospital for Steve, fined two of the local men and helped ourselves to a few fish,' Mirak laughed.

'Did they divorce, then?' Siswan asked him.

'No. They patched it up in the end. Eventually, when the rains came again, the lake filled up and Steve got to use his new rod and reel,' he answered. 'It all boils down to a lack of communication between the locals and the farangs.'

'I can understand why he got angry, though,' a farang customer said. 'I'd have been bloody livid.'

'That's the problem,' Mirak said. 'It's all about understanding our ways. Trouble is, half the time, we don't understand them ourselves. I would have used a net to catch the fish.'

Other customers started with their stories of misunderstandings between farangs and the locals. It seemed as though everyone had a tale to tell. Some funny, others sad. Mirak managed to extract himself from the bar and joined Siswan at a table in the corner where they could talk.

'The bar is doing well, Siswan,' he said, as he sat down opposite her.

'Yes. It's coming on. We still have a lot to do though.'

She told him about the challenge with Apple. She lowered her voice to explain that it had started off as a fixed incentive and he had to lean towards her to hear.

'So, now it's a real challenge?' he asked.

'Yes. Apple set it up with the girls from Mike's Bar,' she explained.

'Well, good for Apple.' He laughed, not unkindly. 'Makes it far more interesting.'

'I suppose it does. Mind you, I was a bit shocked when she did it,' Siswan smiled.

'Of course, you do know I'll have to report this, don't you?' He looked at her.

'What do you mean?'

'Well, gambling's illegal here. As a police officer I have no other choice.' He laughed at her expression.

'Unless, of course, you had an invite as well?' she asked, with a wry smile.

'Ah, well. A day in a spa surrounded by beautiful girls? I suppose I could be tempted to overlook it just this one time.' He smiled.

'No way! I'm not having you staring at all those women!' she said, before she could stop herself.

'Really?' he asked quietly. 'Why not, Siswan?'

Siswan felt herself blush. Why had she said that? Did it matter if he looked at another girl?

Why should she care? Unless, of course, she was falling for him. Allowing herself to like him.

'I don't know,' she said, quickly. 'I don't know why I said that. It was just a joke.'

He didn't say anything. Sat back in his chair. Siswan got the impression that he was helping her. Letting her off the hook. He didn't seem annoyed or frustrated in any way. He didn't want to embarrass her further. He looked around the bar.

'Do you think Apple might win?' he said, looking back to her.

She was thankful for the respite. Pleased that he didn't push her into revealing her true feelings. If he had, she would have withdrawn completely. Perhaps he knew that, or felt it? Perhaps that was why he didn't push too hard? Maybe he knew her better than she knew herself? At that precise moment, Siswan knew, and accepted the fact, that she had really strong feelings for the man sat opposite her. It was the first time she had ever felt the emotions that stirred within her.

'She might,' she smiled at him. 'She's very good.'

'Oh dear, that wouldn't be good would it,' he teased her.

'No.' She laughed. 'I'd have to buy her a new outfit, as well.'

'I could arrange a few visits, if you like?' Mirak joked. 'Put the customers off.'

'No, that wouldn't do. If I'm going to win, it has to be fair,' she said.

They sat in silence for a few moments. Enjoying each other's company. Siswan felt perfectly at ease. The first time she had ever felt at ease with a man.

'So, what does your future hold, Mirak?' she asked, and added quickly. 'With your job, I mean.'

'I think another two years as a detective, then try for promotion. Probably have to go back into uniform for a while,' he told her.

She looked at him whilst he spoke. He became serious when he talked about his work. She could tell he was passionate when it came to policing.

'Did you always want to be a policeman?' she asked.

'Yes. My father was a cop. His father was a cop. It runs in the family,' he answered.

'So, where will you end up? Chief of police?' she smiled, as she asked.

'That would be good, wouldn't it?' He laughed with her. 'No, I don't think so. I'd be happy to make Inspector.'

Siswan sat and talked with Mirak for another hour or so. She skirted any subjects that came too close to revealing her feelings towards him. Feelings that she had now accepted and actually enjoyed.

'Well, I'd better be going now, Siswan,' he told her. 'I have to be up early tomorrow and, unlike you, I need as much beauty sleep as I can get.'

She smiled at his compliment and regretted that he was leaving. The evening had passed so quickly in his company.

'Thank you for coming, Mirak. I enjoyed myself,' she told him.

'I enjoyed it too,' he said, taking her hand. 'Perhaps we could see each other again a little sooner rather than later this time?'

She didn't pull her hand away. Allowed it to rest in his.

'Yes. I'd like that,' she answered. 'You have my number?'

'Yes, I logged it straight after you called. First thing I did.' He smiled.

'Okay. Well you call me next time,' she said.
'Tomorrow?'

'If you like.' She laughed. 'Now go and get some sleep.'

He smiled, squeezed her hand gently, and left with a wave to the customers and the bar girls. Siswan went back to work. She allowed herself a little smile as she started towards a table where a farang sat alone. Occasionally, she thought to herself, it was better to go with the wave. Allow it to push her back into the shallower water. Then, when she found her feet, she could try once more to go deeper. Mirak was a wave she was content to swim with.

*****

At the end of the second month, Siswan, Apple and Mike sat together to tally up the totals from each bar. The three of them met up in Mike's before anyone else turned up for work. Mike acted as the impartial referee. He really didn't mind who won and was enjoying his unbiased position.

'So, Siswan,' he said, as he methodically went over the receipts. 'How do you think you've done?'

'Oh, come on Mike!' She laughed. 'Just get on with it!'

'Yes, hurry up, Mike, the suspense is killing me!' Apple admonished him.

'Okay. Okay. Take it easy. This has to be done right, you know,' Mike said, in mock seriousness. 'We can't have any mistakes.'

Siswan watched him as he slowly went over the figures again. He was looking so much better than when she had first seen him. Rican was fattening him up and he had all but given up drinking alcohol. His eyes smiled more often and his skin had a healthier shine to it. She guessed he was enjoying his life once more.

Apple too, had changed since Siswan had first seen her. The young, dreamy girl had gone. In her place was a woman who commanded respect. A woman who earned respect. The silly girl she had seen a few months before, was now a woman who knew her future. As she watched them both she wondered what they thought of her.

Mirak was in her life now. An important part of it. She wondered how far he would go with her. How long before he became frustrated enough to move on. She knew he wanted to take the relationship further. Knew he would eventually want to sleep with her. That was where the problem lay. With her. She couldn't take that all important step. She had come close once or twice. She had tried to allow him to take her. Had tried to respond to his touch. His passion. She had tried really hard. And failed.

Twice they had become passionate. Both times in his apartment. Both times she had pulled away at the last moment. The thoughts, the memories, wouldn't allow her to relax. To enjoy. To let go and abandon herself to him.

She knew he felt confused. Dissatisfied, even. She wanted to open up to him. To explain the problem. To gain his understanding, his help. She couldn't. The shame of it all kept flooding back into her mind. Her mother had condemned her. What you do is wrong, Siswan. She couldn't block the thoughts. Couldn't prevent the image of her mother entering her mind.

She knew that she loved Mirak. She knew it with all her heart. His warm voice, his laughter. The sparkle in his eyes. She enjoyed their time together. Enjoyed the feel of his hand as he held hers. She loved everything about him. Everything, except one thing. He was a man who wanted her.

She just couldn't give herself to him. It was like giving herself to Bak. Giving herself to the boys in the fields. Don't let them enter you, Siswan. Bak had told her that time and time again. Do whatever they want, but don't let them enter you. Her mother had condemned her.

Siswan pulled her thoughts back to Mike and Apple. This was what was important. The

235

feelings inside her, the emotions, were nothing compared to her dream. Mike was speaking.

'You know, it's a close thing,' he told them. 'I'd better go over the figures again, just to be sure.'

'Don't you dare,' Siswan told him.

'We both love you, Mike,' Apple told him. 'But if you keep us waiting another second, I swear, we'll kill you.'

'Alright, alright.' Mike laughed. 'Siswan, this month Swan's Bar turned over a total of one million, eight hundred and twenty six thousand, four hundred and ten. Not bad, not bad at all.'

Mike paused. Took a drink from his glass of orange juice. Slowly pulled the paperwork from Mike's Bar towards him.

'Mike. I swear,' Apple warned him.

Mike looked at both Siswan and Apple. Two lovely looking girls. Siswan's almost perfect beauty. Apple's radiant cheekiness. He thought of them both as his daughters now. He couldn't help but smile at the concerned expressions on their faces. Both of them determined to win, both of them equally worried that the other would have to lose.

'Okay, well here we go then,' he said to them, as he pored back over the paperwork. 'Apple, this bar turned over a total of one million, eight hundred and twenty four thousand, eight hundred and eighty two.'

He smiled at them both. Saw the slight look of relief on both of their faces.

'A difference of one thousand, five hundred and twenty eight. Sorry Apple,' he said.

'Wow, that was close,' Apple said. 'We almost beat you, Miss Siswan.'

'Yes. Very close.' Siswan smiled back.

She was thinking that it was a little too close. What would have happened if Apple had won? Would she have lost face in the sight of all the girls? She didn't know. Glad that she didn't have to find out.

'So. When do you want to go shopping?' Apple asked her.

'Oh, I didn't mean it, Apple,' she said.

'If I'd have won, would you have insisted on buying the outfit?' Apple asked her.

'Yes. You're quite right. I'm sorry,' Siswan told her.

Apple had grown up completely. Had the girl won, Siswan would have insisted on keeping to the bet. In fact, Apple was exceeding her expectations. She really had expected Mike's bar to flounder a little. As it was, it had beaten the previous months' turnover quite considerably.

'Tomorrow morning?' she asked Apple.

'Great. Meet you here at eleven?'

'That'll be good. Want to come, Mike?' Siswan asked him.

'Oh, yeah. Sure. Now what makes you think I'd enjoy shopping with two women? I don't like shopping with one. I don't even like shopping.' He laughed, in response.

'But you are going to the spa, aren't you?' Apple asked.

'No, keep it as an all girl day. You don't want an old man there, ogling all you sexy girls,' he said, laughing.

'Well, if it's okay with you, Mike, I think both bars did really well so I think all the girls should go, don't you?' Siswan asked him.

'Funny, I was going to suggest the very same thing,' he said. 'Take Rican with you as well, eh? She'd enjoy that.'

'What about the bars? Who's going to open them?' Apple put in.

'I don't think it would hurt if we open late. What do you think, Mike?' Siswan turned to him.

'What are you both looking at me for? You two run the bloody places, you sort it out,' he joked.

In the end it was agreed that they would put up notices in both bars saying that the following Monday was a staff training day and that the bars wouldn't open until nine in the evening.

'So, I'll arrange the spa for next Monday. We'll all meet up here at twelve. That'll give the girls enough sleep,' Siswan told Apple. 'What are we going to have? Mud packs? Body scrubs? Herbal baths?'

'Oh my god, worse than bloody shopping.' Mike laughed, and left them to their feminine discussions.

'You know where he's going, don't you?' Apple asked, as soon as Mike had slipped out of the main doors.

'No. Where?' Siswan was curious.

'To go and get Rican. He hardly ever lets her get a bus or taxi anymore. And never lets her go home alone at night,' Apple told her.

'Well, I knew there was something going on, I just didn't know it was that serious,' Siswan said.

'Oh, yes,' Apple said. 'It's serious alright. Don't be surprised if you're invited to a wedding any day soon.'

'Really? That serious?' Siswan was shocked.

'Yes. Why do you think Mike spends so much time in this bar and not the other one?'

Siswan felt a little out of touch. She had been spending so much time working in Swan's bar, spending so much time with Mirak, that she had lost track of what was going on. She didn't like the feeling. Didn't like the fact that things were happening that she didn't know about. She needed to concentrate on what was important.

*****

Apple and Siswan spent a great time in the local shopping mall choosing a new outfit for Siswan. In the end she selected a cream and light blue blouse and a pair of casual, but well tailored, trousers. Apple had insisted on new shoes and a handbag to complete the outfit.

All the girls enjoyed the visit to the spa the following Monday. They had the choice of herbal or aqua spa therapies. Most went for the aqua spa. It just seemed more fun. When they returned to their respective bars that evening, they all looked fresh, young and healthy.

There were so many girls trying to find work with both bars now that Apple and Siswan were constantly inundated with requests. Siswan was horrified to learn that girls as young as fourteen were trying to apply.

She had been the same age herself when she first approached a bar but, unlike her, most of the young girls that applied were willing to go with farangs. Some already had. They were willing to do anything in order to make money. Money to send home to their families. It made Siswan more determined than ever to concentrate on fulfilling her promise to Sood.

Mirak had contacted her several times and each time she made an excuse not to see him. Her feelings for him were still the same. She wanted to be with him. Wanted to walk along the beach with him, listen to his stories, sit and drink coffee with him. She wanted all those things. The problem was that she knew he wanted more.

She knew she would never be able to have that kind of relationship with him. Perhaps not with any man. She felt guilty that she, in some ways, had led him on. She hadn't known she would react so badly to his embrace. Hadn't known that she would feel revulsion when her body yearned for his touch. It was as though her own mind could not comprehend the cravings within herself.

She wanted him. Wanted him to hold her, to touch her, to feel his caress and yet, at the same time, she could only feel disgust. Disgust at the thought of being touched, being held. Disgust at the thought of touching him, giving him pleasure.

The only way she could handle the mixture of emotions was not to see him. To get him out of her head, out of her heart. She had to focus on work. Concentrate on the business in hand. She didn't need him. She didn't want him. She knew she could manage without seeing him. Knew that the feelings for him would diminish in time.

She threw herself into her work secure in the knowledge that, over time, she would stop thinking about him. Stop wanting to call him. She knew all these things. She also knew that she was lying to herself.

Her mind was in turmoil. One minute she would be able to shut him out of her thoughts, the next he would be the only thing she could think about. She had no idea what to do.

It was Mike who finally broached the subject with her. They were sat in their normal position at the bar after a particularly busy night. The bars were doing well. Apple and the rest of the girls were doing well. Mike was doing well. Even Rican was having a good time. It was only Siswan who seemed to be spending most of her time in a perpetual daze.

'Want to talk about it?' Mike asked her, when they had finished going over the accounts.

'Talk about what?' she said, looking at him.

He didn't say anything. Just sat there and looked back at her. There was a look on his face. Not an unkind, or a 'I know it all' look. Just a look of concern.

'It's Mirak,' she sighed. 'No, it's not him, it's me.'

Again he didn't say anything. Just waited to see if she wanted to explain or not. He was beginning to understand her a little.

'I don't know what I want,' she said, quietly. 'I want him, want to be with him, then I don't. I don't know. It's hard to explain.'

'Sometimes relationships are very difficult,' Mike said.

'Why? Why do they have to be so difficult?' she asked him. 'You and I get on so well.'

'We are friends, Siswan. More than friends, in fact,' he told her.

'Why can't I have that with Mirak?'

'Because he wants a relationship that includes sex?' he asked her, guessing.

'Why does it have to come down to that? We were having a good time.'

'Sex is a part of the relationship between lovers, Siswan. Giving and receiving pleasure with someone you love is just about as good as it gets,' Mike said, with a smile.

'What if one partner hates it? Doesn't need it?' she asked him.

'Then, unless you are both happy with just friendship, the relationship usually ends.'

'Friendship is better, Mike. Don't you think so?'

'Yes, as a matter of fact I do,' he said, with a genuine laugh. 'When I first saw you I thought about being thirty years younger. If I was, then I'd have tried it on with you.'

'Really?' She looked at him.

'Yeah, really. You're gorgeous. But you laid down the rules, and I'm not thirty years younger, so our relationship has developed along a different path,' he said.

'What about Rican?' she asked him.

'Ah, well that's different. She didn't lay down any rules and I could get away with being only ten, maybe fifteen, years younger,' he said and laughed.

'So, you have sex with her then?' Siswan was curious.

'Yes, of course. I may be old, but I'm not past it yet, you know,' Mike told her.

'But does she enjoy it?' Siswan wanted to know.

'This is only between you and me, right? She'd kill me if she found out I'd spoken about our sex life.' Mike looked at her.

'Yes, of course. I'd never let you down,' Siswan said.

Mike looked at her again. No, he thought, I don't think you would.

'Well, there are times when I have to say I have a headache,' he said, with a wink.

'Why?' she asked.

'Bloody hell, Siswan. You don't know much do you? Okay, sometimes she wants it more than I do. Sometimes I have to pretend to be sick, or have a headache, so that she'll leave me alone,' he told her in a whisper.

'You mean she wants sex more often than you do?' Siswan asked, in a normal tone of voice.

'Yes!' Mike whispered. 'Keep your voice down!'

'There's only you and I here, Mike. You took Rican home three hours ago,' she told him.

'Yes, I know,' he looked around, dramatically. 'But walls have ears, you know.'

'Walls have ears?' Siswan looked at him strangely.

'You never know who's listening. That's what I'm saying,' Mike told her.

'Yes, you do, Mike. I am. I'm the only one listening to you.' Siswan started to laugh.

'Oh yes. You say that now. But what if Rican finds out? Then what, eh?'

'Then I guess you're in serious trouble, Mike.'

'Yeah, and it'll all be my fault, as well,' he said. 'The farang is always to blame out here.'

Siswan felt much better. Talking and joking with Mike had put a different perspective on her problems. Suddenly she felt like hugging the old farang.

'Hey, hey. What's this then?' Mike said, as she cuddled into him and lay her head on his shoulder. 'Where's my tough, ruthless bar girl gone?'

Mike put his arm around her shoulders and held her close. Neither of them said anything for what seemed an age. They just held one another. Like father and daughter.

'I love you, Papa,' she told him, finally.

'I know, Siswan,' he said. 'I love you, too.'

Finally, she lifted her head from his shoulder and he slowly dropped his arm. She smiled at him. Her eyes glistened, wet with tears she wouldn't allow to fall. She brushed at them with the back of her hand. Sniffed loudly.

'I'd best be going,' she told him.

'Me too. Rican will wonder what I'm up to,' he said.

They walked to the doors together. Switched off the lights and locked up. She turned to him before he could walk away. Gave him a long, respectful wai. He gave an even more respectful one in return.

'Goodnight, Siswan,' he said to her.

'Goodnight, Mike. Thank you,' she replied, and turned away.

He watched as she strolled down to the motorbike taxis. She was a beautiful woman. The most beautiful woman he had ever seen. But, underneath, she was like a little girl. He smiled to himself, shook his head slowly, and wandered off in the opposite direction.

When Siswan arrived back at her apartment block, Mirak was sat on the steps outside waiting for her.

'I didn't want to come to the bar,' he told her. 'That may have been too embarrassing for both of us.'

His voice was slightly slurred. She could tell he'd been drinking. Maybe to summon up the courage to face her.

'You kept making excuses not to see me,' he said, standing.

'I know. I'm sorry, Mirak,' she told him.

'I don't understand any of this, Siswan.'

'No. Neither do I,' she said, honestly.

A part of her wanted to rush into his arms. To help him. To be with him and feel his touch on her body. Another part of her felt nothing but revulsion at the idea.

'Maybe we could talk about it? Try and find a solution?' he suggested.

She didn't want to continue the conversation outside on the steps. Didn't want to continue the conversation at all. She had to give him something. Some way of understanding. An explanation.

'Let's go inside,' she said. 'We can talk.'

She led him up to the third floor and into her small room. She switched on the light and the overhead fan. Dropped her handbag on the bed.

'Would you like a coffee?' she asked him.

'No. I could do with another drink, though,' he said.

'I don't have any. Only water.'

'Oh yes, I forgot. No alcohol for pretty Siswan.' He laughed.

'Do you want to talk, Mirak? Or just make insults?' She turned to look at him.

'I'm sorry.' He sat down heavily on the edge of her bed. 'I just don't understand, that's all.'

'Mirak,' she said, kneeling down in front of him. 'It's not you. It's me. I can't let go. Don't want to let go. It's difficult to know how to tell you.'

'I thought we were getting along well?' he asked her.

'Yes. We were,' she agreed. 'But I don't want it to go any further. Can you understand that?'

'No. I don't get it. What went wrong?' he asked.

Siswan could easily discern the smell of whiskey on his breath. It wasn't the raw alcohol her father used to drink, but it did enough to remind her.

'Look, Mirak,' she told him. 'I would like us to be friends. Nothing more than that. If you can't handle it, I'll understand.'

'You'll understand what, exactly?' He looked down into her face.

'I'll understand if you want to end our friendship,' she said.

'I don't want it to end, Siswan!' he suddenly shouted. 'I want to take it further!'

'But I don't, Mirak,' she told him, as she started to stand.

He grabbed her by the wrists. Pulled her down again. In front of him. To her knees. He leaned forward to kiss her, but she turned her head and he clumsily ended up kissing her hair.

'Don't, Mirak. Please don't,' she pleaded with him.

'I want you, Siswan. I love you. You know that!'

'If you really love me, Mirak. You'll stop this now and leave. Like a gentleman,' she told him, quietly.

'No,' he said, almost in tears. 'We can sort this out. If you'll just let me.'

He stood, pulling her to her feet at the same time. Holding her wrists he turned and dropped her onto the bed.

'We can get past this, right now,' he said, and lay down on top of her.

She tried to push him away. Tried to struggle out from beneath him. He was too strong. He pinned her down with his weight. With one hand he held her wrists whilst he ripped and pulled at her clothing with the other. He forced her legs apart with his knees. Kissed her again and again on her face, her neck.

'Please, Siswan,' he moaned.

She shouted at him to stop. Tried to use her teeth to bite him. Tried to lift her knees against him. He forced her down with his weight. She felt an anger building within her. The same cold anger as before. She used it.

'Okay, okay, Mirak,' she said, as she stopped struggling. 'We'll do this properly.'

She allowed her body to go limp. Relaxed against him. Allowed his hand to freely explore.

He relaxed the hold on her wrists. Let them go. Started using both hands to undress her. To touch her. She let him. Allowed him to violate her body. Gave him hope that she was finally succumbing to his charms.

'Oh, Siswan,' he groaned into her shoulder. 'You are so beautiful.'

She felt his hands inside her blouse. Inside her bra. The smell of the whiskey. She stretched out an arm. Felt for her handbag. Caught the strap and pulled it towards her.

'That's it,' he was saying. 'We can do this, get over this problem. You'll see.'

She opened the handbag, felt inside for the knife. Found it. Her thumb traced down the length of the handle. Came to the button near the top. Pressed it. Felt the blade spring out.

'What the?'

Mirak felt the sudden pain slice into his arm. Looked and saw the blood flowing through his shirt. He stood up. The pain raced along his nerves.

'What did you do?' he yelled at her.

'I cut you,' she answered.

He looked at her. Made to move toward her. His hand clenched into a fist.

'And I'll cut you again,' she told him.

He stopped and looked into her eyes. Dead. Emotionless. He didn't recognize her. She no longer looked pretty, no longer looked beautiful. She just looked hard. Cold. He grabbed his arm with his other hand. The blood seeped through his fingers.

'What have you done, Siswan?' he asked her, wide eyed. 'What have you done?'

'I'm sorry, Mirak,' she said. 'I wanted to explain, to talk. But you wouldn't listen.'

He didn't say anything. Just looked at her for a few more seconds before turning and storming out of the room. The door rocked back on its hinges.

Standing, Siswan pulled her blouse around her shoulders. Moved to the door. Closed and locked it. She went back to the bed. Dropped the knife. Sat down and cried into her hands. She sobbed. Tears streamed down her face. For the first time in years she allowed herself to really cry. When the tears finally stopped flowing and the sobs stopped wracking her body, she went to the bathroom and showered.

She didn't know what Mirak would do. She had offended him. Hurt him. She expected a reprisal of some sort, but she didn't know what it would be. Half way through her thoughts, half way through her shower, she heard the telephone in her handbag ring.

Drying herself as she walked, she made her way to the bed. She expected it to be him. Expected to hear his voice when she said hello. It wasn't him, wasn't Mirak. She didn't know whether to feel a sense of relief or regret at the sound of Ped's voice.

'Siswan?' her cousin asked.

'Yes. Yes, it's me,' Siswan had to swallow to speak.

'Are you alright?' Ped had heard the strain in her voice.

'Yes. I'm fine. It's late that's all,' she answered.

'I know. I'm sorry.'

'What is it, Ped?' Now it was Siswan's turn to detect the tone of her cousin's voice.

'Your father, Siswan. He died. In his sleep. About an hour ago,' Ped told her.

Siswan didn't say anything for a moment. Her mind raced back in time. To a time when she had lost someone who meant more to her than her father. Someone she had loved, not hated.

'Thank you, Ped,' she said. 'I'll call you tomorrow.'

She switched the telephone off. Sat on the bed. Her thoughts returned to her youth. To a time when the waves had seemed huge.

Chapter 10

Siswan was offered a job at the first bar she tried, but she didn't accept it. She applied late in the afternoon and asked for a day shift. The girl in charge took one look at her and offered her a job that evening.

'You'd make a lot of money,' she said, looking Siswan up and down.

Siswan politely refused the offer. She wanted a job as a cashier, not a bar girl. Eventually she found just the sort of bar she wanted. Not too busy, a little off the beaten track. An open air bar with stools surrounding three sides of a square counter. She couldn't work a day shift as the bar only opened in the evenings, but she was told she wouldn't be expected to go with farangs.

'Start at six, finish when the customers stop drinking,' she was told by the woman in charge. 'You will have to stay sober, make sure everyone pays.'

'Does it get busy?' she asked.

'Not often. Sometimes,' the woman told her.

'What's your name?'

'Nong,' she replied.

'How much will I earn, Nong?' Siswan wanted to know.

'We give you a room to sleep in, four thousand a month and a percentage of any lady drinks you get,' Nong told her.

'Where's the room?' Siswan was very interested.

If the job included a room, she wouldn't need to rent one in the apartment block she had seen earlier. She'd be able to keep the money she had left over. She'd already spent some of it on a new outfit. Black skirt, white t-shirt and a pair of strappy sandals with heels. She looked good in it. Older.

'In an apartment block just a few streets down. You'll be sharing. Two other girls,' Nong said.

'That's okay. I'm used to sharing,' Siswan told her.

Siswan's mind was racing. Four thousand a month! If she earned enough from lady drinks to buy her food, she was going to have a small fortune in just a few months. She decided that she would start sending Ped some money every month. It wouldn't be a lot, but she knew it would help her cousin. One promise fulfilled.

'So, do you want the job?' Nong asked.

'Yes. Yes, please,' Siswan answered.

'You have your ID?'

Siswan pulled the card from her pocket. This would be the first test. Could she pass as an eighteen year old?

'I'll get one of the girls to show you the room. Come back in an hour. Bring your stuff.' Nong passed back her ID card and turned back to stocking the shelves. She'd hardly given it a glance.

Siswan almost ran back to the workhouse. She collected her clothes and bundled them in the old sheet as before. She carried her new outfit, still in its wrappings, carefully over one arm. When she went downstairs Ma was in her usual position behind the old desk.

'I'm leaving,' she said.

'Yes?' Ma said.

'I thought I'd let you know,' Siswan told her.

The old woman gave her a dismissive grunt. It may have been a 'goodbye' or 'good luck', but Siswan didn't think it was either. She turned and walked out through the main door for the last time.

She wanted to go to the beach, to tell Karn what had happened, but she guessed her friend would have packed up and left. She would go there tomorrow. During the day.

By the time she got back to the bar, a young looking girl was sat waiting for her. Nong introduced her as Nok. Nok wore a pair of jeans and a pink shirt and looked Siswan up and down before speaking.

'So, you're going to be the new cashier then?' she said, in a voice that offered little in the way of welcome or kindness.

'Yes. My name is Siswan,' Siswan replied, with a smile.

The girl didn't say anything. Just raised an eyebrow before turning to Nong.

'What room is she going to have?'

'She can share with you and Joy,' Nong told her.

'Three? No way! The room's not big enough!' Nok argued.

Nong suddenly turned on her. There was a flare of anger in her eyes. Siswan was shocked by the sudden animosity in her voice.

'You'll do what I say, Nok!' she shouted.

Nok backed down. Her face showed that she wasn't pleased. She looked at Nong with pure hatred in her eyes. She stood up, looked to Siswan.

'Come on,' she said as she started to walk away.

'Go with her, Siswan. Any trouble, you tell me.' Nong nodded towards Nok's back.

Siswan collected her clothes together and ran after Nok. When she caught up she took a sideways glance at the girl she was going to be living with.

'I'm sorry if I caused you any trouble,' she said.

'I hate that bitch!' Nok replied.

Siswan had to hurry to keep up. The girl strode forward. Her foul mood emphasized in her manner. Siswan didn't say any more. When Nok showed her the room she was surprised at the size. The room was easily three times as big as her room in the workhouse. It was huge in comparison.

Nok pointed to a bed in the corner. A bed with sheets and a pillow. Siswan couldn't believe it. From the way Nok had reacted, she had expected a repeat of the workhouse room. This was wonderful. The walls even had paint and there was a huge array of mirrors fixed to the doors of real wardrobes. There was even a dressing table, with another mirror.

'The bathroom is in there.' Nok pointed to a door. 'You'd better get changed and get back to work.'

'What time do you start?' Siswan asked her.

'Later,' Nok told her, as she stretched out on her own bed. 'You're the cashier. You start early.'

Siswan laid her clothes out on the bed, unwrapped her new outfit, and then made for the bathroom. She was in for another surprise when she looked at the tiled walls, tiled floor and, especially, the shower head protruding from the wall. When she turned the tap beneath it, water sprayed out like rain. The water was still cold, but so refreshing!

Siswan spent a long time getting really clean. She washed herself and then washed her clothes. Finally, when she was spotless, she left the bathroom and walked back into the main room.

Nok was propped up against her pillows watching television. Siswan was fascinated. She'd seen televisions before, of course, but never up close. The images seemed so real.

'Don't just stand there,' Nok said. 'Get to work. The bitch will dock your pay if you're late.'

'Where can I hang my wet clothes?' Siswan asked.

'Why are they wet?'

'I washed them.' Siswan thought it a strange question to ask.

'Well, don't do that again. Just send them to the laundry. We don't want smelly wet clothes hanging around here,' Nok told her, as though she were talking to a child.

Siswan thought about the girls working in the hot shed. The smell of the soap, the heat from the copper cauldrons.

'I prefer to wash my own,' she said.

'If you have to, then put them out there.' Nok pointed to a glass door, almost obscured by a full length curtain.

Outside, Siswan found a small balcony. There was plenty of room to hang her few clothes. She wondered why Nok didn't just wash her own. It was so easy.

She opened up the small makeup box. Sat down at the dressing table and applied her makeup just as the old man had taught her. Not too much, not too little. She made herself look older. When she finished, she dressed in her new outfit and turned to walk out.

'You won't be a cashier for long,' Nok said, looking at her.

'What do you mean?' Siswan asked.

'Oh, nothing,' Nok turned her attention back to the television.

Siswan made for the door. She paused before walking out. There were three beds in the room.

'You said there were three of us here?' she asked Nok, indicating the empty bed.

'Joy.' Nok didn't bother to look up. 'She's with a farang.'

Siswan left the room and walked back to the bar. When she arrived, Nong was still the only person there. The older woman, Siswan guessed twenty-nine, maybe thirty, was setting a small glass, filled with a brown liquid, on the spirit shelf over the bar. Good fortune for the evening. She stepped down and gave a low wai to the image sat on the shelf.

Siswan waited for her to finish. She didn't want to interrupt. On her first night she wanted as much good fortune as the bar could get.

When Nong turned and looked at her, there was a momentary look of surprise in her eyes. A slight shock, even.

'Are you sure you don't want to go with farangs?' she asked.

'Yes. Quite sure,' Siswan answered.

'Okay, but I think they are going to want to go with you!' Nong told her.

Siswan didn't reply. She wasn't too sure what Nong was talking about. The farangs had hundreds, maybe thousands, of girls to choose from. She didn't expect them to want her.

Nong started explaining how the bar system worked and showed her how to keep tabs on the check bins. Each customer got one each. Small wooden cups that Siswan was to put in front of each customer that sat down at the bar.

'When anyone orders a drink, or drinks, put the top copy of the receipt in the check bin,' Nong told her. 'If we get busy, there may be a lot of calls from the girls for drinks. You have to stay on top of it all, okay?'

'Yes. How do I know who's drinking what?' Siswan asked.

'The girls will tell you. Just write out the receipt. Leave the copy in the book,' Nong said.

She told Siswan how lady drinks worked. How the drinks seldom matched the receipt and how to account for each one in the ledger.

'The girls will tell you what to write on the receipt, then place a tick next to their name in the ledger. That way we can pay the girl her commission at the end of the night,' Nong explained.

Siswan didn't see anything very complicated in the way the system worked. The receipts were all hand written. The ledger was just a list of names with spaces beside them. Nothing too taxing.

'If any of the girls order their own drinks, don't bother with a receipt, just jot the drink down next to their name. We can deduct the money from their commission, or their wages at the end of the month.' Nong showed her the previous pages as an example.

When Siswan went back through the ledger the figures, scrawled notes and pencilled jottings looked a mess. There was no way she could make any sense of it all.

'Now, if someone rings the bell,' Nong pointed to the brass bell hanging over the bar. 'Make sure you list all the drinks on the receipt.'

Siswan nodded her understanding. In truth she didn't follow all that Nong told her. The system seemed easy at first sight but, after looking at the ledger again and checking the copies in the receipt book, it didn't appear quite so simple.

'What if one of the girls makes a mistake?' she asked Nong.

'What sort of mistake?'

'Suppose she tells me one thing, but actually pours out something different?' Siswan explained.

'That's why you have to stay sober.' Nong laughed. 'You have to keep your eyes open.'

Siswan suddenly understood that being the cashier wasn't going to be that easy. The system employed by the bar was so simple, so easy, that just about anyone could abuse it. All they needed to do to earn more commission was write an extra tick in the ledger.

'Now, when the delivery boys come, with drinks, peanuts or ice, you pay them from the till and put their receipts in this drawer, okay?' Nong continued.

Siswan looked in the drawer. There was a wad of receipts dating back almost four months. Most of them were just scrawled notes on blank pieces of paper.

'At the end of the night, we pay the girls, or collect from them, deduct all the payments made for the deliveries, add up all the check bin receipts and work out how much should be in the till. If it all adds up we can go home,' Nong told her.

'What if it doesn't add up?' Siswan asked.

'If there's more money than there should be, that's alright, if there's less, it comes out of your wages.' Nong smiled.

Siswan looked into her eyes. The woman wasn't joking.

'How do you check the money against what should have been sold?' she asked.

'We don't,' Nong told her. 'It's not that important, as long as there's a profit.'

'But how do you know if everyone is getting a receipt when they've had a drink?'

'That's your job, Siswan.' Nong laughed. 'That's why you're here.'

That night Siswan met all of the girls who worked the bar. Five of them altogether. Nong, who was in charge, Nok, who obviously thought she should be the leader, Joy, who turned up with a big farang on her arm, Bee, who hardly spoke and Mai, who never seemed to stop.

Nok had changed from her jeans and t-shirt into a tight mini skirt, black, low-cut blouse and a pair of high heeled shoes that looked, to Siswan anyway, as though they would cripple their owner's feet.

Her mood had also changed. It was as though she was drunk. Not angry drunk, happy drunk. Almost silly. Childish, Siswan thought to herself. So different from the tired and sullen girl she had met earlier.

The farang, who had turned up with Joy, drank virtually continuously. Siswan was amazed that any man could drink so many whiskies. By the time he and Joy left the bar, he could hardly stand, let alone walk. Joy laughed to her friends as she staggered away supporting the big foreigner.

'No boom-boom for him tonight,' she told everyone within earshot.

Two more farangs turned up that night. One of them couldn't keep his hands to himself. The girls didn't seem to mind and Bee, who Siswan thought so quiet, happily sat and wriggled about on his lap.

Siswan tried to listen to what the farangs were saying. Tried to understand a little of their language. She didn't understand any of it. The only thing she noticed was that several words were repeated again and again. The same words interjected almost every other word. The more they drank the more she heard the same words repeated.

She kept her eyes on who was drinking what. Kept the ledger and receipt book up to date and, when she needed to go to the toilet, even locked the books in the cash drawer. She was determined not to make any mistakes. She couldn't afford them.

At the end of her first night she and Nong added up the receipts against what was in the till. It all tallied.

'Well done, Siswan.' Nong smiled at her.

'It wasn't so hard.' Siswan smiled back.

'No, it was a quiet night,' Nong said, almost with a sigh.

'How often does it get busy?'

'It used to be every night,' Nong told her. 'Now, who knows? Sometimes, when we expect a quiet night, it gets really busy.'

'The two farangs tonight,' Siswan asked. 'They kept using the same words again and again.'

'All the farangs talk that way, Siswan. They swear all the time,' Nong told her.

'What are swear words?' she asked.

'Oh, words that the farangs use to express themselves,' Nong replied.

'What do they mean?'

'Nobody knows anymore. Even the farangs don't know. The words are just a part of their language.' Nong laughed. 'They were certainly interested in you, though.'

'Really?' Siswan was shocked. 'I didn't notice.'

'You were too busy. Their eyes followed you everywhere and the things they said.'

'What things? What did they say?' Siswan was curious to know.

'Oh, you know. Sex. That sort of thing. One of them said he'd never seen such a good looking bar girl.'

'But I'm not a bar girl. I'm a cashier,' Siswan said.

'Doesn't make a lot of difference to the farangs.' Nong laughed. 'They think they can buy any girl they see.'

'Well, not this one,' Siswan said, emphatically.

'Don't be too sure, Siswan,' Nong told her. 'I've seen many a young girl swayed by the lure of farang money.'

Siswan didn't reply. She knew in her heart that she wouldn't be swayed. Wouldn't be lured. There was no way to prove it. Just wait and see, she thought.

'Anyway, it's time to go,' Nong said. 'Let's lock up.'

Nong showed Siswan how the big wooden boards slotted across the back of the bar to secure the optics, stereo and television. The boards were fairly flimsy and the small padlocks holding them in place would be easy to remove if someone wanted to steal anything.

After saying goodnight to Nong and offering her a wai, Siswan walked back to her new room. The sound of Nok, snoring in her sleep, welcomed her as she opened the door.

The following morning, Siswan awoke early as usual and made her way to the beach to meet Karn. The old woman was pleased to see her and happy to sit and listen to Siswan's account of her first night in the bar.

When she spoke of Nok's change in mood, Karn nodded in confirmation of what she knew.

'Ya Baa,' she said.

'What's that?' Siswan asked.

'Methamphetamine. A drug. Some of the girls take it to stay awake or to put them in a good mood. Some can't work without it. Problem is, after the effects have worn off, you sleep all day long,' Karn told her.

Siswan didn't understand why anyone needed to take a drug in order to work, but at least now she understood why Nok had still been snoring that morning.

'A lot of the girls don't like what they do, Siswan. Some get drunk, others take drugs. Then it doesn't seem so bad,' Karn added.

'But if they don't like it, why do they do it?'

'To pay the family. Take care of their children. All sorts of reasons. Maybe their boyfriends or husbands make them do it,' Karn said. 'Of course, there are also girls who enjoy what they do. Usually, they're the ones who don't need drink or drugs.'

'Did you take drugs, Karn,' Siswan asked, quietly.

'No. I didn't,' the old woman answered. 'That's not to say I enjoyed what I did though,' she added, with a laugh.

'So, what happened? Why are you working the beach now?' Siswan asked.

'When I was young, and attractive to men, I came here to make money. I had a child and a family to support. Nothing too expensive. All I had to do was provide enough for food, clothes. The basics, really. It was easy then. Not too many girls worked the bars,' Karn told her. 'It was frowned upon by everyone. No one liked, or respected, a bar girl.'

'Has that changed now?' Siswan asked her.

'A little, yes,' Karn said. 'It's complicated. A bar girl loses respect from men. No man wants to pay a dowry for a bar girl. No family wants a bar girl to marry into it.'

'So, she becomes an outcast, then?' Siswan questioned.

'For a while, yes. But if she makes a lot of money, returns to the village and buys back her respectability, then she becomes acceptable once again. It all depends on how much money she can make.'

'Did you make a lot?' Siswan asked.

'Would I be working a beach, if I had?' Karn laughed. 'No, I made the biggest mistake of all.'

'What was that?'

'I married a farang,' Karn told her.

'Why was that so bad?'

'He didn't have a lot of money. When we went to the village, for him to meet my family and for me to collect my son, he couldn't afford to buy my respectability,' Karn said, wistfully. 'It was different back then. Now, lots of girls take farang husbands.'

'What happened?'

'Oh, we stayed together,' Karn said. 'You see, unlike some of the girls, I didn't marry him for money. I married him because I loved him.'

Siswan looked at her old friend. Without thinking, she reached out her hand and placed it on top of Karn's.

'What happened to him?' she asked.

'He died twelve years ago,' Karn told her, with a smile. 'He was a good man, Siswan. He had a kind heart and laughed easily.'

'Did he swear a lot?'

'How do you mean?'

Siswan told her about the two farangs in the bar. What Nong had told her about the way they spoke.

'No,' Karn said, with a shake of her head. 'He didn't use those words. I hear the farangs talking now. They don't know I can understand them. It's not good, what they say about the locals.'

'You understand the farangs?' Siswan asked, in surprise.

'Yes, of course!' Karn laughed again. 'I was married to one for over thirty years.'

'Can you teach me?' Siswan asked.

'Only if you're willing to learn.' Karn looked at her.

'Yes. I'm willing,' Siswan said, truthfully.

*****

For the next year, Siswan worked the bar during the nights and, during the days, spent a lot of her free time with Karn learning English.

When she wasn't with Karn, and whenever Joy and Nok were out of the room, she would turn on the television and watch the news programs. She began to learn about her own country. The politics, the superstitions, the problems and the apparent solutions. The first thing she discovered was that the country was run by men. Women were subservient. Second class. But things were changing. Slowly.

Whenever she could, she read the local newspapers and, after a few months, started reading the ones printed in English as well.

When she walked down to the beach or the bar, she would read all the shop signs, the bar signs, the restaurant signs. She read them again and again. If a sign changed, Siswan was the first to know.

She came across a small shop that sold secondhand books. They were cheap and, when she took them back, the shopkeeper gave her half her money back against another. She read only those books that were in English. Simple ones to begin with, then more complicated. Any problems she had, she resolved with Karn.

She listened to the conversations in the bar, on the beach, or sat outside the coffee bars. She paid particular attention to how the farangs interacted with one another. How they gesticulated as they spoke. Their mannerisms.

One thing she learned very quickly was that, unlike the locals, the farangs were spatially aware. They had a circle around them that they didn't like anyone entering. It was complicated to learn.

The area around the farang, the no-entry zone Siswan called it, was about half a meter. Only really close friends, children, or, in the case of the male farangs, attractive members of the opposite sex were allowed to enter it.

When strangers, or street traders like the persistent tailors, approached within the zone, the farangs stiffened. Became defensive. They didn't like it. Didn't like the physical contact. Siswan could immediately spot the signs.

Once, when she had been sat outside the coffee bar, she had witnessed just how hostile a farang could become regarding his no-entry zone.

She had been sitting watching an Indian tailor plying his wares. He was working for the shop next door to the coffee bar and was obviously new to the game. As the farangs walked towards him along the pavement, he would step directly in front of them and use some inane comment to gain their attention.

'Hello, my friend. Where you from?' Was one of his favourites.

Each time he did this, the farangs would awkwardly move around him with their eyes averted. The looks on their faces told Siswan that they weren't happy with the man invading their space. They deliberately avoided his outstretched hand.

Whenever a local walked toward him, however, the tailor moved out of the way. He'd quickly learned that the locals had no problems with no-entry zones and would quite happily walk right over, or even through him, as though he didn't exist.

Siswan had been watching him, and the farangs he annoyed, for about an hour when the incident happened. A young looking farang couple were happily ambling along the road looking into the shops. As they approached, the tailor jumped directly in front of them and gave his latest opening gambit.

'Hey, English! How are you?' He held out his hand for the man to shake.

Immediately, the young couple stopped smiling and, with eyes averted and heads bowed, made to move around the tailor.

'No, thanks,' the man mumbled.

The tailor made the mistake of moving in closer and pressing the back of his hand gently against the farangs chest.

'Good suits, mate!' he said, in a mock imitation of a London accent.

Suddenly, the farang raised his head. He looked the tailor directly in the eyes and spoke in a voice like ice.

'I said, no thanks.'

That was when the tailor should have backed off. He didn't. A mistake he would regret for a long time.

'Hey, man. What's your problem?' he said, again using his fake accent and flashing a grin.

The farang brought his head further up, pulled it back and, with as much force as he could muster, brought his forehead down onto the tailor's nose. Siswan heard the sound of the nose breaking under the force of the head butt from where she sat. It was a sickening sound.

In the bar, the no-entry zone was more relaxed. The more drunk the farangs became, the less distance they seemed to protect. Siswan had been amazed, one evening, to see a particularly drunk farang wandering around hugging all the other farangs he came across. They hadn't minded either. They just laughed, swore at him in good humour, and carried on drinking, or talking, as though nothing had happened. He had even kissed one or two on the cheek as he slurred about how happy he was to see them.

Slowly but surely, Siswan learned. She didn't use her knowledge to actually talk to any farangs. It was easier to pretend ignorance. That didn't mean that she didn't understand what they were saying, however. In fact, as time passed, she understood them all too well.

One evening in particular, she had almost spoken up for herself. Almost revealed what she knew. She'd had to bite her tongue to stop herself from berating the foul mouthed farang that was pestering her.

He'd arrived early and alone. A fat man in his fifties by the look of him. Nong had been making an offering to the spirit shelf, asking that the bar do well that night. Siswan had been busy loading new optics and ensuring that the bottles of beer were cold in the ice box.

'Hello, sweetheart,' he had called out, amiably enough. 'A cold beer.'

Siswan had smiled, taken a bottle from the ice box, and passed him his drink after sliding the bottle into a rubber sleeve.

'You made that look easy,' he laughed. 'Used to putting condoms on are you?'

Siswan knew exactly what he had said. She'd heard it many times before. Every time a farang said it, he thought he was the first. She just smiled, as though she hadn't understood, and passed over his check bin.

'You weren't here last year when I came,' he said.

Again, she just smiled and got on with her work.

'What's up with you?' he said. 'Can't you talk or something?'

It was Nong who answered. She'd finished her prayer and came over to sit next to him.

'She's new here,' she lied. 'Can't speak English. She's just the cashier.'

'Well, she ain't going to be 'just the cashier' for long!' He laughed. 'Not after tonight, anyway!'

Siswan had heard that before as well. Over the months she just ignored the comments made towards her. The other girls would take care of him when they arrived. That was their job, not hers.

Unfortunately, even after the girls arrived and assailed him with their formidable arsenal of charms, he was still interested in her. Even when Nok danced on the bar top, gyrating her hips as seductively as she could, the farang kept his attentions firmly focused on Siswan.

'So, you don't speak English,' he said to her. 'I'll bet you understand money though, eh?'

Siswan concentrated on her job. She deliberately ignored looking at the man, kept herself busy, just as she had before when men wanted to gain her attention. He would give up eventually.

'Hey, Nong!' he shouted across the bar. 'Tell the virgin I'll give her five thousand to be first.'

'No, you cannot, Robert,' Nong answered with a laugh. 'She does not go with farang!'

'She'll go with one eventually,' Robert told her. 'She may as well make some real money doing it.'

Nong moved along the bar and spoke to Siswan in their own language. The language of the bar girls.

'Five thousand is a lot of money, Siswan,' she told her.

'No it isn't,' Siswan said, quietly.

'It's more than a months wages,' Nong argued.

'Five thousand?' Nok had lowered herself off the bar and stood with Siswan and Nong. 'Don't be stupid. Take it.'

'No,' Siswan told them both. 'Never.'

Nong turned back to Robert who was still leering at Siswan.

'Cannot, Robert,' she repeated. 'Another girl?'

'I don't want another girl, Nong!' he raised his voice. 'I want that little bitch.'

'Sorry, Robert. You cannot,' Nong said. 'You must look at another.'

'What the hell's the matter with her?' Robert asked. 'She's a bloody bar girl. Too good to go with a farang eh?'

Nong smiled and walked away from him. Everyone could see that he was becoming angry. Losing face. No one wanted to be with him.

'Bollocks to you, you little bitch!' he shouted at Siswan. 'You'll open your legs for enough money.'

Siswan didn't look at him. Ignored him completely. Inside she felt her anger growing. Rising from deep within her body. She looked at the heavy ashtray on the bar in front of her. She wished she still had her knife.

'I'll give her ten thousand,' the big farang shouted across the bar. 'But for that I want her jacksy as well.'

None of the girls paid him any attention. They looked the other way. Tried to welcome new farangs to the bar. Nobody stopped. Robert was too noisy. Too aggressive. No one would come to the bar whilst he was there. Even Nong was getting angry.

'He is going to ruin business tonight,' she said to the other girls.

'Siswan should go with him,' Nok replied. 'She could just give him short time.'

Siswan overheard the conversation. She knew that the girls would blame her for the big man's behaviour. It wouldn't be his fault. It wouldn't be down to the fact that he was an overbearing, loud mouthed bully. No, it would be because she wouldn't go with him. Never the man's fault.

'I'm not going to go with him, Nok. I'm not going to go with any farang,' she said, quietly. 'I don't care what you think.'

'Well, you're stupid. How can you make enough money?' Nok almost spat the words at her.

'I make enough,' Siswan told her, without looking up.

'You could make a lot more!' Nok shouted. 'Your family must think you are useless. A stupid buffalo!'

It was the worst insult Nok could think of to use against Siswan and one that the girls knew only too well. To be called a buffalo was to be called, fat, ugly, stupid. An animal.

Siswan didn't reply. Her face showed nothing. The insult washed over her as though it hadn't been stated. The anger, however, rose within her. Unheard and unseen.

Having watched the discussion, Robert burst out laughing. He hadn't understood the words, but he'd understood the body language. The angry interaction between the two girls. He enjoyed the fact that they were arguing. He rose from his barstool, walked around the counter and leant over in front of Siswan.

'See what you've done now, you little bitch?' He grinned at her. 'Even your friends think you're stupid.'

For the first time since he started his tirade, Siswan looked at him. He had obviously drunk too much. His white skin was blotchy, his complexion pallid. She guessed he drank too much every night. She was tempted to speak to him, tempted to tell him he was an ugly man with a bad heart. She didn't. Instead she bit her lip.

'Ten thousand for your first time?' He leered. 'It's a good deal.'

Siswan felt the anger. Felt the familiar rush of hot blood rise to her face. She glanced at the ashtray.

'Oh, no you don't,' he smirked. 'No ashtrays!'

For a big man he moved quickly. His hand reached out and pushed the ashtray out of her reach. It didn't matter to Siswan. The glance had only been a feint anyway.

She had considered the ashtray, but it was useless as a weapon. Too bulky. Difficult to grasp quickly.

The only reason she had looked at it was to distract him. To make him follow her eyes. As he did so, and even before he had brought his arm back from pushing the ashtray away, she hit him on the side of the head with the beer bottle she held in her hand. Her sting was as fast as any scorpion.

He went down. Blood spurted from the gash in his scalp. He fell heavily against the barstools, knocking several over.

'Siswan!' Nong shouted.

None of the girls moved. They were shocked. Surprised at the sudden explosion of violence. They looked to the farang and then up at her. She stood quietly. Looking down at the prone figure lying on the other side of the bar.

'He's had enough to drink,' she said to the security guard who came running over to see what the problem was. 'He fell off his stool.'

No one questioned what she said. No one disagreed. The calmness of her voice, the coldness within it, brooked no argument. She turned to Nok.

'If you ever call me a buffalo again,' she said, with a voice like cold steel. 'I will cut your face open.'

She sat back down. Started checking the ledger. Carried on with her work as though nothing untoward had happened. Slowly, the anger within her receded.

From that moment on, not one of the girls, not even Nong, and especially Nok, ever joked, or berated her, for not going with a farang again.

Eventually, the time came when Siswan had to put all that she had learned into practice. She and Karn were sat on the beach together when the decision was made. They had sat together so many times. The old woman had taught Siswan all she knew. They had drawn words in the sand, practiced the different sounds groups of letters made, and spent many hours speaking together in the foreign tongue.

'It's time for you to start talking with the farangs,' Karn had told her.

'Yes. I suppose I have to try at some stage.' Siswan smiled.

'You'll be fine.' Karn looked at her. 'You're better than I ever was. I never saw the things you've taught me.'

Siswan had not only learned how to speak and read English, she had pointed out the subtleties of the language to Karn. The gestures, the body language. The meanings that were sometimes hidden within the words.

'I still feel nervous about trying,' Siswan said.

'Don't start in the bar. Talk to someone in the coffee shop.' Karn smiled at her. 'It'll be easier.'

'What do I say?'

'I don't know, girl!' Karn laughed aloud. 'Ask someone the time!'

'Okay. I'll do it,' Siswan said. 'I'll be back in a minute, okay?'

Without waiting for an answer she stood and walked up the beach to the road. Before she crossed it, she saw a farang walking towards her. She waited. This was it. Her first ever real conversation with a farang.

As the man approached, Siswan moved across the walkway to intersect him. He looked like a nice man. His eyes, a deep blue, appeared to be smiling at something.

'Excuse me, sir,' Siswan said, in her best English. 'Do you have the time, please?'

The man stopped walking. Looked her up and down. It seemed to Siswan that he took a long look at her breasts before his gaze returned to her face. She suddenly realized the position she had put herself in.

A lone farang. A young girl approaching him from the beach. It reminded her of the night she had watched Sood for the last time. She felt her face flush. She averted her gaze from his face. She couldn't believe how stupid she had been.

'It's just after three,' the farang told her, with a smile. 'And I'm sorry, very sorry actually, but I already have a girlfriend.'

Siswan didn't say anything else. She ran back down to the beach and collapsed on the sand next to Karn.

'Oh, my god,' she laughed to the old woman. 'You'll never guess what happened.'

'He thought you wanted sex,' the old woman smiled.

'How did you know?'

'Well, before you ran off, I tried to warn you.' Karn chuckled. 'A young girl, coming off the beach, talking to a farang? What did you expect him to think?'

'Do they all think every girl is for sale?' Siswan asked, lying back on the sand.

'Yes,' Karn answered.

'Why?'

'Because, Siswan. In this town,' Karn explained. 'All the girls are for sale!'

'Not this one, Karn,' Siswan told her, seriously. 'Not this girl.'

Karn looked down at her young friend. The expression on Siswan's face didn't allow for further comment.

'Maybe not.' Karn smiled down at her. 'Maybe not.'

That was the last time that Siswan sat on the beach with Karn. The last time that she would enjoy her time with the old woman. Two days later, when Siswan returned to the beach to meet her friend, a woman she had never met before was

279

there. A younger woman who told Siswan that she was Karn's niece.

Karn had passed away in her sleep two nights ago. The same day that they had joked about Siswan's first proper conversation with a farang.

Siswan had spent so much time with Karn, so much time talking and learning, that she had become used to the old woman's presence. Had never thought about her not being there, on the beach, whenever Siswan went to see her.

Now she was gone. Like Sood. Siswan was alone once more. She spent a week mourning the loss of her friend. She didn't speak to any more farangs for that week. Hardly spoke to anyone. Every day she went to the beach and watched the waves race towards the shore. So many obstacles.

Every day for a week, she watched the waves and said prayers for Karn. Spoke of her kind heart. Her love for a farang Siswan had never met. She said prayers for the old woman's life, her help and her friendship.

A woman who had gone against the tide. Who had struck out for the calm waters beyond the surf. A woman who had married a farang for the right reason. Siswan would miss her and, in her memory, as well as Sood's, she repeated her promise to the sea.

A week after she had been told, Siswan stopped mourning for the loss of her friend. She stopped praying, stopped feeling sorry for herself.

It was time to act on everything Karn had taught her.

Chapter 11

When Siswan saw Mike the following day, she told him about the death of her father. He offered his condolences and tried to comfort her. She was clearly upset.

'I'm sorry, Siswan,' he said to her, and placed his arm around her shoulder.

'Thank you, Mike,' she said.

In truth, Siswan was more upset over what had happened between her and Mirak. She had accepted the death of her father far more readily than she had accepted the loss of Mirak. She knew she had hurt him. Offended him. She had expected him to call, but he hadn't. Perhaps he had finally given up on her?

She didn't expect him to forget the cut she had given him, though. Surely there would be some reprisal, some negative reaction to her anger?

Siswan was troubled by her own reactions to Mirak's advances. Although she had strong feelings towards him, even loved him, she couldn't bring herself to allow him to touch her. To allow the natural feelings of sex to flow. She wanted him. Felt the desire within her own body but, when those feelings arose within her, something stronger, more malevolent, took over. She desired him, wanted him so badly, needed to feel him against her nakedness. At the same time, she felt revulsion. Disgust at the thought of his nakedness against her. Within her.

It was as though another mind lay within her own. A mind that came to the fore whenever a man reached for her. 'Don't let them enter you, Siswan,' it said to her. And the voice she heard was that of her brother.

'Siswan?' She heard Mike say.

'Sorry, Mike. I was miles away.' She turned to him. 'What did you say?'

'That's okay. It's understandable.' He smiled.

She looked at the farang who had become like a father to her. A kind man. A man who wouldn't hit a woman. Maybe she could talk to him, open up to him? He thought her sadness was for her father. He didn't know. Perhaps she could tell him?

'Thank you, Mike,' she told him again.

'I was just asking about, you know, the funeral arrangements?' he asked, almost apologetically.

'Oh, yes,' she said. 'I called Ped this morning. The cremation will be in two days. An auspicious day.'

'Yes,' Mike said, thoughtfully. 'Funerals are always auspicious.'

She almost laughed at his sombre mood. He didn't understand. Why would he? She knew that the farangs didn't have the same religious beliefs as her own people.

'No. I mean that it's an auspicious day for the monks. A lucky day on which to ascend to heaven, Mike.' She smiled, not unkindly.

'Oh, I see,' he said. 'When will you be leaving?'

'Leaving?' The thought hadn't crossed her mind.

'Yes. To go to the funeral?' Mike said.

'I'm not sure I'll be going,' she said, quietly.

Mike looked a little shocked. He didn't say anything for a few minutes. When he did, his voice sounded concerned.

'You have to go, Siswan,' he said. 'He was your father.'

'You don't understand, Mike. You're more of a father to me than he ever was,' Siswan told him.

'Yes. But he was your real father. You owe it to your family, Siswan,' he replied, quietly.

'I owe my family nothing, Mike.' She sounded angry. 'Nothing at all.'

Siswan couldn't stop herself from becoming annoyed. If it hadn't been for her father, Bak might have been a better brother. If it hadn't been for Bak, she wouldn't have had to do what she did in the fields. If it hadn't been for her mother she wouldn't have had to leave the village. If it hadn't been for her mother, none of this would have happened. If her mother had been stronger. If she had removed her father's sting instead of accepting her lot in life. Why had her mother been so weak? Why had she condemned her instead of helping her?

Suddenly, Siswan found herself sobbing. Tears streamed down her face. She tried to stop them. Force them away. They wouldn't stop.

She felt Mike's arm again as he held her. She felt him pull her towards him, into his chest. She didn't pull away. She didn't resist. No inner voice spoke to her. No thoughts of revulsion filled her mind. She allowed her arms to wrap around his big shoulders. She pulled herself in closer to him.

She cried and cried into the shoulder of the man who should have been her father. The shoulder of a man who cared for her in a way she had never known before. This was the first embrace she had ever had from a man that didn't involve sex.

'I'm sorry, Mike,' she said at last.

He pulled back, looked down into her face. The tears had removed the little makeup she had applied around her eyes that morning. She looked beautiful. Young and beautiful.

'Are you alright?' he asked.

'Yes,' she sniffed. 'I'm okay now.'

She took her arms from his shoulders, wiped at her eyes with the back of her hand. She felt better. She looked up into Mike's concerned face.

'I'm fine, Mike,' she said, trying to smile. 'I feel a little foolish but, other than that, I'm fine.'

'Would you like a friend to come with you, Siswan?' he asked.

She knew what he meant. He didn't need to explain. What would they think, though? In the village. What would they think if she returned with a farang? Would they condemn her again? Would her mother condemn her?

'Yes, Mike,' she said, with a real smile. 'I'd like that a lot.'

To hell with the village. To hell with what they thought. To hell with her mother. Karn had returned with a farang. A farang she had loved. Not for money, for love. Siswan would do the same. She loved Mike as a father. She would not be ashamed of him. She would not be ashamed of herself.

'There's something I'd like to do on the way, Mike,' she asked. 'If that's all right with you?'

'Of course.' He smiled. 'No problem. When do you want to travel?'

'We'll go up on the day of the funeral. That way we won't have to stay the night,' she told him.

Two days later Siswan and Mike set off in a hired car. Apple confirmed she would be able to cope with the two bars whilst they were away. The bars were doing so well that there really wasn't a lot for her to do. Just keep an eye on things and make sure the customers were happy.

'You know how to do the cash deposits at the bank?' Siswan had asked her for the third time that day.

'Yes. I'll take care of it, Miss Siswan,' Apple had dutifully replied.

Eventually Mike had managed to get her to go home and get a few hours rest before he collected her in the early hours of the morning.

Even so, she didn't get much sleep. Mirak hadn't called. She hadn't seen or heard from him since the evening of the argument. She wasn't surprised really. She doubted if she would ever hear from him again. Couldn't blame him for walking away. She was tempted to call him, to try and patch things up, but what would be the point? Eventually it would get back to the physical side of their relationship, or the lack of one, and then the same argument would flare up again.

She knew that there was no future with Mirak, perhaps no future with any man, and it made her sad. Mike was the only man who she felt comfortable with and he was old enough to be her grandfather. Anyway, she didn't look upon Mike as a man. Not a man in a sexual way.

When he turned up outside her apartment block she was already showered, dressed and waiting outside.

'Am I late?' Mike asked her, as he reached across and opened the passenger door.

'No. I couldn't sleep much,' she answered as she climbed in.

'Well, this journey will make you sleepy. It's a long way,' he told her.

She remembered the journey she had taken with Tad and Song so many years before. It had been a long way in the cab of that old truck. The car Mike had hired was far more comfortable and a lot faster.

'How long will it take us?' she asked him.

'Oh, we'll get there about one, maybe one-thirty. What time did you say the funeral was?'

'Three.'

'We'll make it.' He smiled at her.

Siswan settled back into the seat as Mike steered their way out of town and onto the main highway. She didn't really know why she had agreed to go to the funeral. There was no need for her to show her respects. She didn't have any respect for her father or his memory. There was something though. Something deep inside her that wanted her to go. To show up in the village as a successful woman? A woman with enough money to buy her respectability back? She didn't know. Maybe she just wanted to see her mother again. To question what she had said all those years ago. To make her pay for what she had said. No, it wasn't that. She expected nothing from her mother. Nothing at all.

Suddenly it dawned on her. The reason she had agreed to go was to get away from the pain the loss of Mirak had caused her. To keep busy. To stop the thoughts. That must be the reason. There couldn't be any other.

The road stretched out before them. Not as an unknown future this time, but as a known past. A past that defined who she was; who and what she had become. She had learned the ways of the farang and had made their world her own. For now, at least. Mike's words brought her out of her reverie.

'How old was your father, Siswan?' he asked her.

'I'm not too sure,' she answered after a moment's hesitation. 'About fifty I think, maybe a little younger.'

'My god, he was young,' Mike stated.

'Yes. But he drank all the time, Mike. Too much whiskey.'

'Even so, that's no age,' Mike said.

'He lived too long,' she said, coldly.

She told him of her childhood. Told him about the nights she had lain awake listening to her mother's cries and her father's ranting. He listened without speaking as she told him what her life had been like in the village. The visits to the temple. The harsh upbringing. Her lack of education. Everything. Everything except what had happened with Bak. She was too ashamed. Too wrapped up in the guilt of what she had done. Her mother had condemned her. What you do is wrong, Siswan.

When she finished, Mike didn't speak. He drove with a fixed expression as though he were contemplating what she had told him. Trying to understand the life she must have lived. Finally, as though he had accepted what he had been told, he spoke.

'I can understand why you wouldn't want to go home,' he said, quietly.

That was all he said. There was no need for her to reply. No need to discuss it further. In her own mind she still questioned what it was that was making her take this journey. Making her travel back in time to face the stares of the villagers. The remarks they would make about her. She was about to confront a wave so large, so immense, it threatened to engulf her, and yet she was still going.

As they approached the outskirts of the town, Siswan remembered the way to the park where she had slept under the big blossom tree. She remembered the night she had killed a rat that came too close. She remembered the boys and their illicit drinking. She remembered the old man and the fight under the low hanging branches that had threatened to trap her.

She gave Mike directions as he slowly manoeuvred the car through the busy streets. Eventually they came to the road beside the park and he pulled over. Cut the engine.

She sat and looked out of the window. The park looked the same. The small lake sat languid in the afternoon sun. The tree she had slept under didn't look so big now. The branches hung heavy with pink blossoms and she imagined she could smell their fragrance as she sat and stared.

Memories flooded into her mind. The smell and taste of the water from the lake when she washed herself and her clothes. The search for work and for food during the days. Fighting off the dogs to be able to scavenge from the rubbish bins. It all seemed so distant now. So far removed from the noise and lights of the bars. She thought about how she had felt those first nights away from home. How small she had seemed. How insignificant to the world around her. How lonely.

She turned her head and looked along the sidewalk. There were no small restaurants there yet. Too early. Too hot under the glare of the sun. They would be there later though. When the sun began to dip below the horizon. She wondered if the old woman would be there. If she still worked the same spot on the dusty paving slabs.

'We'd better get going, Siswan,' Mike said, softly.

'Yes,' she replied, pulling her thoughts away from her past. 'Yes, we should.'

They drove away from the town and into the countryside. The roads were familiar to Siswan now. She had walked the same route to get away. In order to feel clean.

'Just pull over here, Mike, please,' she asked when the car was nearing the outskirts of the village.

Once more, she sat and looked. The small pond really did look small now. The fetid water lay still, hardly a ripple to disturb its glass-like surface. The muddy brown banks were dry and hard looking as they slipped down to meet the green coloured water.

A sudden splash startled her. A circle of ripples moved outward toward the banks. The circles became larger, wider as they stretched across the pond. A fish had broken the stillness of the picture. The only movement in an otherwise fixed moment of time.

She remembered the times she and Bak had played there as children. A time of innocence. A time of laughter.

'Okay, Mike. Let's go,' she said, turning away from the pond.

As they drove slowly past the first of the houses she saw people look up. Look to see who was passing in the shiny new car. Something to talk about in the otherwise dull evenings.

At Siswan's direction, Mike drew up outside her old house. There were people in the garden. People she recognized from her youth. Would they recognize her? She didn't know. Didn't care that much. The chanting of the monks from inside the small downstairs room marked the beginning of the funeral ceremony.

As they approached the weather beaten wooden door she turned to Mike. It would be bad enough for her to walk in alone. Already she could hear the murmurings of those gathered outside. 'Siswan', she heard them say and 'farang'. Mostly farang.

'I'll wait here, Siswan,' Mike said, as though reading her thoughts.

She smiled up at him. Reached out and squeezed his arm. More for the villagers to gossip about.

'Thank you, Mike,' she said, before turning and entering her old home.

Inside lay her father. Placed within a plain wooden coffin that was more like a box than a coffin, he was in the centre of the small room. A yellow-robed monk sat to one side chanting the prayers and rites necessary for the soul to attain heaven.

To one side of the monk, at a respectful distance, sat Ped. Her cousin had her hands raised in prayer and her eyes closed. She didn't open them as Siswan entered the room. To the other side of Ped sat her mother. The woman who had condemned her.

The sight of her mother filled Siswan with emotions. She suddenly wanted to cry. To stand in front of the gathered family and cry. She held the tears back. Stood in the entrance of the room she just stared at her mother.

The woman looked older. Much older than the six years that had passed since Siswan had last seen her. She looked worn and broken. Ped had told her that her mother was better. That she had even started to go to the temple again. Siswan couldn't see that woman. She couldn't see a person strong enough to even stand, let alone make the journey to the temple to pray. What she saw was an empty, broken body. A body that had grown thin and frayed. She almost allowed a cry to escape from her throat.

The monk stopped chanting. The prayer was over. Ped lowered her hands, opened her eyes. When she saw Siswan a startled sound escaped her lips. Her mother, too, lowered her hands and looked at Ped to see what had startled her. She followed the young woman's eyes and caught sight of Siswan standing in the doorway.

At that moment, the moment that their eyes met, Siswan understood why Ped had told her that her mother was getting better. It was in her eyes. The watery faraway look Siswan had remembered was gone. The eyes that looked at her were alive. Alive and aware of what they were seeing. Her mother's eyes were those of a younger woman. A woman who wasn't yet defeated. A woman who had come back.

'Siswan,' her mother said.

A single word. Spoken so quietly. Almost whispered. Siswan. Her name spoken from the voice of her mother. A voice that had condemned her so many years ago.

Now Siswan understood what it was that had made her come back for her father's funeral. Now she understood why she was here. Why she was willing to risk being ridiculed by the villagers. Why she risked the stares, the gossip, the possibility of further condemnation. With that one, whispered word, her mother had made it clear.

It had nothing to do with running away from Mirak, nothing to do with buying back her respectability, nothing to do with showing off her success. The only reason she had come back was to gain redemption. Redemption for her sins. Redemption for having done what she had done with Bak, with the boys in the field. Redemption for the old man in the park, for every sin, great or small, that she had committed in order to survive.

There was only one person in the whole world who could give her the redemption she so desperately wanted. One person who would be able to tell her that it hadn't been her fault, that she hadn't had a choice. The same person who had condemned her. The same person who had told her that what she did was wrong. Only one. The woman she now stared at. Her own mother.

Siswan crossed the floor on legs she didn't trust. She felt light headed. Faint. She never took her eyes off her mother. Didn't look at the dead body of her father. Didn't look at her cousin or the other members of the family gathered in the small room. She needed her mother. Wanted to feel her touch. Hear her words of forgiveness.

She fell to her knees. Lowered her head to the floor in front of the old woman. Silently she prayed for the touch, the words that would redeem her soul. Redeem herself.

She felt her mother's hand on her shoulder. Felt the weight of her arm as she leaned out to touch her.

'Siswan,' her mother whispered, again. 'Oh, my Siswan.'

Siswan looked up into her mother's face. Tears were running down the old woman's cheeks.

*****

The cremation took place in the temple. Her father's body had been placed on the back of a truck and Siswan, holding her mother's arm as though she would never let it go, had walked slowly behind it.

Paper flowers of white, yellow and blue had been placed around the bloated and unrecognizable figure of her father. The flowers, so pretty in the afternoon sunshine, did little to eradicate the ugliness of her father's face. A face swollen in size and blotched from years of whiskey consumption. She didn't know this man they were to burn. Didn't allow herself to even think about him.

As she walked behind his body, the only thing she cared about was the woman at her side. She had come back from wherever she had hidden herself. Come back from the place where her father's fists had sent her. That was what mattered to Siswan.

'Where have you been?' her mother asked her.

Siswan told her a version of her life. Told her how she had found work with the farang that followed behind them in the car. Told her a sweetened story of how she had been lucky to find such a good and honest employer. She omitted anything that lay blame on Bak or the family.

'We don't know where Bak is,' her mother told her, in her quiet voice. 'But I'm glad you have returned. Your father will be pleased you are here.'

Siswan didn't reply. Didn't say what she thought of her father. What he had done to her mother. What he had done to them all. She was happy to be with her mother. Happy to be walking beside her to the temple.

After the ceremony, after the fires had consumed what was left of her father, Siswan helped her mother into Mike's car.

'We can drive back, Mama,' she said. 'It's too far for you to walk again.'

They drove back in virtual silence. Only once did her mother speak in the car.

'Is this farang your husband?' she asked.

'No Mama,' Siswan said with a smile. 'He is my friend. A good friend.'

As they drove away from the village that evening, Siswan felt happier than she had in a long time. Happier than when she had last left her home. She had managed a conversation with Ped even though she hadn't wanted to leave her mother's side.

'I'll send you some more money,' she had told her cousin.

'She was asking about you for the last three days. I'm glad you came back for her.' Ped smiled.

'Thank you, Ped.' Siswan had hugged her. 'Thank you for looking after her.'

'She's family, Siswan. I had to help my family.' Ped smiled, and hugged her back.

The family had all gathered in the garden that evening to eat a meal in honour of her father. Siswan had looked at them all. Years before, they had gathered in her garden. Years before, they had said and done nothing to stop the beatings her mother received. To stop the man they were now honoring. She said nothing. Held her peace and contented herself with her mother's company. It didn't matter anymore.

Mike had sat in the garden and ate with her and her family. He hadn't said much. Hadn't needed to. His very presence gave her strength. Finally, after they had said their goodbyes, he turned to her.

'Are you glad you came, Siswan?' he asked.

'Oh, yes.' She smiled at him. 'Thank you, Mike.'

'Well, I didn't do very much. Just drove the car.'

'Mike, you don't know how much you did. You'll never know.' She put her arms around him.

She didn't care that the family were watching this show of affection. Didn't care that their beliefs disallowed such public displays. She smiled up at the big farang.

'Now you truly are my Papa, Mike.'

He smiled back, opened the car door for her to climb in.

'If that's true, it means Rican is going to be your stepmother.' He closed the door before she could reply.

She had to wait until he had walked around the car. Had to wait until he had smiled and waved to her family. Had to wait whilst he slowly and deliberately took his time getting in behind the wheel.

'What did you say?' she asked him.

'Oh, sorry. Didn't you know?' He grinned.

'No. I didn't know!' she admonished him. 'When did you decide that?'

'Well, I was going to tell you the morning you told me about your father. It didn't seem right then,' he told her.

'That's wonderful, Mike,' she laughed. 'Can I be a bridesmaid?'

'Well, I thought a maid of honour,' he smiled. 'You and Apple.'

'No, Mike. A bridesmaid,' she laughed.

'What, you mean?' he asked, incredulously.

'Yes. Why not?' She smiled at him. 'Do you mean to tell me that you've never met a bar girl who's a virgin?'

Mike just looked at her for a moment. She didn't say anything. Just looked at him with a smile on her face. She waited for what she had said to sink in. Now you're just as shocked as I am, she thought to herself.

'I didn't know,' he said, as he drove. 'I should have guessed.'

'How could you guess?' she asked.

'You never go with a man. The trouble with Mirak,' he told her.

'Ah, yes.' She turned serious. 'The trouble with Mirak.'

'What are you going to do about him?'

'I don't think there's much I can do. I really hurt him,' she said, quietly.

'Oh, I don't know, Siswan. Us men are pretty thick skinned you know.' He smiled. 'He'll come back. If you want him to.'

'I'm not sure that I do, Mike,' she told him. 'It just makes life so complicated.'

'It makes life worth living, Siswan,' he said. 'There ain't much else besides love.'

'Apart from the money, Mike. There's always the money.'

Mike didn't say anything in reply. He just smiled and kept driving down the dark and dusty lanes. She remembered Karn. She hadn't thought about the money. Not when it came to her farang.

'Maybe there's more, Mike,' she said, quietly.

'Yes, Siswan. There's more. You'll see.'

They continued on in silence. When they came to the main town, Siswan asked Mike to return to the park. There was something she wanted to do.

When they pulled up alongside the small lake once again, the road had changed dramatically. Rows of small restaurants and cafés lined the sidewalk. People were everywhere; walking, jogging, even a few riding bicycles. So different from the day when the heat of the sun kept most people away.

'Here, Mike,' she suddenly said. 'Stop here please.'

She climbed out of the car and walked a few paces down the sidewalk. The first thing she saw was the old, rusting motorbike and sidecar. She was certain it was the same one. She looked along the sidewalk.

The old woman was stood at her small grille when Siswan approached. She looked up at the young woman stood in front of her.

'Yes?' she said, expectantly.

'Hello.' Siswan gave her a wai. The old woman smiled in reply.

'Do you want to eat?' she asked.

'Can I work for you?' Siswan asked, in all innocence.

The old woman cackled. She revealed black stumps of teeth and a yellow coated tongue.

The teeth were even blacker than Siswan remembered.

'Why?' she asked.

'I have nowhere to go. I need a bed, somewhere to shower. Food,' Siswan told her.

The old woman didn't reply. Her face looked puzzled as though she was remembering something. Something from her past.

'I know you,' she said, hesitantly. 'I think I do.'

'I know you,' Siswan told her.

Siswan reached into her handbag. Pulled out her purse. Whilst the old woman watched, she counted out ten, one thousand notes.

'This should cover the rattan mat I took from you,' she said, handing the money to the surprised old woman.

'What?' The woman looked at the money, then back to Siswan.

'Yes. I owe you a new one.' Siswan smiled. 'And I owe you a young girl's thanks.'

Without waiting for a reply, she turned and walked back to the car. Settling herself back in the passenger seat she turned to Mike.

'And sometimes, Mike,' she said. 'Just sometimes, it's all about the money.'

It was just after two in the morning when Mike pulled up outside Mike's Bar. There wasn't room to park so he dropped Siswan off and went to find a place for the car. The long journey back had been uneventful and, as far as Siswan was concerned, thankfully so. She'd had enough emotional stress for one day.

When she entered the bar she found it in full swing. The girls were all busy, the drinks were flowing and the music was blasting out like there was no tomorrow.

It's good to be back, she thought to herself and, smiling, headed for the bar where she could see Lon chatting away to a good looking farang.

'Where's Apple?' she said to the girl, after nodding and smiling to the farang customer.

'Oh, hello, Miss Siswan.' Lon smiled and offered a wai. 'She's up at your bar. I mean Swan's Bar.'

Siswan had told the girls often enough that she didn't own either bar. Mike was the owner. Call the bars by their names. She let it go this time.

'Okay, I'll walk up. Everything alright here?'

'Oh, yes. Very all right!' Lon answered, with a grin and a slight nod towards the young farang.

Siswan smiled back. She couldn't blame Lon. The guy was very handsome.

'If Mike comes in, tell him where I've gone.'

She turned, walked back towards the doors. She could see all the other girls serving drinks, talking and joking with the customers. They were doing well. Everything looked as it should be.

As she walked along the crowded street she could spot the bars that were doing well and those that weren't. The difference was the girls. It was always the girls. She passed one small bar. Three customers sat drinking. They wouldn't stay long either. Who could blame them. The four girls who worked the bar sat outside looking bored.

Dressed like the young prostitutes they were, they sat and smoked cigarettes. Too bored to even talk to one another let alone their customers. As she neared, a farang walked past the bar.

'Welcome!' One of the girls sang out, in a long nasal sounding voice.

To Siswan, it didn't sound like a welcome at all. More like the wail of some banshee. Enough to frighten off the most hardened drinker. The farang walked past without giving a second glance.

It was the same in other bars. Even if the girls were pretty or attractive they weren't getting much custom. It's all about the attitude, Siswan thought to herself. Show the customer the good time they could be having without being obvious. That's why she didn't allow the girls to sit outside. Didn't allow the banshee wails of 'welcome' to permeate the bars. The girls were inside, talking to the customers. Making them feel really welcome.

That's what it was all about. Make them feel they're important. Don't pretend either. After all, they were important. The most important people in all the world.

She made her way to Swan's bar. Followed the man who had walked past her earlier, in fact. Followed him all the way to the front door and into the noise beyond. She allowed herself a small smile of satisfaction as he held the door open for her to enter.

She found Apple surrounded by customers. Three men and two women were all listening to her tell a tale of bar work.

'And, to end a really bad night, he didn't even buy me a drink,' she shouted to them above the noise.

The laughter that followed, as well as three offers of another drink, told Siswan that Apple was in control. She looked around. The other girls were all working well. Drinks were being sold as quickly as the girls could pour them. The two cashiers were beating out a steady rhythm on the cash registers. Two more girls, wearing skimpy miniskirts, were running around serving bar food and collecting the empty plates. The customers were enjoying themselves. The place was in full swing.

So different from the sombre mood of the afternoon. A world away from her village. A different universe. How much money did a bar like this contribute to a village like hers, she thought. How many thousands were sent home each week to keep the families fed?

'Hello, Miss Siswan. How was it?' Apple asked her in a concerned voice.

'It went well, Apple,' she said. 'Very well, in fact.'

'Things are okay here.' Apple raised her voice over the noise.

'Yes. I can see,' Siswan replied. 'Only one thing wrong, Apple.'

The young girl looked worried. She glanced quickly around the bar to see what it might be that had upset her boss.

'What is it, Miss Siswan?' she asked.

'When, exactly,' she asked. 'Were you going to tell me about Mike and Rican's wedding plans?'

Apple smiled with relief.

'I did tell you not to be surprised,' she said.

'Isn't it great!' Siswan laughed. 'And, we're to be bridesmaids!'

Apple looked at her. She'd never seen her boss looking so happy. So radiant. It couldn't just be about Mike's wedding. There had to be something else.

'Has Mirak called?' she asked.

'No,' Siswan said. 'I haven't heard from him.'

'Oh. I'm sorry.' Apple suddenly felt foolish.

'That's okay, Apple. Don't worry about it.' Siswan smiled. 'Let's meet up with Rican tomorrow to discuss dresses.'

'Yes!' Apple laughed again. 'Pink, or maybe light blue.'

'Hold that thought, Apple.' Siswan laughed. 'I'm not going looking like icing on a wedding cake.'

The two girls laughed at the idea before walking back to the bar arm in arm. There were customers to serve. Drinks to be sold. Business first. Always business first. Siswan had never felt happier.

In the morning when Siswan, Apple and Rican were sat around the kitchen table discussing wedding plans, Siswan's telephone rang. It was Mike.

'Where are you?' he asked.

'Talking to your future wife,' she told him.

'There's a problem.' He sounded serious. 'You need to come to the hospital.'

'Oh, Mike. What is it?' Her tone made Apple and Rican stop talking.

'It's Lon. She's hurt,' he told her.

'How? What's wrong?'

'She's been beaten, Siswan,' Mike said. 'Beaten badly. The police are here with me now.'

'I'm on my way,' she said, and hung up.

'What is it?' Apple asked.

'Lon. She's hurt,' Siswan told her. 'I'm going to the hospital.'

'I'm coming with you.' Apple wasn't asking.

The two of them raced outside and called a taxi. By the time they got to the hospital they were desperately worried.

Siswan couldn't help remembering the handsome face of the farang Lon had been with the night before. Had he done something? What could he have done?

Mike stopped them both at the entrance to the ward.

'It's not good,' he told them. 'Be prepared.'

When they entered they saw Lon lying on the first bed they came to. A tube ran from her nose to a respirator stood beside the bed. Her arms were covered in bandages and a tube connected her left one to a bag of blood hanging from a stand.

Her face was a mass of bruises and small cuts. Her eyes, although closed, were swollen and red. The lids looked as though they had been burned. The white sheet that covered her body had slipped off slightly, revealing a cut and bruised leg. A uniformed police officer sat in a chair at her side.

'What happened?' Apple was the first to find her voice.

With a nod of his head Mike alluded to the officer who stood before he spoke to them.

'It may be better to talk outside,' he told them.

Before turning, Siswan glanced once more at the face of Lon. She remembered such a pretty girl, a girl who laughed and smiled. Not this. Not a face that looked so much like the dead face of her father.

Outside in the corridor the police officer spoke succinctly and quietly. He told them all that he knew and what he knew made Siswan feel sick to the stomach. In her mind she pictured the dead face of Sood. Cuts had covered her face. Bruises had revealed where she had been beaten. The open gash around her neck testament to the way she had died. But even those wounds, those vicious signs of a brutal attack, had not been as bad as what she was being told. What she had just seen.

Only once before had she known of an attack on a bar girl. Once, in all the years she had worked the bars. That had been different. She hadn't really known the girl that well. Hadn't thought of her as one of her girls.

As the officer spoke, her mind cast back to the last time something like this had happened.

The last time a girl got more than she bargained for from a farang.

Chapter 12

The evening had started quietly enough. Nong had taken the night off, so Siswan opened the bar at six and made an offering to the spirit table herself. She prayed that the evening would bring good fortune to the bar and plenty of customers.

When the girls turned up at ten there were already two farangs sat drinking cold beers. Joy and Nok homed in on them as soon as they got there.

'Hello. What your name?' Joy asked the first of them.

Siswan watched as the girls flirted, joked and cajoled with the farangs. She had spent the last hour talking politely with them. They had been surprised to discover that she could speak good English and had been asking her questions about living in her country. That changed as soon as the girls arrived.

Siswan didn't understand the girls' attitude towards the tourists. Sure, she knew they wanted to make money. They all did. But it was the way they went about it. They didn't so much charm the men, as attack them.

She remembered what she had learned from watching the beach traders. The farangs preferred to buy from those that didn't push too hard. Those that didn't try to force them into buying something. It was the same with the girls.

The ones that launched into an all fronts attack were seldom the ones that went home with an attractive farang. They usually ended up with none at all or, at the very least, the ugliest or drunkest.

Siswan had already learned that the farangs liked to window shop for a while. They liked to stand back and look at the goods they were being offered before they bought.

To the local men it didn't matter so much. They just wanted sex. Short time. The farangs wanted more.

The two men smiled and joked during the onslaught, but Siswan noticed the signs of disinterest before the girls did. It was in their body language. The smile of one was a little strained. He raised an eyebrow to his friend who, in turn, nodded almost imperceptibly to the check bin.

It was a shame. She had been enjoying their conversation. Siswan had been in the bar almost two years now. She'd learned to speak with the customers as though they were people instead of just money machines. She enjoyed their company. Had made a few friends, a few regulars.

The two farangs, who were now calling for their bill, were new to the country. Perhaps later, after they got used to the ways of the girls, they would come back. Be more susceptible. Siswan doubted it. Joy and Nok were too pushy. Too forceful in their attempts at getting a drink.

Siswan smiled to the two men as she handed them their bill. A smile of apology.

'Thanks, Siswan. Nice to meet you,' one of them pointedly told her.

'Maybe we'll see you again,' the other one said.

'I'd like that. Thank you for coming.' She offered them a wai as they walked away from the bar.

'Why do you do that, Siswan?' Joy asked. 'They didn't even leave a tip.'

'No, they didn't. But they came, bought a few beers and they are customers,' she replied.

It was a waste of time. The girls just didn't get it. They probably never would.

'They were sticky shits,' Nok said in distaste. 'Didn't even buy us a drink.'

Siswan looked at the drug addicted girl. A black sleeveless t-shirt. A pair of denim shorts that left nothing to the imagination. Too much makeup. Her hair unkempt and lacklustre. She looked a mess. The drugs gave her deep dark circles below her eyes. Her mouth seldom smiled. She smoked cigarettes by the dozen and, Siswan was sure, didn't shower often enough. Joy wasn't much better.

'They're only farangs, Siswan,' Joy said. 'Why do you show them respect?'

They'd had the same discussions many times. The girls had their view and she had hers. She didn't tell them that the two farangs had bought her three drinks that evening. Two of which she hadn't needed to pour.

'Just tab us for it, Siswan,' they'd laughingly told her. 'You don't need to drink it.'

Siswan just couldn't understand why it was that the girls thought it was all about the sex.

Admittedly, a lot of the time it was, but not all the time.

The western men liked a bit of a chase. A bit of a game. They knew they could just buy a woman. They all knew that. They weren't stupid. But that didn't mean they didn't enjoy the fantasy of actually wooing one. The make believe that, somehow, they had managed to pull a beautiful, sexy, young and, above all, willing, girl from the bar. It was all about the game. Sometimes the farangs played it better than the girls.

Siswan could see how it worked. Could tell when a man was genuinely interested in a girl and when he wasn't. The signs were obvious.

'Why don't you go with a farang, Siswan?' Mai asked her. 'Then you'd know what a bunch of sex maniacs they are.'

'That's true,' Joy added. 'Go with one. Then you'd know.'

Siswan just looked at them as they wandered to the corner to sit and chat amongst themselves. She didn't care what they thought. She wasn't going to go with any men. Farang or otherwise.

She overheard Mai telling the others that she was late. She should have started her period a week ago and was worried that she was pregnant.

It was one of the fears of working the bars. The worst was HIV, but getting pregnant ran a close second. Sometimes a condom split or the farang didn't like wearing one. Siswan could never understand that.

Very often the girls complained that a farang had insisted on not wearing a condom and the girl had to take the morning after pill. It made them sick and very few could work the following night. She didn't understand the farangs either. Condoms protected against disease.

When Siswan had first started working in the bar, she'd been puzzled that the girls managed to work every day of the month. In the end she'd asked Nong about it.

'They use the sponge,' Nong answered.

'What sponge?' Siswan asked.

Nong had gone to her handbag, taken out a small, oval shaped sponge. It looked a bit like the one Siswan used to apply foundation except that it was slightly conical in appearance.

'What do you do with it?' she asked.

'When you have a period, you push it inside,' Nong told her. 'It stops the blood for long enough. The farang doesn't know the difference.'

Siswan had been shocked. Shocked that the girls would go to such lengths to continue working. To continue earning.

Even now, even though Mai was concerned about her late period, she was still in the bar. Still willing to work.

Three farangs approached. The girls all moved towards them. Smiled at them.

'Welcome!' they called in their long, drawn out, sing-song manner. 'Welcome!'

The farangs allowed themselves to be drawn in. Siswan recognized one of them. He'd been there a few times before.

'Hello, Siswan,' he smiled at her, as he took a stool.

'Hello, Steve.' She gave a wai. 'Haven't seen you for a while.'

'Just got back,' he told her. 'Been home to earn some more bar fine money.'

'Well, you'll be more than welcome to spend it here,' she said and laughed, easily.

Steve was an easy guy to get along with. He knew the score and always paid his way.

'My friends, Thomas and Harry.' Steve introduced the two men with him. 'Met them in The Tiger Bar. Told them I'd show them the friendliest and best looking cashier in the whole town.'

'That's nice of you, Steve.' She laughed. 'Why did you come here then?'

'Ah, Siswan. Modest as ever!' He laughed with her.

Siswan shook hands with all three of the men. It was Harry's hand that lingered too long. She spotted the sign immediately. His palm was too clammy as well. Like shaking hands with a dead fish.

'So, gentlemen,' she asked. 'What will it be?'

'A beer for me please, Siswan,' Steve told her.

Thomas asked for the same. He seemed quite nice. A newbie as far as Siswan could judge. He was still a little embarrassed by the sights and sounds of the bars. He wouldn't be for long, though, Siswan thought. A few drinks and the inhibitions soon fell away. It was Harry who waited for her to look at him before ordering.

'I'll have you, sweetheart,' he said with a laugh.

'Really, Harry?' she asked him, staring into his eyes. 'Can you afford me?'

'Whatever it takes, darling!'

'More than you'd be willing to give, Harry,' she said, smiling.

'I told you before.' Steve butted across. 'Siswan isn't for sale.'

'What a shame.' Harry allowed his eyes to linger over Siswan's breasts. 'What a bloody shame.'

In the end, Harry ordered a beer and the three men started what was to be a long drinking session. After an hour they had each consumed enough to make them easy prey for the bar girls. Even Thomas was enjoying the attention Mai was giving him.

Harry was in a deep and meaningful conversation with Nok that seemed to mostly consist of him sliding his hands all over her body. Nok didn't mind. Not in the least. She quite openly allowed his searching fingers to wander wherever they wanted. After all, it was her job. Whilst he was spending money, ringing the bell and running up his tab, he could touch anything he wanted.

Steve sat at the bar and attempted a conversation with Siswan. The noise of the music blasting out from the huge loudspeakers made it a little difficult.

'So, Siswan,' he shouted. 'When are you going to marry me?'

'What was that, Steve?' Siswan laughed.

'I said, when are you going to marry me?'

'Oh, I thought that was what you said. Couldn't be sure though. The music is very loud.'

'You're not going to answer me are you?' He laughed.

'No, Steve.'

'Was that an answer?'

'Yes.'

'You will?'

'Will what?'

The conversation carried on in that vein for quite a while. Siswan enjoyed Steve's company. He was easy to deal with and he was spending a fortune.

'I suppose I'll have to ask Joy, then?' he said, finally.

'Good idea, Steve.' Siswan laughed back. 'She's looking for a good farang husband.'

The reality was that most of the girls were. The dream in the laundry had been about money in a pocket. The dream amongst the bar girls was that a good farang, a farang with a good heart, would come along and take the girl away from all this.

Of course, in the dream, a good heart meant a farang who had a lot of money and didn't mind spending it. The dream always had the clause that the farang would take care of the girl, her child or children, as well as the rest of the family. The dream didn't come true very often.

Siswan knew of one girl who had married a farang. He had a very good heart indeed. Very big. He'd fallen in love with the girl and asked her to marry him. Three months later she was back working the bars.

It hadn't worked out. After the initial lust had died down he'd sent her packing. Told her he didn't like her family or her two kids. Didn't see why he had to support her whisky drinking father and her fat, lazy mother. The reality of life was never included in the dream.

Steve turned his attentions towards Joy. Siswan didn't mind. Nor did Joy. Even Steve was happy with the situation. He knew he'd never get Siswan to come out from behind the bar. Never.

She tallied up the ledger. The girls were doing well. The three farangs were out for a good time and, as always with farangs, a good time meant lots of alcohol. Siswan, herself, had already earned more from drinks that evening than she had from her wages.

Harry rang the bell again. Drinks all round. She decided a cocktail called 'sex on the beach' would go down well. Orange juice for herself though.

The sound of the bell brought more customers. Well, not exactly customers. More like freeloaders. If a bar had a party of revelers, who were ringing the bell often enough, it would always attract those farang who were out for a cheap night. The cheap charlies.

Several men now sat around the bar, sipping from their cheap bottles of beer, whilst the unsuspecting merry makers continued to ring the bell. Continued to buy a round for everyone.

Siswan despised the farangs who did that. They were mostly long timers. Farangs that worked in the country as English teachers, diving instructors, or some other job that didn't make a lot of money. They would frequent the bars almost every night, sipping from their bottles of beer, whilst keeping an ear open for the sound of a bell ringing.

It was even worse when one of the girls had a birthday. All the balloons would be the giveaway. The girls would order an array of colourful balloons to decorate the bar and a buffet of food for everyone to enjoy. They would pay for it all out of their own pocket as well.

The whole idea was that the girl held a party for everyone. The bar would get busy and the bell would be rung often throughout the night. At midnight, all the balloons would be burst to celebrate the birthday and also to ward off any evil spirits from attaching themselves to the girl for the following twelve months.

The parties always attracted the freeloaders. Free food. Free drinks. They could sit and drink all night without ever putting their hands in their pockets.

When all the decent customers, as well as staff, pinned money to the girls dress as a sign of good luck, and also to help her pay for the food and drink she had provided, the freeloaders would skulk off into the night. They had spent the whole night drinking, eating, even groping the girls that didn't know them too well, and then they'd move off to find another free drink, and maybe another free grope, at some other bar.

Siswan didn't like them. She didn't like people who just took and never gave. When the bell rang again she pointedly served anyone who was joining in and ignored the freeloaders.

'Hey,' one of them shouted above the noise. 'Where's my drink?'

'What did you order?' she asked.

'No. From the bell,' he told her. 'Free drink for everyone.'

'Yes.' She looked at him. 'But not for you.'

'That's the spirit, Siswan!' Steve had overheard the brief conversation. 'Best you clear off to some other bar, mate.'

Siswan smiled. She was glad that Steve had noticed. He knew the tricks well enough. Now he knew that Siswan wouldn't cheat him he'd be even more inclined to drink at the bar.

'Thanks, Siswan,' he shouted over.

'You're welcome, Steve.' She smiled.

Siswan never cheated the customers. Even when the girls had told her she should overcharge the drunk ones, she never did. She had learned straight away that the farangs didn't mind spending their money. Didn't mind buying a few girly drinks. Didn't mind too much about anything. What they hated though, what really got them angry, was being ripped off. It didn't matter if they spent several thousand in a night, didn't matter one bit. As long as they didn't get cheated.

She knew of one bar that had regularly ripped off the customers. When the farangs were drunk enough, and called for their bar tabs, the girl would very often add a hundred, maybe two, to the total. If the customer did check, the girl would just smile and mumble an apology. Those bars never had regulars. Once they knew the bars that cheated, the regulars never went back. The bars soon went out of business once word got around. The farangs were loud, sometimes ill mannered, occasionally downright offensive, but they weren't stupid. They weren't stupid at all.

It didn't take long for the other cheap charlies to discover that Siswan wasn't going to be playing their game. They finished their beers, paid the small tab, and left. The two other customers who had joined up to enjoy the three revelers were paying their way. No problem.

'Hey, Siswan!' Harry shouted over. 'Come out and enjoy the fun!'

'And who would serve the drinks, Harry?' she shouted back, with a smile.

She watched as Harry slipped a finger inside the crotch of Nok's shorts. She shook her head and returned to serving more drink.

The public scenes of sex had shocked her when she had first started. The groping, kissing and touching had been an eye opener. Now she was used to it. It happened all the time. A hand on a leg. A hand up a skirt, inside a blouse, down the back of a pair of jeans. It was all part of the bar scene. The girls didn't mind and the farangs thought it was all very funny.

Amidst much laughter, one or two would see just how far a bar girl was willing to go before she dragged herself away from the probing fingers. All part of the game. The game between the sexes. Between the races.

Money was what it was all about. Money was the prize. If a farang was willing to pay enough, he could see his wildest fantasies come true. Two in a bed, three in a bed. Whatever. It was all about the money. One farang she had met when she first started had summed it all up for her.

'We're like kids in a sweet shop, Siswan,' he'd said. 'The only difference being is that we're not kids and the sweets aren't sweets.'

Thomas, who Siswan had guessed would indulge himself after a few drinks, was really getting into the concept. He had Mai wriggling her behind all over his crotch and, at the same time, was feeling up the back of Joy's thighs as she drooled all over Steve. No one seemed to mind. Least of all Joy who was enjoying the attention.

Siswan was still surprised by the girls sometimes. When the bar was quiet, and they had time to sit and talk amongst themselves, all she ever heard them do was bemoan the farangs. They'd each take turns in telling their tales of debauchery, each trying to outdo the others as to how awful their experiences had been.

Many times Siswan had heard them say that they were leaving. That the life was killing them. That they hated being sex objects to drunken old fools who thought the girls actually liked them. Many times she'd listened as they moaned about the farangs who were taking Viagra, the ones who couldn't get enough, the ones that wanted anal sex as well as vaginal.

From what she'd heard she would have guessed that the girls hated farangs, hated them with a vengeance, but here they were again. A few drinks inside them, a dose of ya baa for Nok, and they were all over the farangs. As though they couldn't get enough.

The evening finally ended at three in the morning. Steve, who could hardly stand, was escorted home by Joy, who could hardly walk. Harry, who'd made another vain attempt at buying Siswan, finally wandered off with Nok and Bee each supporting an arm. Thomas, the quiet man, staggered off with Mai in search of a place to dance.

Siswan cleaned up the mess left by the revelers, secured the wooden boards and added up the cash against the totals in the book. A good night. A very good night. The girls would be pleased with their cut of the lady drinks.

Before making her way home, Siswan called to the bank and used the twenty four hour deposit drawer. It wouldn't do to be carrying that much money around with her. She called for a motorbike taxi and returned to the apartment block. At least she had the room to herself that night.

When she turned up for work the following day, Nong was already there. The older woman looked worried.

'What happened last night?' she asked, as Siswan approached.

'It was a good night. Very busy,' Siswan told her. 'Why?'

'The police called. Mai got hurt,' Nong said.

There was always a risk of getting hurt. All the girls knew it. There had been many stories. Sometimes a farang went too far. Sometimes what fueled his desire was something that the girls didn't enjoy. He could get angry. Things could get out of hand.

'What happened?' Siswan asked.

'I'm not too sure,' Nong said. 'The police called. The cleaners in the hotel found her. She was beaten. Quite badly, I think.'

'Where is she now?'

'In the hospital. I should go,' Nong said. 'To see her, I mean.'

'Yes. You go,' Siswan agreed. 'I'll take care of things here.'

Whilst Nong was gone the other girls turned up. They looked tired. Worn out from the night before. Only Nok seemed awake, and that was drug induced.

'Where's Mai?' she asked Siswan. 'Got lucky with that farang, I suppose.'

'No,' Siswan answered. 'She's in hospital.'

Bee and Joy suddenly took an interest as well.

'What happened?'

'I don't know. Nong has gone to see her,' Siswan told them all.

'Did she get beaten?' Joy asked.

'It seems so, yes.' Siswan took control. 'Until Nong gets back we won't know. It's no good talking about it until then.'

The girls moved back to their favourite corner. There really wasn't any point in discussing what had happened. All they could do was wait for Nong. Up until then it was just business as usual.

When Nong did arrive, they were all eager to find out the news.

'She's not too bad,' Nong told them. 'The cleaners in the hotel overreacted because of the blood.'

Nong told them the whole story. Mai and Thomas had gone off to find a night club, but the farang had been too drunk to dance. They'd had another drink and then made their way back to his hotel.

Mai had gone into the bathroom to shower whilst Tom had virtually collapsed on the bed. When she'd come out, he was asleep. She'd covered him with the sheet, removed his shoes and climbed into the bed beside him.

When she'd been in the shower her period had started. She had been really pleased, but also a little worried that Tom wouldn't like it if she couldn't have sex. She'd gone into the bedroom to get the sponge out of her handbag, but when she saw the farang fast asleep she didn't bother. If he wanted her in the morning she could slip it in then. She tucked a pad into her panties and very quickly fell asleep.

Apparently, while she slept, Tom woke up and started touching her up. By the time she awoke he was already pushing into her from behind. He obviously hadn't noticed the thin pad as he'd pulled down her underwear. She was half awake and still pretty drunk from the bar. She forgot about the sponge.

When Tom finished, he rolled out of the bed and went to the bathroom to shower. The next thing Mai knew, he was shouting that she was a dirty slut and hitting her across the arms and legs. When she turned to confront him he laid into her with his fists. She was too startled to do anything about it and, even before she could cry out, the blows had beaten her almost unconscious.

The next thing she remembered was the cleaner lady waking her up and crying about all the blood on the bed. When the cleaner saw her face she called the police.

'Was she cut?' Nok asked.

'No. Just bruised and dazed. The blood was from her period. It was a heavy one,' Nong told them.

'I knew a guy that didn't like that,' Joy said. 'He wouldn't go near me when I was on.'

'Most men don't like it,' Nong said. 'That's why we use the sponge.'

'The bastard,' Nok put in. 'How'd he like to bleed every month?'

'The most important thing is that Mai is okay,' Nong said. 'She's badly bruised and has a hell of a bump on her head, but she'll live.'

'What is it with men, anyway?' Bee said. 'Don't they know a woman can't do anything about it?'

'It's only blood,' Joy said.

'Yeah. I'd like to see them put a rag in their assholes every month,' Nok said.

'In their assholes?' Joy asked.

'Well, they haven't got a vagina,' Nok pointed out.

'Yeah, but wouldn't it be better if they just bled out of their dicks for a week?' Joy asked.

'Well, okay. But they should also have something big shoved in their assholes. That's what they expect us to do,' Nok pointed out.

'Did they catch him?' Siswan asked, whilst the rest of the girls contemplated Nok's suggestion.

'What? Oh. Yes, they caught him,' Nong replied. 'Apparently, he left the hotel early in the morning. Packed up all his stuff and moved to another one. The police tracked him down.'

'Good!' Joy said. 'I hope they put him in prison.'

'That won't happen,' Siswan said, quietly.

'How do you know?' Nok turned on her. 'You don't know!'

'He'll be fined. Told to leave. If he pays enough he won't even have to do that,' Nong put in.

'That's not fair,' Bee said.

'Life isn't fair, Bee,' Siswan said.

'But, what about Mai. What about her?' Joy asked.

'She'll stay in hospital for another night,' Nong told them.

'Then what?' Nok shouted, angrily. 'Then what happens?'

'She'll have to pay the hospital bill and either come back to work or go home,' Siswan said.

'Doesn't anyone care what happens to her?' Joy asked, quietly.

'No, Joy,' Siswan said, flatly. 'No one cares what happens to a bar girl. Why should they?'

'Because we're human. Because we have feelings. Because we can get hurt as well,' Nok pointed out.

'Who cares?' Siswan said.

Nok rushed at her. Made to grab at her throat, her hair. She was almost crying in rage. Spittle sprayed out of her mouth as she shouted.

'You don't fucking care! You don't give a shit!'

Siswan easily slipped out of the way of the girls hands. Easily ducked the clawing fingers. She didn't fight back. Didn't lash out at the girl. There was no need. No need to fight because it was over before it started. Nok sank to her knees in front of the bar. Tears rolled down her cheeks.

'Nobody gives a shit,' she said, quietly. 'Nobody gives a fucking shit.'

Joy and Bee helped her to her feet. Sat her down on a bar stool. Siswan got her a drink of water. She held the glass out to the distraught girl. A few moments passed before she spoke.

'The only people we have on our side, Nok,' she told her. 'Are ourselves. There's no one else.'

Nok looked up at her through her tears. She drank some of the water.

'I didn't want to do this,' she said, between sips.

'No.' Siswan looked at all of the girls around her. 'I guess you didn't. It just seemed an easy way to make money, didn't it.'

None of the girls spoke. None argued. The money. It was all about the money and sometimes, just sometimes, the price they paid was high.

'Okay,' Nong said. 'Let's go back to work.'

There was nothing else they could do. Nothing else that mattered. Siswan knew that all the shouting, kicking and screaming in the world wouldn't do any good. You chose your life. You lived your life.

It was about an hour later that Steve came to the bar. He looked awful. As he approached he gave a wai to each of them in turn. He knew their ways.

'I am so sorry,' he said to the girls. 'I am so very sorry.'

'It's not your fault, Steve,' Nong said to him. 'Sit down. You don't look so good.'

'I only found out about it this evening,' he said, taking a seat. 'I didn't know. I'm so sorry. How's the girl? I don't remember her name.'

'Why would you remember, Steve?' Siswan asked him. 'She was only another bar girl.'

'Oh, don't be like that, Siswan,' he said apologetically. 'You know I don't think like that.'

Siswan didn't believe him. Not for one second did she believe that he cared. He was a nice enough guy. Was always polite, always bought a drink for the girls. Nice enough. He was no saint though. He still took the girls. Still had sex with them.

'No, I know that, Steve,' she smiled at him. 'Her name is Mai.'

'How is she?'

'She'll be fine. We'll take care of her,' Siswan said, in a voice loud enough for all the girls to hear.

'Well. If there's anything I can do?' Steve asked.

There's loads you can do, she thought. You can pay the hospital bill. You can go to the police. You can cause a stink over this. A stink that the authorities would have to listen to. You could make sure that Thomas gets what he deserves.

'No. There's nothing you can do, Steve,' she said.

Steve sat awkwardly for a few moments more. She could tell he wanted to buy a drink. A drink to calm his nerves. A drink to take him through another night in paradise. She didn't offer any help.

'Well, I'd better be going,' he said.

'Okay, Steve,' she smiled. 'Thanks for coming.'

'I didn't know, Siswan. Honestly I didn't,' he said, before leaving the bar and walking away.

Mai was sent home the following evening. Nong and Siswan met her at the hospital entrance and took her back to the apartment. Her face was a mass of black and blue bruises. One eye was so swollen it was almost closed.

'I don't think I can work tonight,' she joked to Nong.

'No. Maybe tomorrow?' Nong joked back.

Siswan helped Mai into her room. Sat her on the bed. She looked into her face.

'Are you alright?' she asked, as she held the girls hands.

'Yes. I'll be okay,' Mai said. 'I don't remember much. Just his voice shouting at me.'

Siswan didn't reply. Just sat there on the edge of the bed and held her hands. She wanted to give Mai time. Time to talk if she needed to.

'I should have used the sponge,' she said, quietly.

'No. It was his fault, Mai. His alone,' Siswan replied. 'He was wrong. Just a fool of a man who got scared at the sight of blood.'

'I'm not pregnant though,' Mai tried to smile at her. 'That's good.'

'Yes,' Siswan said. 'That's very good.'

'I took his shoes off. He wore them on the bed.' Mai leaned into Siswan's shoulder.

Siswan felt the sobs rather than heard them. Mai cried without any noise. Normally so talkative. A girl who talked so much. Now, as she cried into Siswan's arms, she didn't make a sound. Siswan held her tightly.

'I'm sorry,' Mai said, after a few moments.

'That's okay. You don't have to be sorry about anything,' Siswan said, looking into her face.

'I didn't expect him to do that,' Mai said, wiping away the tears. 'He seemed like a nice man.'

'They all do,' Nong put in. 'They all seem nice.'

'Wasn't bad looking, either,' Mai continued.

'Maybe, but he didn't have a good heart did he?' Siswan told her.

'No. That's for sure,' Mai almost laughed. 'He didn't even pay me.'

All three girls laughed together then. The crises was over. Mai was going to be fine. Siswan was amazed at her courage. Amazed at all the girls, really. The life they chose, or found themselves in, wasn't an easy one. At first it seemed an easy route to take. An easy path to follow. They could make a lot of money. A lot of money to please their families. A lot of money to change their lives. It seemed so easy. At first.

Once they'd been doing it for a while, they learned that it wasn't so easy after all. That there wasn't as much money as they had first thought. The families soon got used to the little they sent home. Got used to it and wanted more. Demanded more. Once you became a bar girl it was difficult to stop. And of course, there was always the dream. The one in a million chance that a farang with a good heart would come to take you away. The dream that kept them going. Kept them turning up night after night. The dream of the man with a good heart. One in a million.

The problem was that nights like the one Mai had been through happened all too often. One in ten thousand? One in a thousand? The odds were definitely in the favour of the nightmares. Not the dream.

'You'll be alright, Mai,' Nong told her. 'We'll soon have you chattering away in the bar again.'

'Oh, no,' Siswan groaned, and they all laughed again.

'Oh, don't,' Mai said. 'It really hurts when I laugh.'

The three girls looked at one another for a few seconds before bursting out in gales of laughter. The more Mai groaned in pain the more all three of them laughed. They couldn't stop. Even in pain, Mai giggled uncontrollably. Siswan felt pains in her sides and she still couldn't stop laughing. Finally, with tears rolling down her face, Mia pushed them both out of her room.

'Get out! Before you kill me!' she shouted through the pain. 'Out!'

Nong and Siswan finally stopped giggling by the time they got back to the bar. They both agreed that Mai would be fine and spent the night serving farangs as usual.

'She'll be back within a week,' Nong stated to the others. 'You'll see.'

As it happened, Mai never returned to the bar, or any other bar come to that. When Bee got home that night she hadn't noticed anything unusual. Mai had been tucked up in bed, fast asleep. At least Bee had assumed she was asleep.

It wasn't until half way through the following morning that anyone knew that something was wrong. Siswan had got up, early as usual, and had headed for the beach. She hadn't seen anything wrong.

It was when Nok awoke a few hours later that the awful truth dawned. She had opened her bedside drawer to discover that her whole stock of ya baa was missing. About thirty tablets all in all.

Mai had taken every one of them and had died in her sleep the night before. When Bee had pulled back the sheet they had seen the staring eyes. The bruised face even more darkened by the congealing blood. A thin line of vomit had trickled from the corner of Mai's mouth and had trailed onto the pillow.

When the car came to take her body to the hospital, Siswan had asked one of the men what would happen to her.

'Her family will be told,' he'd said.

Siswan wondered what the family would do. Would they give her a good funeral in the temple? Hold a party in her honour? Call all the friends and relatives around to celebrate the life of a girl who had taken care of them for so long?

She wondered how the family would be able to pay for such a funeral, such a party? Now that the bread winner was gone? How would they manage now? Did Mai have a sister who could take her place? A brother who could earn as much as she could? Siswan didn't think so. She didn't think there would be a party. She didn't think anyone would be invited to celebrate the life of a bar girl.

The following day Siswan bought herself a new knife. She chose a fairly small blade but one that looked evil. It had a curved edge, a sharp point and a serrated back. With the press of a button the blade slid out from the handle. What had happened to Mai wasn't going to happen to her. Not without a fight.

Chapter 13

Mike, Apple and Siswan listened in horror as the police officer told them what had happened to Lon. The police suspected she was the victim of a gang that had operated in the country before. A gang that made video films for sale via the internet. Torture tapes they were called.

There had been two similar attacks in the last twelve months. One on the south coast and one in the north of the country. It seemed that the films were sold illegally and made a lot of money.

Siswan couldn't believe how anyone, in their right mind, could bear to watch one, let alone actually purchase the tape.

The police officer told them that three farangs had been seen renting a house on the hill overlooking the resort town. The house was remote enough so that any noises or disturbances wouldn't be heard. That was where they had found Lon. She had been lucky.

A local man, who was employed by the letting agency to clean the pool and carry out general maintenance, had called early that morning and noticed the door was ajar. When he'd gone in, he had found Lon barely alive and had called the police. There was no sign of the farangs.

'If he hadn't called early, she most certainly would have died from her injuries,' the officer told them. 'He'd gone early because his wife wanted him to go to the market with her in the afternoon.'

'What did they do to her?' Siswan asked.

'I think it will be better to speak to the doctor about that,' he told her.

'Where is the doctor?' Mike asked. 'I want to speak with him.'

He wandered off down the corridor in search of a member of staff. Siswan noticed how distraught he looked. How his shoulders sagged when he walked.

The police officer told them he wanted to speak with Lon as soon as she was up to it. They needed to catch this gang before they struck again. All they had at the moment was a name registered with the letting agency.

'We suspect that's going to be false.' He shook his head. 'Fake passports, identity cards, even birth certificates, they're just so easy to buy.'

Siswan and Apple promised to call him as soon as Lon awoke. As soon as she could speak. They thanked him for his help before he left.

When Mike returned with the doctor they began to understand just how bad Lon's injuries were. Siswan translated all that he said to Mike. Several times her voice almost cracked as she told him what the doctor was telling them.

'She was beaten badly. About the face, stomach and back. They probably used a stick or other blunt instrument,' the doctor said, as though reading from a list. 'She has a great deal of cigarette burns on her body. Two fingers from her left hand were amputated. We have the fingers in cold storage. Three toes were cut off her right foot. We have those as well. She has four fractured ribs, one of which punctured her right lung. Her nose is broken and several teeth are missing. She may have swallowed those as we believe she was gagged at the time. There are bruise marks around her neck that would suggest a gag was used.'

The doctor cleared his throat. The list read like something from a horror movie and he wasn't finished.

'She was repeatedly raped, anally as well as vaginally. Her right arm is fractured as well as her left wrist. We believe a serrated knife, or small saw, was used to cut her in various places. There are signs of electrical burns on her stomach and neck. Basically it's a miracle she's still alive.'

The three of them looked at the doctor in shock. Mike found his voice first. He made demands that Siswan translated for him.

'I want her moved to a private room,' he said, quietly, but forcefully. 'She's to have a nurse with her at all times. I want the best treatment possible for her. Get specialists in. Counsellors. She has to have everything. Everything possible.'

'Yes, of course,' the doctor said.

'I'll pay,' Mike told him.

'So will I,' Siswan added to the translation. 'Whatever it takes.'

When the doctor left to get things organized, the three of them returned to Lon's side. The girl looked more dead than alive.

'What do we do, Miss Siswan?' Apple asked.

'There's not much we can do,' Siswan answered, quietly. 'Just hope and pray.'

'I'd like to get my hands on those bastards,' Mike said.

'We all would, Mike,' Siswan leaned over, held his hand.

'What's the matter with men?' he asked no one. 'What the hell is the matter with us?'

Apple and Siswan said nothing. They didn't have the answer.

It was another three days before Lon recovered enough to be able to help the police. She gave a horrific account of what had happened. Siswan sat with her the whole time. By the end of the interview both girls were crying. Siswan wondered if she could have been as brave as Lon.

When the police finished, Siswan joined them in the corridor outside Lon's private room. Her nurse was allowed back in to sit with the injured girl.

'Will all that help?' Siswan asked one of the officers.

'Yes. It will,' he replied. 'We'll get them, don't worry. We're already talking to police in other countries.'

'If you catch them, will they be tried here? Will they go to prison here?' she asked.

The two officers knew exactly why she wanted to know. Prison life was hard in their country. Harder than most. Especially for foreign sex offenders.

'Yes,' the most senior officer said, emphatically. And repeated 'We'll get them.'

Siswan had considered calling Mirak. Asking for his help. Considered it, but then told herself she was being silly. There wouldn't be anything he could do and, anyway, she questioned her reasons for wanting him involved.

All she could was visit Lon as often as possible and carry on working. Apple was coping well enough. She ran Mike's Bar with her usual efficiency. It was Mike, himself, that worried Siswan.

He was spending almost all of his time at the hospital annoying doctors and staff alike with his constant nagging. He wanted to know everything. Wanted to be kept informed of Lon's progress. Kept trying to improve things.

In the end, Siswan called on Rican's help to get him away from the place. He had his wedding to organize, things to do in the bars. He couldn't do any more in the hospital.

When Rican finally convinced him to go back to the bar he wandered around aimlessly. As though he could no longer justify what he did for a living. As though, in some way, he were to blame for what had happened to Lon.

'You aren't responsible, Mike,' Siswan told him.

'She worked here, didn't she?' he said, morosely.

'She could have worked anywhere. Any bar. Any town. She was just unlucky, that's all,' Siswan tried to explain.

'Unlucky?' Mike said. 'Unlucky to have been a bar girl in the first place? Unlucky to have been born in a god forsaken country that allows bar girls? That does nothing to stop the trade?'

'Yes, Mike. All of those things, and more. Sometimes people are lucky, sometimes they're not. That's life,' Siswan told him. 'All we can do now is make sure she gets good treatment and isn't left alone.'

'And afterwards, Siswan?' Mike asked. 'What happens to her afterwards, when she can leave the hospital, what then?'

'Then she'll go home to her family, Mike,' Siswan told him.

'A family that sent her here in the first place?' he said, scornfully.

'Yes,' Siswan said. 'The same family.'

Mike looked at her. Shocked at the calmness in her voice. The acceptance of all that had happened.

'Christ, Siswan. They tortured her!' he shouted.

'Yes. And you're right, Mike. This has to stop.' She indicated the bar around them. 'We have to stop it.'

'What the hell can we do, Siswan? We're the perpetrators for Christ's sake.'

'We can do something, Mike,' she told him. 'We already have.'

'What?' he asked. 'What have we done?'

'Our girls, Mike. They earn really good money. They don't have to go with so many farangs. They can pick and choose. They get good wages and time off. It's better, Mike. It's not good, but it's better,' she said.

'Tell that to Lon, Siswan,' he said.

'Lon was unlucky, Mike,' she countered. 'I don't like it any more than you do, but if we give up, if we stop trying, how many more girls will get hurt?'

'Siswan, what the hell are you talking about? We don't help the girls, we make money from them.'

'Yes. We do,' she said, quietly. 'There's a reason, Mike. A reason for making so much.'

'What reason?' he asked.

Siswan told him of her dream, her goal. Why she wanted to earn so much. Why she worked in the bars. The promise she had made to Sood and Karn. It took a little while for her words to sink in. After sitting quietly for a few moments Mike turned to her.

'And you honestly believe you can do it?' he asked.

'Yes,' she said. 'Someone has to at least try. Someone has to care.'

'But, hell, Siswan. That's a hell of a task,' he said.

'I can start it, Mike. Other's will help,' she told him. 'It'll grow. Maybe it'll take the rest of my life, even longer, but someone has to start.'

'Well, I'll be,' he said. 'I never guessed.'

'No,' she smiled. 'It isn't something I discuss too much. Not around here.'

'Well, Siswan,' he smiled back. 'I don't know how many years I have left, not too many I'm sure, but I'll help as much as I can. So will Rican. I know she will. We owe that much to Lon.'

She smiled. Leaned towards him. Kissed him on the cheek.

'All it takes is money, Mike. A lot of it!'

Four nights later Mirak came into Swan's Bar. He walked immediately to where Siswan stood talking to customers.

'I just heard,' he said, interrupting her conversation. 'I'm sorry.'

'Thank you,' she said. 'I didn't expect to see you again.'

'I've been north. Working,' he told her. 'An old case.'

'I was going to call you,' she said.

'You should have.' He smiled. 'I wanted you to call.'

'I'm sorry. It's just that,' she started.

'It's okay, Siswan. You don't have to explain,' he told her.

'But I'd like to try, Mirak,' she said.

'No,' he said. 'You don't need to. I only came to offer my condolences.'

He turned to leave. To walk away from her. She couldn't let him. There were still feelings for him. Deep within her.

'Mirak,' she said, quickly. 'I'm sorry.'

'So am I, Siswan,' he replied, before turning and walking out of the bar.

She couldn't blame him for leaving. Couldn't blame him for not wanting to be with her. She had hurt him, both physically and emotionally. She had to let him go. Had to remove him from her mind. She had so many other things to do.

Between visiting Lon and running the bars, Siswan had her hands full. All the girls knew what had happened and it took all her efforts to convince them that the same wouldn't happen to them.

Eventually they settled down. Apple helped immensely. Siswan didn't know what she would have done without her. She was an example to the other girls and made it easier for Siswan to calm them down.

She and Apple very often went to see Lon together. The girl was recovering. Slowly she was coming to terms with what happened to her and, although still weak, was able to ask how the bars were doing. Siswan soon realized that Lon needed to be told every detail. Everything that happened each night. It was her way of keeping sane. Her way of staying in touch with her life. Siswan and Apple spent hours at a time recounting the smallest of details.

Life continued that way for the next three months. The nights in the bar, with the bright lights, the loud music, the laughter and drinking, contrasted so vividly with the hours spent sat with Lon. The sterile environment of the hospital versus the sullied atmosphere of the bars.

When it came time for Lon to leave the hospital, her father turned up to collect her in a battered old pickup. Siswan, Apple and Mike were all there to see her off.

'You will keep in touch won't you, Miss Siswan?' Lon asked.

'Yes, of course.' Siswan smiled and hugged her.

'And you too, Mike.' Lon looked to him.

Mike was finding it difficult to hold back tears as he looked at her.

'Of course,' he said, and wrapped his arms gently around her shoulders.

Finally, after hugging Apple and promising to call as often as she could, Lon climbed into the passenger seat beside her father who hadn't said a word.

They could all see how close to tears she was. Not only was she leaving her friends, but she would be returning to the village in shame. A bar girl who had got what she deserved. Unable to buy her respectability, she would have to live the rest of her life as an additional burden to her family.

Siswan turned to Mike. There were tears rolling down his cheeks as he watched the pickup make its way into the traffic.

'She'll be the first, Mike,' she told him, and took his arm.

'Yes.' He sniffed back the tears. 'She has to be. Let's get this scheme of yours moving.'

'What scheme?' Apple too was wiping tears from her eyes.

As the three of them strolled back to the bar, Mike and Siswan told Apple all about it. By the time they arrived at the door she was convinced.

'Well, you can count me in,' she told them. 'I have a lot saved up now.'

'It'll take hard work,' Siswan warned.

'Yes, it will. Let's get started,' Apple replied.

*****

Two months later Siswan had two visitors in one night. The first was Mirak and she was surprised to see him as he walked across the crowded bar to reach her.

'Hello, Mirak,' she smiled at him.

'I need to speak with you. Somewhere private,' he said, without greeting her.

'What about?' She was puzzled at his abruptness.

'Somewhere private,' he repeated.

She led him into the small back room where the kegs were stored. The coolers rattled in the corner, but it was quieter than in the main bar.

'What's this about, Mirak?' Siswan turned to face him.

'You, Siswan,' he said, taking a notebook from his back pocket.

He flicked through the pages. Stopped when he reached the one he needed.

'When did you arrive here?' he asked.

'I told you, about six years ago, nearly seven now,' she answered.

'And where did you stay?'

'Mirak, if I'm in any kind of trouble, if you need to question me, then I think you ought to do it somewhere a little more formal,' she said quietly.

'Okay. I'll tell you. I was working on an old case. An unresolved case. Sometimes we go over them before filing them away for good,' he told her.

She didn't say anything. Her stomach was sending signals she didn't like. There was something in his manner. Something different about him. She couldn't figure out what it was. Almost as though he found this as unpleasant as she did.

'An old man in a park, Siswan. A young girl who ran away. I often wondered how you got that scar on your arm,' he told her.

'Why didn't you just ask? Most people do,' she answered, as calmly as her beating heart would allow.

Was it all over? Had she come this far to be thrown back by a wave she couldn't possibly overcome? Would her promises to Sood, to Karn and now to Lon, all be in vain?

'I didn't want to, Siswan. I didn't want to pry into your past,' he said.

'But you did though, Mirak. You did pry didn't you?' She looked at him.

'I didn't know it was you until now, Siswan,' he told her. 'Of course I could have proved it anyway. You left blood traces all over the place. A simple enough test. The old man died in the hospital two days after you ran away.'

'So, what happens now?' she asked.

She knew then that it was all over. If the old man had died then she would be charged with his murder. There was no way she could prove he had attacked her.

'We could go two ways with this, Siswan,' Mirak said.

'Two ways?' she said.

He looked at her. He didn't smile. Hadn't smiled from the moment he'd arrived. He seemed troubled. As though he were being torn in two.

'This could all be forgotten. I could just file it away and it would never come to light again.'

'Or?'

'Or, I could hand the case to my superiors, allow them the honour of arresting you. That would do well for my career.'

'And what would it take for you to file it away?' she asked, even though she had guessed the answer.

'Five million,' he told her, without enthusiasm.

She couldn't stop the look of distaste that showed on her face. The man she had once loved was stood in front of her demanding money. He was nothing to her. Just another man. Another man who wanted money.

'I'm taking a big risk for you, Siswan,' he said.

'Okay, Mirak,' she said. 'It'll take a few days to arrange. I'll call you.'

'Alright,' he said.

'Once you have the money, you'll give me the file?' she asked.

'Yes, that can be arranged,' he said.

'Okay. Three days. I'll have the money. You bring the file. No file, no money,' she stated.

He didn't say another word. Just turned and left. Leaving her alone. The noise of the coolers suddenly seemed too loud. She was so angry, so annoyed! It took several minutes before she was able to walk back out into the main bar. All that she had done. All that she had been through. It could all be ruined by something from her past. The obstacles she had surmounted seemed nothing in comparison to what was facing her now.

She had five million, just about anyway. She could borrow some from Mike, or Apple, if she needed to. But what if he came back for more? What if he made a copy of the file? She wasn't sure she could trust him. He had seemed so strained tonight. Not his normal confident self. What had been going through his mind?

Her second visitor called just as she was closing the bar. The customers had left, some with girls, others alone, and she was about to lock up and walk down to see Mike. As she reached up to lock the inner door, it was pushed back against her.

'We're closed,' she said, before looking at who was trying to get in.

'Not for me, Siswan,' a voice replied.

She looked up. Mirak had surprised her when he had called earlier, but the shock she got as she stared into the face of the man who stood in front of her almost caused her to cry out. She put a hand to her mouth and stared at the face of her brother. A face grown older and more mean, but a face she knew so well.

'You remember me, don't you, Siswan?' he asked.

'What do you want, Bak?'

'Oh, just a chat. You know, catch up with the family.' He smiled.

'Well I'm just leaving,' she told him.

'Yes. Off to meet your farang boyfriend. He's a little old, don't you think?'

'He's not my boyfriend. He's my boss and he's expecting me,' she said.

'He'll wait a while, Siswan. We need to talk.'

'What about? I've nothing to say to you, Bak.'

He pushed further into the bar. She couldn't prevent him from walking in. He was bigger than she remembered. A real man now. Not some teenager who acted like one.

'But I have things to say to you, Siswan,' he told her, as he walked to the bar.

She followed him. What else could she do? She had listened to Mirak. Listened to his threats and demands. Now she had to do the same with her brother. She knew it would boil down to money again. That's what it always came down to. Money or sex. The two things men thought about more than anything else. As she followed she slipped her knife out of her handbag and into the back pocket of her trousers.

'Okay, Bak. I'm listening,' she told him.

Stepping behind the bar he poured himself a whiskey. He smiled at her as he did so, daring her to complain. To protest.

'You went to the funeral.' It was a statement rather than a question.

'Yes,' she said.

'I didn't know he'd died until a few days ago.' He sipped the whiskey.

'No one knew where you were,' she said.

'Oh, I've been to a lot of places, Siswan. Learned a lot of things,' he told her.

She didn't answer. Didn't need to. He was going to do the talking. She could tell from his manner that he wasn't interested in what she had to say. She just had to listen.

'You've got rich from what I taught you, Siswan,' he told her. 'Made a lot of money from your farang friends.'

'You taught me nothing, Bak,' she said, the familiar anger building up within her.

'A lot of the girls I taught are now making a lot of money,' he looked at her and grinned. 'Oh, you weren't the last, Siswan. I have a lot of girls who are thankful for the things I taught them. So thankful that they pay me.'

'So, you're a pimp now?' she sneered.

'Call me what you like. It doesn't matter. The girls look after me,' he said.

'So, if you are being looked after, what do you want from me?' she asked.

'Oh, they're good girls. Do as they are told. But they can't earn much, Siswan. Not like you,' he told her. 'You've got a good thing going here with your farang.'

'I'm not giving you anything, Bak. I told you before. I don't care what happens to you!' She was angry now.

'You owe me! You left me with nothing. I had to fight to survive. I had to struggle in the city to make a living!' he shouted in reply.

'You mean you had to find some other poor girl to work for you!' She spat the words at him.

'You bitch,' he shouted again. 'You left me with nothing, not even a mother to take care of me. You took her away!'

Without warning he struck her across the cheek with the back of his hand. She just managed to turn her head. Just managed to divert most of the blow. To avoid the pain.

'This is what you left me with, Siswan! This!'

He was pushing the back of his hand in her face. Showing her the scar that she had given him so many years before.

'You deserved it, you bastard.'

As she shouted at him her hand slipped behind her. Felt for the knife. She pulled it from her pocket, pressed the button and whipped the small blade at his face. She was fast. As fast as a scorpion, but he was faster this time.

Pulling his head back, away from the vicious blade that threatened to cut him, he brought his hand around. Caught her wrist as it passed by his eyes. Twisted it violently. She cried out, dropped the knife.

'I was expecting that, little sister,' he told her. 'Like I told you, I've learned a lot.'

He let go of her wrist, picked up the knife, examined it.

'Nasty,' he said with a grin. 'Just like its owner.'

She held her wrist with her other hand. Looked at him. He was a man now. Faster. More controlled than he had been the last time she had cut him.

'Now this is what you should be using, Siswan,' he said, reaching behind his back. 'An automatic. Nine rounds. Not much good at a distance, but close up, close like this, it's a real killer.' He pointed the gun at her face. 'Up close like this, it would cause a real mess,' he told her, grinning.

'What do you want, Bak?' she asked him, quietly.

'I want what's due to me, Siswan,' he smiled. 'I want what's mine.'

'What?'

'Oh, let's call it a partnership. That's good isn't it? A partnership.'

'Mike owns the bars. I don't own anything.'

'Well, we can soon deal with Mike,' he told her.

At the thought of Mike getting hurt, Siswan almost gave up. Almost agreed to whatever Bak wanted. She could do it. She could warn Mike, get him to go away. He had enough money. He and Rican could set up somewhere else. She almost agreed to everything. In the end, she didn't need to.

'Who are you?' Bak said, looking past her shoulder.

She turned, looked to where her brother was staring. Mirak stood in the doorway. He had a large brown envelope in his hand. He ignored Bak's question.

'Siswan. I'm sorry. I need to talk with you again,' he said.

Siswan looked at his face, back to her brother's. She didn't know what to do. For the first time since leaving the village, she didn't know what to do. She felt powerless. The more she looked at the two men the more she believed that she couldn't tell them apart. One became the other. They looked the same. They looked like men.

Just two men in a world of millions. How could she ever overcome so many? How could she have ever held a dream in her heart? How did she have the nerve to make promises to her friends that she didn't have a hope of fulfilling?

'I can't,' she whispered.

'That's right. She's busy now. Come back later,' Bak said to Mirak.

Mirak obviously hadn't seen the gun. Hadn't seen the look of shock in Siswan's eyes. Hadn't heard the veiled threat in Bak's voice. He couldn't have. He couldn't have noticed all those things and still walked towards her.

'I just want a quick word,' he said.

'I told you, she's busy! Fuck off!' Bak shouted at him.

He kept coming. Kept walking towards where she stood. He kept his eyes on hers. Didn't look at Bak.

'I'm warning you!' Bak pulled the gun up, pointed it at Mirak.

Siswan didn't see all that happened in that moment. She saw Mirak drop the envelope, saw the pistol the envelope had concealed. She heard the bang next to her ear, saw the flash from the barrel. She ducked away. Down in front of the bar. She put her hands over her ears, squeezed her eyes shut.

She may have screamed, she didn't know. The noise from the gun was so loud! It wasn't like the films on television. It wasn't a mild explosion of sound. It was a bang. A bang like a thunderclap of noise that threatened to deafen her. Even as it died away, left her ears ringing, another bang. Then more. Even louder than the first. The smell of burnt smoke. The ringing sound.

She crouched low by the bar. Didn't know what was happening. The buzzing in her ears grew less. Faded enough for her to take her hands away. She opened her eyes. She was still in the bar. Her eyes took in the legs of the stool she had fallen beside. She looked around. Slowly. Afraid of what she may see.

Bak lay to her right. His eyes were open. At first she didn't see what it was that looked different about him. At first he looked just like he always had in her mind. A boy. A young boy who liked to laugh as he caught fish in the pond.

As she stared her eyes finally understood what was different. The hole in his forehead. The blood running from the back of where his scull should have been. She could see grey and white glistening under the red veil that poured out of the back of his head. He stared at the ceiling with a gaze that would last forever.

She looked over to where Mirak had stood. He was lying on the ground   clutching his stomach. She saw the revolver lying beside him on the floor.

Staggering to her feet, she went to him. Went to the man she had once loved. She fell to her knees at his side.

'Mirak!' she cried and reached out to him.

He turned, looked up at her. His face was white, the blood drained away from it. His eyes were half closed in pain. Blood ran through his hands and spilled onto the floor.

'Siswan,' he groaned.

'Mirak. I'll call for help,' she cried at him. 'Wait. Wait for them.'

She ran back to the bar, clutched for her handbag. Grabbed her phone. She dialed the number as she reached him.

'Get the envelope,' he rasped at her. 'Get the envelope.'

She reached over him. Picked up the brown envelope he had been carrying. One side was covered in his blood.

'Siswan,' he said, weakly. 'Siswan, I'm sorry.'

'Don't talk. Just be strong. Help is on the way.'

She spoke quickly into the telephone when her call was answered. Told the woman at the other end to send an ambulance. Told her a policeman had been shot.

'Get rid of the envelope,' he told her, as he rocked back and forth on his side.

She looked inside. It was the file. The file he had threatened her with earlier. Why had he come back early? Three days, he'd said. They had agreed three days.

'Siswan,' he whispered. 'I love you.'

'I love you as well, Mirak,' she replied.

She didn't know if was the truth. She didn't know what to think. She stood. She wasn't sure what to do. Get rid of the envelope, he'd said. She ran back towards the bar, towards the small cellar. She saw her knife lying on the floor near the bar. Picked it up.

She put the envelope and the knife at the back of the shelf that held the pipes for the beer kegs. No one would see them there. She ran back to Mirak, fell to her knees once again. She held him. Took his head in her hands.

'Thank you, Mirak,' she said to him. 'Thank you.'

She didn't know why he'd done it. Why he had changed his mind. All she knew was that he had. He'd come back to her. To give her the file. To say sorry.

The ambulance and the police finally arrived. All the time Siswan held Mirak's head. Stroked his face. Waited with him. He hadn't spoken again. Nor had she. There was nothing to say. Nothing that would help. He had come back. That was all that mattered.

When she was gently taken aside by the medics, Siswan knew they were too late. She had heard the last breath Mirak would ever take. She had heard it and still held him. Still stroked his face. She would never understand him. She would never get the chance. Suddenly, Mike was there. Holding her.

'Are you alright?' he asked her.

'Yes, Mike,' she said. 'I'm okay. Just shocked.'

'When they said there had been gunshots,' he tailed off.

She clung to him. Held him as though she was scared he'd leave her. Bak dead. Mirak dead. She started to cry. Softly into his shoulder. She cried, not so much from the sadness of their deaths, but from the relief that it was all over. The noise. The blood.

The police asked her a few questions. She told them her brother was drunk. Angry at having missed their father's funeral. She told them he had pulled a gun, was going to shoot her. Mirak had turned up just in time. Just in time to save her.

The police believed her story. They knew Mirak had been going out with her for quite a while. It wouldn't have been unusual for him to meet her after work. They didn't ask any other questions. Didn't bother to search the place. After all, she was a good customer. Paid them more than any of the other bars.

When they left, when she had assured Mike that she was fine. When the bodies had been removed and she was alone once more, she went to the cellar. Retrieved the knife and the envelope.

The papers contained all the information regarding the attack in the park. The old man had been a known drunk for many years. He had been in trouble with the police several times. Once related to an attack on another young girl. She used one of the ashtrays to carefully burn each piece of paper. Her past was over.

By the time she left the bar the morning sun was beginning to rise over the horizon. Instead of making for her small room, she strolled down to the beach. To the spot where she and Karn used to sit.

The beach was deserted. As the sun rose higher she could make out the waves racing towards the beach. They just kept coming. One after the other.

She allowed her mind to go back to when she had left Nong's Bar. The weeks she had spent looking for the next bar. Looking for the next step she knew she had to take to make her dreams come true.

Eventually, that step had brought her to Mike's Bar. She had spent several weeks checking over the place. Making certain it was right. She had listened to the conversations between Tam and the rest of the girls. Had overheard them as they gossiped outside. She had been right. The bar needed help or it would close. She had made her move.

She remembered the first night she had spoken to Mike. The first night she had told him how she could help him. It all seemed like a lifetime ago.

She remembered Karn. Sood. Lon. Mai. She remembered them all. Bar girls who came for the money. Came to sell themselves. Sell their bodies. Sell their souls.

She looked to the waves. Now the future lay before her as clear as the day that was dawning around her. She had spoken with her mother again. Laid to rest the resentment she had felt towards her. She had Mike, Apple and Rican to help her now. To help her achieve her goal.

Siswan brushed the sand from her hands as she stood. She walked down to the water's edge and strolled along feeling the coolness of the water on her feet. The future beckoned. She walked towards it.

Chapter 14

For the next three years Siswan worked the bars. Her, Mike and Apple bought two more during that time; Apple's and Rican's. Within just a few months, all four bars were doing well. All four employed only the best girls and all four competed each month to see who was making the most money.

For all of them now, it was all about the money. That was the only thing that mattered. They took care of the girls that worked well. Got rid of the ones that didn't. They had a shared goal, a goal that they all wanted to achieve. They were ruthless about it.

When Mike and Rican had married, Siswan and Apple had been there as bridesmaids. In the end, they didn't get to wear the dresses they had each dreamt about. Even Rican had married wearing an outfit she had hired.

Mike was the only one who was allowed to spend anything on himself and even he had complained.

'I don't need a new suit,' he stated, as the girls all fussed around him.

'Oh yes you do, Mike.' Rican laughed.

'Yes, Mike. You do,' Siswan and Apple agreed.

Mike's idea of a decent suit was the old one he still owned from the days he had first arrived. It had long since given several meals to the moths that had frequented his old room above the bar.

'Well, why can't I hire one?' he questioned.

'There isn't a hire shop for men,' Siswan pointed out.

'Yes, and they certainly wouldn't have one big enough for you if there was,' Rican said.

'That's your fault,' he said and laughed with her. 'I keep telling you I don't need feeding anymore.'

In the end the wedding had been a huge success. The reception was held in Mike's Bar. It would have been sacrilege to hold it anywhere else. Lots of customers turned up as well as all the staff and several other bar owners that had befriended them over the years.

Mike had beamed at everyone. He was the proud owner of four bars, a new bride and had the two best looking bridesmaids anyone had ever seen before. He paraded them as though they were his daughters, and neither of them minded in the least.

Although Siswan and Apple had insisted, Mike and Rican refused to go away on a honeymoon.

'We're in paradise. What's the point of going away,' he told them, with a laugh.

'Well, you have to take some time off,' Siswan told them.

'Yes, you can't be expected to work all night and still have enough energy left,' Apple said.

The other three had looked at her in silence for a moment. Then they had all four burst out laughing.

'Well, you know what I mean,' Apple told them.

'I've got enough energy, young lady. Don't you worry,' Mike told her, and wrapped his arm around Rican who blushed.

Two weeks after the wedding, Mike arranged a meeting between the four of them. He and Rican had some news they wanted to tell them about.

'You're not pregnant already are you?' Siswan asked, in pretend shock.

'No.' Rican smiled. 'Not yet anyway.'

'Not ever,' Mike butted in. 'I'm too old for any more children.'

'You never told me you had children,' Rican turned to him.

'I meant these two.' Mike nodded towards Siswan and Apple.

'Oh. That's all right then.' His wife smiled.

'And that's what we want to talk about,' Mike told the two girls. 'Rican and I have been thinking.'

'What about?' Apple asked.

'About a will. My will,' he replied.

'What for?' Siswan cut across. 'You aren't about to die.'

'Calm down, Siswan.' Mike laughed. 'I have no intention of dying just yet, but we have to sort things out. I'm older than you. A lot older. I'll probably go first. We need to make sure everything is sorted properly.'

'What do you have in mind?' Apple asked.

'Well, as long as Rican is taken care of, I'm going to leave everything to you two,' he told them.

'Why not to Rican? I don't understand,' Siswan said.

'I don't know about business, Siswan,' Rican told her. 'How would I know?'

'Look, we've already talked about this,' Mike said, taking his wife's hand. 'Rican trusts you two as much as I do. If anything happens to me, we have to make sure the plan still goes ahead.'

'But Rican, you can still do it with us,' Apple said.

'No, Apple. If anything should happen to Mike, I wouldn't know what to do,' Rican told her. 'I'm a cook. That's what I know.'

'Well, it doesn't matter anyway. You aren't going to die for a long time. I don't know why we're talking about it,' Siswan said.

'It will make me happy that everything is sorted, that's all.' Mike smiled.

'Okay. If it will make you happy and stop you talking about dying,' Apple agreed with Siswan.

That had been three years ago and Mike hadn't died in the meantime. On the contrary, his marriage to Rican was having the reverse effect. He seemed younger than when Siswan had first walked into his bar.

Siswan had been keeping her eyes and ears open over the previous few months. She had been reading the papers avidly. Searching all the local adverts posted on the internet. Finally, she found what she had been looking for. She couldn't wait to show the others.

'Look,' she said, as they all gathered round. 'What do you think?'

She unfolded the newspaper in front of them and they all craned forward to read the advertisement she pointed out.

'It's got thirty rooms and it's far enough outside of the town. What do you think?' She looked at each of them in turn.

'It looks good, Siswan,' Mike said. 'Just what we need. Have we got enough money?'

'We've got enough to buy it,' she told them. 'But that's all. We'd need to keep the bars going to run it.'

'How much are we making a month now?' Rican asked.

'Just over three million a month,' Siswan told her. 'It's enough to keep the place running. We'll have to get it registered and rely on donations pretty quickly.'

'Well, that's that then,' It was Rican who spoke. 'We'll go and look at it tomorrow.'

Mike turned to his wife. If there had been any hesitation on his part it would have been because of her. Because he was worried about the hard work he was getting her involved in as well as the risk of losing everything. He leaned towards her, kissed her on the cheek.

'Tomorrow morning, Siswan? About eleven? I'll make the call,' he said and smiled.

Siswan could have kissed him right then and there.

'Apple?' She turned to her friend.

'Oh, yes! Let's get started,' Apple said.

Mike made the call early the following morning and set up an appointment with the agent. Rican said she didn't need to go. She had groceries to organize and she wanted to go over some new recipe ideas with the other three cooks. She told Mike that whatever he decided was fine by her.

Siswan met Apple and Mike outside her apartment block. She was really excited. This was the start. The start of the promise she had made to Sood and Karn. The last of the big waves.

They took a taxi to the hotel. It was situated a little out of town in a secluded road that looked down across the hills to the sea beyond. There was a small swimming pool, thirty bedrooms, all with their own bathrooms and, on the ground floor, living quarters for the staff. The staff rooms weren't big, but there were three separate bedrooms. Enough for the four of them.

'If we all moved here, we'd save even more money,' Apple suggested.

'You and I can, Apple,' Siswan said. 'Mike, I want you and Rican to keep your apartment.'

'Don't be daft,' he told her. 'Rican won't mind.'

Siswan smiled at him. He was so much the gentleman. He never worried about himself. She knew he loved the apartment she had found for him.

'It's not that, Mike,' she said. 'I just don't think it's right to have our Papa living with us. Do you Apple?'

'No way!' Apple grinned. 'We'd have to be in by ten every night!'

All three of them laughed. To get home by ten would be a real luxury.

'What about you, Apple?' Mike asked her. 'With, er, men I mean?'

'Oh Mike. Haven't you noticed?' she scolded him. 'I haven't been with a man for over a year. I think I've had enough of them.'

'Right. Well, if you must know, I had noticed. I just needed confirmation, that was all,' he said, huffily.

'Oh, sure,' Siswan giggled. 'Come on then, let's make a decision. Do we want it or not?'

'Yes,' Mike said.

'Yes!' agreed Apple.

'Okay. When we see the agent, tell him we'll think about it. Tell him we'll ring him in a few days with an offer,' Siswan told Mike.

Two weeks later they bought the hotel. Siswan had negotiated through Mike to get the price down by almost ten per cent. Three months later, her and Apple moved into the staff quarters.

Almost as soon as she had put her clothes away Apple ran into Siswan's room.

'Can I call her?' she asked.

Siswan knew what she was talking about. They had discussed it many times before. Both of them had been keeping in touch with Lon via the telephone and mail. She had managed to find some work in one of the factories near her village. She was paid a pittance and what she did earn she had to give to her father. Life hadn't been too good for her since she'd had to leave the bars. Her spirits remained high, but both Siswan and Apple knew she was lonely and miserable.

'Yes. Get her here,' Siswan answered. 'She'll love it!'

When Lon arrived, she was the first bar girl to be offered a place in the home. After their first advertising campaign, using the local media and the internet, twelve girls turned up. Two had young children, three others were addicted to drugs to such an extent they could no longer work. One had been attacked by her employer and was cut extensively around the mouth and nose. All of them needed help. All of them were suffering. None were turned away.

When Mike informed Siswan that the authorities needed a name to register as a charity she gave him the one name that she had always dreamed about using.

'Baan Sood, Mike,' she told him. 'It means Sood's Home.'

A month later they were given their registration. Sood's Home became a refuge for bar girls who, for whatever reason, had had enough. Those that couldn't work anymore. Those that found themselves in trouble.

Rican left Mike's Bar, found another cook to replace her, and worked full time at the home. She worked tirelessly tending to the girls needs. Siswan campaigned constantly, using the press, the internet, and anything she could think of to get the necessary publicity. Mike discussed the home with all the other bar owners, farang and local. He managed to convince them that the home was worth investing in, that they owed the girls who needed help, a chance to recover. A chance to start again.

The four bars supported the home. They made enough money to ensure it kept open whilst other funds were being sought.

Eventually the funds did start coming in. Money was donated, sometimes anonymously, sometimes amid a great fanfare of publicity. More and more money started reaching the home.

The rooms began to fill. Twelve girls became twenty, twenty became forty. They were given medical care and counseling. Education programs were made available to them. They were given food, clothing, a good bed and as much time as they needed to heal. That was the most important aspect of the home. The girls were allowed time. Time to recover. Time to step away from their lives. Time to think.

Before long the home had a steady stream of visitors. Teachers, who kindly offered a few hours of their week. Nurses and doctors who all gave their help free of charge. Sheets and blankets were donated. Soap, toothpaste, food. Everything the girls needed was made available.

Siswan was amazed at how many people were willing to help. How many people were willing to offer their support, both their time and their money. She was amazed at how many farangs wanted to help. Both those that lived locally and from overseas. It seemed that she had tapped into something she hadn't expected. Something she didn't even know existed. It was Mike who explained it to her.

'You've pricked a conscience, Siswan. A huge conscience. Farangs have been coming here for years, decades even. They've all indulged. They've all been a part of a bar girl's life at some time or another. Now they see a way of repaying. You've offered them a way to make retribution. A way to ease their guilt,' he told her.

'I didn't set out to do that, Mike,' she told him. 'I just wanted to help.'

'You are. You're helping the girls and you're helping the men who use them. Both sides win,' he said.

Siswan received countless letters and emails from farangs who wanted to help. One letter summed up what Mike had told her. She had a copy printed and framed. She hung it in the foyer for all to see and read.

To Sood's Home.

I served in the Army and was stationed in Asia for four years. I met a girl who worked in a bar when I was on a two week pass. She was a beautiful girl and her name was Lin. I was a young man then, and foolish. I spent the whole of my two weeks with Lin and she took care of me well. I gave her some money. It wasn't a lot. Not compared to the money I earned at the time. I never saw her again.

I finished with the Army and returned home. I married a lovely lady and had three children who are all grown up and living their own lives.

I'm an old man now, and just as foolish. My wife died two years ago from cancer. I'll be following her soon. I heard about your work from a magazine article and looked for more information on the internet.

You see, after all these years, I still remember Lin. I remember her smile and her laughter. I remember her long dark hair and how soft it felt. I remember how she took care of me. The little things she did. Things she didn't need to do.

I loved my wife, and I believe I was a good husband and father, but I never did forget my little Asian bar girl.

I hope the enclosed helps you to take care of girls like my Lin.

Even the bar girls, themselves, helped. They started making small donations. They saw it as a good investment. If they were ever in trouble, they'd have somewhere to go, somebody to take care of them.

As those girls in the home became stronger, as they became well and fit, they were helped to find work. Many of them ended up working in one of the four bars owned by Mike. They were never expected to go with farangs.

They could earn enough to survive without taking any risks.

On a few occasions, the families of girls who had taken refuge, turned up to demand the return of their daughter. She hadn't sent home any money. Her baby was starving. The bills needed to be paid. Siswan would arrange for the girl's baby to be brought to the home. She would only concern herself with the welfare of the girl and her child. The rest of the family were told, in no uncertain terms, to find a job. Earn their own money.

If they became violent, the police were called. They always came. The home was too high profile to be ignored and anyway, Siswan was still a very good customer.

Eventually Siswan and Mike opened more homes in other towns. More centres to help bar girls in need. The donations poured in. Very often, the girls who had received help, were the ones that were employed in the centres.

When Mike died in his sleep, seven years after the formation of Baan Sood, there were twelve homes up and running. He and Siswan owned a total of sixteen bars that earned enough money to support the project. In his will he left all that he owned to Siswan and Apple with the proviso that they take care of Rican.

He had been like a father to Siswan. More than that. He had been a friend to her. She cried at his funeral. Not tears of sadness. Tears of joy that she should have met such a kind and selfless man.

Afterwards, after the guests had left, Siswan walked down to the beach alone. She sat on the sand where her and Karn had sat so many times before. She sat and said a silent farewell to the only man that she had ever truly loved.

She watched the waves. They kept rolling in. Kept rushing towards her. She knew now that they would never stop. She smiled as she watched their progress.

Her life had changed on the day of her twelfth birthday. She hadn't chosen that change. Hadn't asked for it. Where would she be now if her life had taken a different course? If Bak hadn't touched her? If her father hadn't beaten her mother? If her mother had been stronger? Would she be married now? With a child of her own? Would her husband beat her as her father had beaten her mother?

She didn't know. She had walked away from her village as a young girl determined to take control of her own life. There was still so much to do. So many girls who needed help. Her and Apple were already looking at buying two homes upcountry. Homes that may prevent the girls from ever getting here.

She looked at the waves and allowed herself a small smile. All in all, she hadn't done too badly. Not too badly at all...for a bar girl.

The End.